THE MUSTANGERS

Other novels by Alfred Dennis

Chiricahua
Lone Eagle
Elkhorn Divide
Brant's Fort
Catamount
Yuma
Rover
Sandigras Canyon
Yellowstone Brigade
Shawnee Trail
Fort Reno
Ride the Rough String

To see more books by Alfred Dennis visit
www.alfreddennis.com

THE MUSTANGERS

by

Alfred Dennis

Walnut Creek Publishing
Tuskahoma, Oklahoma

The Mustangers

This novel is a work of fiction. Names, characters, places, and incidents are
either the product of the author's imagination or are used fictitiously. Any
resemblance to actual events, locales, organizations, or persons, living or dead, is
entirely coincidental and beyond the intent of either the author or the publisher.

ISBN: 978-1-942869-07-8
Second Edition Revised, Paperback
Published 2015 by Walnut Creek Publishing
10 9 8 7 6 5 4 3 2
1. Western 2. Action/Adventure 3. Historical Fiction

Books may be purchased in quantity and/or special sales by contacting the
publisher;
Walnut Creek Publishing
PO Box 820
Talihina, OK 74571
www.wc-books.com

This book is dedicated to my children
Carl, Kim, Kevin, Goldie, and Michael

Introduction

Arkansas Territory, the year is eighteen hundred and forty six. The smell of gunpowder drifts across the mighty Arkansas River as the feud between the Stallings and the Pike families escalates, claiming even more lives.

For five long, bloody years, the hatred and feuding raged across the rugged peaks and valleys of the Ozark Mountains. Two men, Ben Stallings and Levi Pike, both strong, unforgiving men, elders of their clans, drove the bloodbath onward. Men who would not forgive any encroachment into their family's lives or onto their lands.

Love and jealousy touched the trigger, igniting a tinderbox and starting the two families feuding. Ben Stallings and Levi Pike were never friends, but they were neighbors with a grudging respect for each other's possessions and land. Both elders have many brothers and they all have sons, ranging up and down the river. The two huge families remain separated by the Arkansas River, and that alone keeps the quarrelsome young men of each family away from one another, except on trading day in town.

When young Eli Stallings snuck off and eloped with Sarah Pike, without her father's permission, Levi Pike swore vengeance and damnation on the marriage. He claims the girl was kidnapped and taken against her will. He knew no self-respecting Pike would marry a Stallings.

Ben Stallings didn't like the notion of his son Eli, marrying a Pike either, but the lad was headstrong, just like his pa, so there was no arguing him out of courting the girl. Eli lied and told his father he had Levi Pike's permission to call on his daughter. Ben was as surprised as the Pikes when he learned they eloped in the middle of the night.

Zeb Pike, the older brother of Sarah Pike, spread the word all over the county, up and down both sides of the river. The marriage would never take place and if they marry, his sister would be a widow before the sun sets.

The happy newlyweds were coming from the Methodist Preacher's home, where they were quietly married, when Zeb Pike's prediction came true. Eli Stallings was blown from his wagon seat as they drove home by someone hiding, in the woods, near the edge of town. People say they could hear Sarah screaming all the way into town.

Eli Stalling's death marked the beginning of the Stallings and Pike feud. Two days later, Zeb Pike and his brother Levi Junior went down before the fast guns of Ben Stallings' second oldest son, Corey Stallings. They could not prove if Zeb Pike killed Eli Stallings, but he had made the threat for all to hear. That was proof enough for the young Stallings. The feud exploded with a vengeance from behind every tree, rock, and dark trail. The Stallings, Pikes, and their kin, could not ride the mountains in safety. Ambush and death awaited any who dared stray far from the safety of their homes.

For five bloody years, bodies were found along the remote wilderness trails. No one was safe. Even innocent travelers were killed for being in the wrong place at the wrong time.

Finally, Ben Stallings looks across his supper table and realizes his sons, who had numbered nine, were now down to five. Only his oldest Caleb, then Corey, Samuel, Colby, and Lambert, the youngest, were left. The older Stallings, the patriarch of the family, has aged over the last five years. His deep blue eyes still spit fire and hate, but he loves his sons. He decides he will no longer lose any of his children or kinfolk. Eli, Pate, Joshua, and David were all killed.

Corey was wounded three times, almost dying the last time he was ambushed. Out of all his sons, Corey was the most like him; big, strong, and hard as nails. Corey retaliated against the Pikes every time one of his brothers or cousins was ambushed. The young Stalling was no back shooter. All of his victims went down in front of his smoking guns, knowing who their killer was. Their mother, rest her soul, passed that spring. The local doctor said her death was from plain heartbreak over the loss of her sons, and knowing how the feud changed her beloved Corey.

Ben Stallings looks around the table to where his daughter is serving their breakfast. His eyes blink sadly. It seems like only yesterday, she was a girl of seventeen years, about to marry Kyle Evans. The feud claimed

Kyle's life too, shot in the back by Zeb Pike and Manny Sharps on the streets of Collinsville, just days before Eli was murdered. She has aged and now she is a quiet, dispirited recluse, talking only to her immediate family. Corey killed Zeb Pike and his brother, two days after Eli was killed. It was a stand-up fight on the streets of Fort Smith. Corey Stallings could not prove it, but he knew Zeb Pike killed Eli, the same way he shot Kyle in the back, only days earlier. Five years later, Ben Stallings decides the killing must end.

CHAPTER 1

The Stallings' log cabin and farmstead was cleared and built from the wild mountainous terrain of the Ozark Mountains. It has taken men with strong backs and iron hard muscles, to work this land, men like the Stallings, men that fear only God himself. Once, the farm was a beautiful and peaceful home, nestled in the fertile valleys, lying alongside the beautiful Arkansas River. A serene and tranquil homestead with rich, fertile soil, taking only hard work and toil to make it productive. The place was peaceful before the trouble with the Pikes. The bloody feud erupted into a full-fledged warfare, leading up to killings on both sides.

Lithe and graceful, Judith Stallings stands before the hot, wood cookstove, preparing breakfast for her pa and brothers. Above the hissing of the side meat, frying in a large cast iron skillet, she can hear her father outside, pacing the plank front porch. He strides heavily back and forth in deep concentration, as the boards under him moan with each step he takes. Something is on her father's mind this morning. What, she does not know, but she is aware when her pa starts pacing the floor, he is brooding over something deep and troubling. She hopes it doesn't lead to more killings. Despite her beloved Kyle, the man she was to marry, being shot down on the eve of their wedding, she wants no more killings.

At her beckoning, Ben Stallings enters the snug, warm room and takes his seat at the head of the table. All bow their heads as he asks grace and finishes the blessing with a holy amen. Forks and knives rattle as the young men at the table start eating. Slowly, one by one, the noise subsides as the men stop what they are doing. They turn their attention to where their father sits staring at his plate, his chin resting on the knuckles of his big hands.

Ben Stallings is a tall, rawboned man, with enormous strength and energy. It was said, in his youth, he could out wrestle and whip any three men in the Ozarks. A hard man he is, but also a fair man with his neighbors, a gentle giant that could turn mean when trouble arises and warrants it. His eyes look around the table, stopping and studying each vacant chair where once his wife, daughter and nine sons sat, eating and laughing. Now, five of those chairs sit empty. The feud with the Pikes has taken four of his sons and his beloved wife.

The biggest of the young men puts his fork down and looks across at his dad. "What's wrong, Pa? What's on your mind?"

"It's over." The words rush out, taking the others by surprise.

"What's over?" Caleb, the oldest, asks and looks curiously into the hard face of his father.

"The feud, that's what." Ben Stallings looks around the table. "I'm crossing the river today and have a talk with Levi Pike."

"You're what?" Corey Stallings swallows a mouthful of coffee, staring incredulously at the older man.

"You heard me boy, I'm gonna cross the river this morning and try to make peace with Levi Pike."

"Why?" The word crosses the table cold as ice. Corey Stallings is as tall as his pa with the same dark, handsome features and strength.

"I've lost all the sons, relatives, and friends, I aim to." Ben Stallings stares across the table at his son. "You yourself are lucky to be alive, shot three times from ambush, and the knife cuts you took from Caudell Pike or the Mathis boy dang near done you in both times. They would have killed any ordinary man."

"They didn't kill me, and neither Caudell nor Pate Mathis are gonna be cutting on anybody, anymore."

"Like I said, you were lucky, now it's finished." The older man studies his second son. "Ain't you killed enough boy or is what they say about you true, you love it?"

Of all the sons, only Corey dares to stand up to his father. The rest are not exactly afraid of their pa, but they respect him enough to keep quiet. Not Corey, arguing has gotten him several whippings until he turned eighteen and told his father that he would no longer subject himself to any whippings, unless he wants to use his fists. Since then, there has been an uneasy truce between the two strong-willed men, until this morning.

The two men respect each other, but the older Stallings doesn't hold the same soft feelings for Corey that he has for his other sons. He feels the coldness in the boy, the coldness that caused many a man's death. Looking at his son is like looking at death. He has known many bad men in his time, but Corey is the meanest of the lot when he is provoked, and it sure doesn't take much to provoke him. The warmth he holds for his other sons is different from what he has with Corey. Yes, he is his son, and it is true, he depends on him more than the others in troubled times. People in town call Corey a cold-blooded killer, a man not to cross. In his own way, Ben loves Corey, but he cannot love the killer he thinks his son has become.

"You cross the Arkansas and you're a dead man, Pa." Corey adds the pa, as a sign of respect. "You hear me, they'll kill you sure."

"I already sent Reverend Bishop to set up a meeting between me and Levi Pike."

"I don't know Pa, them Pikes are as mad as a stirred up hornet's nest." Caleb, the oldest son shakes his head. Caleb is the oldest and he is also the most levelheaded of the family. He is so quiet and peaceful that some dare to go so far as call him yellow, regretting the words when Caleb finally gets his dander up.

"What's it gonna prove? I'll tell you, nothing." Corey stands to his full height, towering over everyone at the table, slamming his huge fist down on the wooden top. "Nothing!"

"I'll be going, soon as the Reverend sends word, and that's final." Ben stares over at his wild son. "I'm still running this family."

Corey glances around the table, finally letting his eyes rest on Ben Stallings. "If them Pikes have their way, it could be final alright, maybe even fatal."

Breakfast finishes without further mention of the matter. Only Corey's dark scowl shows the slightest hint the conversation ever took place. Lambert, the youngest of the Stallings clan, walks back through the door.

"Amos Stone is coming up the lane, Pa." The youngster stands in the doorway, staring down the sandy road.

Ben Stallings stands up and looks over at Corey. "Reckon, that'll be word from the Reverend."

"You want me to side you?" Corey rises from the table, pushing his coffee cup and saucer away from him.

"No." Ben shakes his huge head. "I'm trying to make peace here, not have another killing."

Caleb walks to the barn with Corey and watches as he saddles his bay horse. "Where you headed, brother?"

Corey looks down the road to where his pa and Amos Stone are passing from sight. "He don't want me, but I ain't gonna let him go alone."

"You want me to ride with you?"

"No Caleb, this is a looking job, not a shooting one." Corey shakes his head. "I can handle it."

The Reverend Joseph Abernathy Bishop stands at the low water crossing on the Arkansas as Ben Stallings walks his horse into the shallow murky water. Levi Pike waits alongside the preacher on the sandy banks, his eyes searching the woods behind the oncoming rider. He trusts the word of Ben Stallings, knowing him to be a man of honor, but the rest of the bunch, he isn't so sure of. He wouldn't trust that no-account killer, Corey Stallings, in the same room with a dead skunk.

The preacher's bony hand clutches a bible and extends it for both men to see plainly. Hardly ten feet separate the two patriarchs of the feuding families as Ben Stallings dismounts heavily from his horse. Checking the two men over closely, Reverend Bishop makes sure there are no weapons on either man. That was his one stipulation when he was asked to set up the meeting. He knows both men have hair-trigger tempers, and both lost sons and close relations in these mountains and valleys. As emotional and heated as it is, it wouldn't take much to have the banks of the Arkansas running red with blood.

Levi Pike studies the big man in front of him. They have known each other as young men when they traveled west to Arkansas on the same wagon train. They fought Indians and renegade white men side by side, sharing the same food and hardships together. He came to like Ben Stallings and respected him more than any man he has ever known. Pike himself, was always a loner, not a sociable man. Nevertheless, he has been neighborly in his dealings with Ben Stallings, at least before the killings started.

"Alright Stallings, you called this sit down. What do you want?" Pike's voice is hard as flint.

"Levi Pike, we've been fighting nigh on five years; I'm through."

"You're through? Just like that, you're through?" Pike looks the man up and down. "You gone yeller?"

Stallings big hands ball into fists. "Is that what you think, Levi?"

Pike shakes his head slowly. "No, I've known you too long Benjamin Stallings, you ain't yeller, but then what is it?"

"I've lost all the sons and nephews I aim to, that's what it is." Ben stares hard at Pike. "No more senseless killings, losing loved ones. I'm finished, I tell you."

"How do you expect me to keep the peace on my side?" Pike shakes his head. "My people have been bled and they've tasted blood. No, they will never quit killing you Stallings, never."

"Nor will mine."

"Then, what do you propose?"

"I'm pulling out. I just want your word there will be no more killings, once my family departs these mountains."

"Your boys agree to this idea, do they?"

"They don't know yet, that I'm leaving Arkansas." Ben looks across the river. "I haven't told them."

"I see, what about Corey? You think you can handle him?" Pike lets his eyes drift back along the far bank.

"He's my son." Stallings draws himself straight. "He'll do as I say."

"Corey Stallings is a mad dog killer. He'll do as no man says, even you Ben Stallings." Pike spits. "He's mean clear through, a killer and you're a knowing it."

"This feuding has made him the way he is."

"Has it Ben?" Pike questions, "Has it?"

"What are you saying, Pike?"

"Corey killed my sons Zeb and Levi five years ago when he was just seventeen. Before that, it was the Mathis lad. What was he then fifteen, sixteen? No telling how many he's killed these past years. I'm telling you, he's a crazed killer and he ain't leaving these mountains alive. You hear me Ben Stallings, alive!" Spittle flies from the tall man's lips as he snaps the words out. "I'll not lie awake at night and wonder when he'll be back. I can't let my sons go unavenged."

"The Mathis boy pulled a knife on Caleb. Corey stepped in to help his brother and was cut badly. The Mathis boy's death was of his own doing, and you know it, Levi Pike."

"What about Zeb and little Levi, and all the others, were their deaths an accident too?" Pike steps forward. "Corey killed them all, shot 'em down in the street, he did."

"And Zeb killed my Eli, your own son-in-law. It has to end, Levi. I'm asking for your help to stop the killing now, today." Ben looks hard at the tall man. "Either help me, or I'll go get my gun and we'll finish it here, right now."

Pike runs his long fingers over his face, trying to calm down. "Your place, who's taking it over?"

"I'm having a sale this coming week. The highest bidder gets it and my cattle." Stallings looks over at the preacher. "All wanting to come in peace will be welcome."

"Alright Ben, I want to see the killings stopped before we lose all our sons, but on one condition."

"That being?"

"You deliver Corey Stallings to stand trial for my boy's deaths, then and only then, will we have a truce."

"No!" Stallings voice turns cold. "There will be no trial. I'm selling out next week, like I said, and then me and mine are leaving these mountains forever. Corey will be with us and he won't be back. He will not stand trial now or ever, and if I hear of one killing, I'll be back and there won't be a Pike left living when I'm done."

"You mean when Corey Stallings is done, don't you Ben?" Pike looks over at Ben. "You'd turn that crazed killer loose on us, wouldn't you?"

"You heard me Levi Pike, if one more of my people die violently, after we leave these parts, I'll do whatever it takes to stop the killings."

"Alright, I agree, the killings must stop before we're all dead." Pike shakes his head. "I've lost most of my sons, and now it seems I've lost my only girl."

"Your word Levi Pike; swear it on the good book." Ben nods at the Bible, Preacher Bishop holds.

"Only if you do likewise, Ben Stallings."

Corey Stallings watches from the wooded hillside as Reverend Bishop holds out the old, frayed, well-read Bible, and both men place their hands on it. He nods. Maybe it was as his Pa said. Possibly, the feud is over. He will have to see, trusting a Pike is something he will never do. The bitterness and bloodshed runs too deep and passionately in his veins.

"Will she be leaving with you, Ben?" Pike walks to where his horse stands, ground tied.

Ben studies the moving river for a second and then looks to where Pike stands. "I reckon that'll be her choice, Levi. I don't know for sure. She hasn't said one way or the other."

"Well, if she do, take care of her for me, please."

"You have my word on it, Levi Pike."

"Ben, how'd it ever come to this?" Pike doesn't wait for an answer before mounting his horse and riding off. "White men killing one another like dogs."

Ben mounts and crosses the Arkansas. He stares down at the small dirt trail that runs alongside the river. It is midsummer, and the flowers are blooming, their petals of blue, yellow, and red, waving in the light wind. The fragrance on the air smells fresh and sweet. Ben is deep in thought. He never hears the grey squirrel's bark, scolding him from the safety of a huge oak, as his gelding trots past, following the sandy road.

Riding up alongside Ben, as the older man comes jogging down the narrow trail toward home, Corey notices something distracts the big man. His horse matches pace with the other, while Corey waits, letting his pa meditate before speaking. Only the saddle leather squeaking or the occasional horse snorting breaks the silence.

Corey cannot contain his curiosity any longer. "Is the feud over, Pa?"

"It is." Ben looks over at his one son that is almost his own self, made over. "We're selling out and heading for Texas."

"Texas?"

"Yep, I traded for a fair size chunk of that country several years back for a song, now we're gonna try our luck there." Ben mumbles absently, deep in thought. "He asked me why we killed one another like dogs."

"Who did?"'

"Levi; Levi Pike."

"Is that what we did?"

Ben looks over at Corey. "Yes, I guess we did, at that."

"They started this feud Pa, not us." Corey won't back up an inch on the subject. He never has and he never will. Maybe what they say is true, he's a killer. It doesn't matter; he hates the Pikes with a passion.

"Well, it's over! We're heading for Texas and as far away from this mess as I can get the family."

"And do what, chase buffalo?" Corey is shocked. He never, in his wildest, figured to be heading for Texas. Arkansas is all he knows.

"We're gonna be Mustangers boy, Mustangers." Ben looks over at his son. "They tell me horses run loose all over Texas, thicker than fleas on a hound's back."

"Mustangers?" Corey looks over at the older man. "What in the world is a Mustanger?"

"We're gonna catch wild horses, break 'em, then sell 'em to the highest bidder."

"Mustangers?" Corey shakes his head. "First we gotta get outta here with our hide in tack. You think the Pikes are gonna let us just ride out of here, scot-free?"

"Told you, Levi Pike gave his word. I've never known him to go back on it, not once."

"What about his boys, nephews, and who knows who else?"

Ben nods. "Funny you should ask, he said the same about you."

"I've only killed when I had to, you know that."

"Do I Corey? I wish I did know that for certain." Ben looks into Corey's eyes for the longest. "It would bring me some relief boy."

Corey's face grows hard. He is tired of the remarks, the accusations of him being a crazy killer. His enemies accusing him of being a killer is one thing, but his own father. Yes, he has killed and everyone in the valley knows, but only after he was attacked first or when one of the family was killed.

CHAPTER 2

Texas, people call it the land of hope, the land of new beginnings. Nevertheless, it is an untamed land, full of wild Indians, outlaws, Mexicans, buffalo, wild horses, and rattlesnakes. If it doesn't bite, it will shoot and with the war with Mexico still fresh in everyone's memory, no one trusts anybody, especially strangers.

Corey sits his long-legged bay horse, as he looks out across the muddy water of the broad Red River, the pathway to Texas. Across the Red, lies a beautiful land, a land where a man could spread his wings and grow.

Even sitting here on the banks of the river, he cannot believe his father sold out and now they are heading southwest, into the great wide expanse of land. He shouldn't have agreed to go, but his father gave his word that he and his would leave Arkansas if the Pikes would call off the feud, which especially meant him. Corey would not go against his father, at least for the present. He would leave Arkansas, but if he needs to, he could always return later.

The sale of the Stallings' homestead went peacefully. Many hill people arrived by wagon or horseback for the sale early in the morning. Many came to buy, but most came out of curiosity. They heard the feud was finally over, but they heard that many times before. Federal marshals, local constables, and friends from far away, everyone tried to stop the feud and the killings, but to no avail. No one figured the so-called settlement would be any different.

Riley Gant, a cousin to the Pikes, bought the farm and cattle, and took possession the next morning as the Stallings loaded their wagons and rode away from a lifetime of hard work. He stood there unarmed, under a huge bois d'arc tree, relieved the Stallings family finally disappeared around a bend in the dirt road, on their way west. Riley shutters slightly as he remembers the way Corey Stallings looked at him with those cold hard eyes of his, as he rode past him. Riley never fired a shot in anger at anyone during the feud, but he knows that means nothing to Corey Stallings. He believes, as others do, the man is a bloodthirsty killer.

Levi Pike was invited to the sale, but he had the good sense not to show. It would only take one wrong word, from either side, to start the feud again. It doesn't matter if it is Pike or Stallings, if he and his boys are present at the farm, trouble could erupt.

The morning after the farm sold, the tall patriarch of the Pikes sat hiding in a small grove of trees with two of his sons, as the Stallings' wagons and outriders approached, on their way southwest to Texas. Corey Stallings rides far ahead of the wagons, so Pike lets him pass before riding out from his hiding place. He knows how trigger happy the hotheaded Stallings boy is, and he doesn't inadvertently want to start the feud all over.

Ben Stallings kept his word, now Pike will keep his. There will be no more killings. Kicking his horse forward, Pike rides to the middle of the dirt road, then waits as the wagons stop before him.

He raises his hand when several rifle barrels point in his direction. Motioning for his sons to stay where they are, Levi rides close to the wagon, Ben Stallings and a girl are driving.

"You kept your word, now I'll keep mine." Pike stares hard into Ben's face. "There will be no more killings if I can help it."

"Remember Levi, one killing and I'll be back."

"I heard you." Pike looks over at the girl, which was his main reason for coming. "Sarah gal, you gonna go with them?"

Red headed, green-eyed Sarah Pike nods her head at her father. "Yes Papa, I'm a Stallings now. I married Eli and this be my family now. I'm obliged to go with them."

"I'm sorry gal, truly sorry about your man." Pike drops his eyes. "You'll always have a home here if you've a mind to return to your folks."

"I love you Papa, but I'm a going." Sarah looks ahead at Corey. "I'll never forget you and mama."

"Sarah, I didn't mean for your man Eli to be killed."

"I ain't faulting you none, Pa."

Nodding, Pike looks back at Ben. "I've come to warn you, one of my boys, Travis, has lit out. I couldn't stop him from leaving, don't know for sure what he be up to, no good I reckon, but he'll be waiting somewhere ahead I figure."

"Where does that leave us, Levi?"

"Travis is dead set on killing your boy, Corey. He and Zeb were brothers." Pike pulls off his worn-out felt hat. "Being twins, I reckon they were closer than brothers."

"He's somewhere ahead, waiting for Corey?" Ben looks over at the surrounding woods, "Is that it?"

"I figure, you do what you have to do, Ben Stallings. The boy went back against my word." Pike looks behind him, down the road. "I'll not be holding it against you. I told him the fighting and killing was finished."

"I remember the twins, when they were small." Ben looks down at Levi. "They were something."

"I warned Travis to let it go, but he wouldn't listen to me. Well, he's made his bed, now let him lay in it." Pike looks down at the ground. "He and Zeb looked alike, but they were different as night and day. Travis is a good son and he always listens to me, except in this. Zeb was like your boy, bad clear through."

"I'm sorry, Levi. We are both to blame for the killings, but I don't hold you responsible for the death of my boys. We should have stopped it sooner."

"Maybe, but what's done is done. Good-bye Ben Stallings". Pike kicks his horse and trots east, without looking back.

Ben looks over at Sarah as the wagon starts forward. "Why are you going with us, gal?"

The girl looks down at the backs of the horses. "I loved Eli, and my family killed him. I love my folks, but I can't stay with them."

"It was your brother that killed Eli, not your folks."

"Yes, but Papa knew Zeb threatened to kill Eli. Papa, Travis, and Zeb argued about it the night before."

"Travis didn't want Eli killed?"

"No."

"Then why is he coming to kill Corey?" Ben looks across at the girl.

"Corey killed Zeb. He figures family honor or some such nonsense." Sarah looks over at Ben. "If you don't want me, I'll be leaving."

"No Sarah, you're a Stallings now. You are family and we want you to stay with us." Ben looks ahead to where Corey sits his horse. "Don't get any ideas about him girl, he's no good."

"Papa Ben, he's your son, he loves you."

"Maybe he does at that, in his own way, but he's walking death to any man that crosses him, maybe even me." Ben spits. "He'll be no good for any woman."

"You're wrong. Corey is a good-hearted man, I can tell." Sarah looks over at Ben. "He's so soft and gentle with Colby."

"With Colby yes, but Colby's different." Ben agrees. "You just watch if Travis shows up. He won't be so gentle."

Corey studies the wide river crossing, letting his black eyes take in every tree where a man could be waiting in ambush on the other side. They have traveled far, crossing the wild, untamed Indian Territory, following this well-traveled road leading straight into a low water crossing. Once they cross the river, they will be in Texas. For centuries, this was a natural crossing for many buffalo and wild horses. The crossing has no quicksand or deep holes of water to trap a wagon wheel or an unfortunate rider. Its low banks made entering the water and coming out easier on the teams pulling the heavy wagons. He can see where the road exits the river on the far side and heads due southwest, into the flat, plains country of Texas.

He studied the map Ben carries, several times. It shows the way to the hill country where their land should be. He figures it is two hundred miles or better, if the map is accurate. He has never been in Texas before, but he figures with no major problems and at the speed they are traveling, it should take no more than ten or twelve days to arrive there.

Corey thinks back to the rough map sketched on deerskin and the paper that supposedly is the deed to the great land track. They say Sam Houston made the deed, the conqueror of Santa Anna and the first

President of Texas. Shaking his head, he kicks the bay into the knee-deep water of the Red.

It could be a wild-goose chase. The dang deed probably isn't worth the paper it was written on. It doesn't matter as Ben Stallings supplied two huge wagons with everything they need as they head into Texas and that is all there is to it. When the old man makes up his mind, he is like a mule and nothing will change his direction. Well, maybe it's for the best. He wouldn't have to look over his shoulder or behind every bush for a hidden Pike. Corey Stallings doesn't mind the killings, better them than himself, but he was sure tired of being shot at or knifed.

He could swear by the good book, except for Zeb Pike, he did not start any fights, not that he hasn't been in several. Others didn't believe it and said differently, but Corey honestly knew Zeb and the ones with him who killed Eli was the only fight he ever intentionally looked for or provoked.

The bay is almost halfway across the Red when two riders come into sight on the far bank. Corey recognizes the tall shape of Travis Pike and the red headed Manny Sharps, a cousin to the Pikes. Pulling his horse in, Corey looks back at the wagons and motions them to pull up. Here is another confrontation, which is not of his choosing. Travis Pike came for him personally so this is his fight alone. There is no use letting the wagons move closer into rifle range because the women are riding in the front wagon seats. Letting the wagons come closer would place them in danger, directly in the line of fire.

Ben Stallings sits on the tall wagon seat and stares at the broad back of his second son, looking on across the river to where the two riders sit. Two against one, they have Corey in the middle of the river, with no way out.

"It's my brother Travis, and that no-account cousin of ours, Manny Sharps." Sarah holds her hand up to shade her face. "I'm sorry, Papa Ben."

"It'll be alright gal, ain't your fault."

"Yes, it is, if I hadn't married Eli, all this wouldn't have happened."

"Did you love him, girl?"

"No woman could love a man more." Sarah nods. "He was the apple of my eye."

"Then you did right." Ben pulls out his long barreled Kentucky Rifle and checks the priming.

"They're too far, Papa Ben. That squirrel gun can't reach way over where they are."

"I know, gal. They're outta range for sure, but I might scare them and mess up their aim."

"Manny Sharps is my cousin for sure, and he's a bad one if he's got the deadwood on you. Face-to-face, he's a coward." Apprehension shows on her face. "Not like Corey, he's a brave and gentle man."

"You must see something in him I don't." Ben looks at her curiously. "I agree, he's brave, but gentle, I sure wouldn't say that. Girl he's a born killer."

"I can see the good in him. You don't because you haven't looked close enough."

Ben watches as the three riders across the river face one another. "This could be bad, girl, real bad."

Sarah nods, causing a red curl to fall across her face. "Travis and Manny brought this here trouble to you, Papa Ben. Whatever happens, they brought it on themselves. Let Corey handle it alone, and don't blame him later."

Ben looks over at her and uncocks the hammer of his rifle. "Tell me Sarah, why don't you want me to try to help?"

"If Corey wanted your help he wouldn't have stopped the wagons over here out of range." Sarah's eyes never leave Corey's back as she speaks.

Ben studies her face for several seconds, nodding slowly before looking ahead, across the river. "Alright Sarah, but like I said, don't set your sights on him, gal. I don't think he'd be good for any woman, not now anyhow."

Making sure the wagons, and his brothers, are staying where they are, Corey kicks his horse forward, through the shallows and splashes ashore. He can see Travis and Sharps still have their rifles slung across their backs. Only the butts of their revolvers are close enough for them to bring into action quickly. He knows Travis, he isn't a coward, and he would make a fair fight of it. He also knows Manny Sharps, the Pikes' cousin who lives far from Arkansas. Corey knew him when they were kids. Supposedly, he's a hard man and killer now, but it could be just rumors. This is their first meeting as grown men and it looks like their last, at least for one of them.

Thirty yards separate the three men as they rein their horses to a halt. Travis is the spitting image of Zeb Pike. He should be, as they were identical twins. Even when they were little, no one could tell them apart.

"We've come for you, Corey Stallings, for killing Zeb." Travis spits a stream of tobacco onto the ground as he speaks.

"Travis, snakes like your brother Zeb need killing." Corey drawls slowly. "Don't get killed over the likes of him. You're too good a man."

"Those be harsh words against a dead man." The one known as Manny grins at Corey. "A man shouldn't talk bad about the dead."

"Manny Sharps, long time no see, but this ain't none of your business." Corey doesn't bother to look at the man. "I hear Hatton Evans has business with you."

"You remember me do you? That's good, and it is my business," Sharps grins wickedly. "We're gonna kill you, then I'll take care of Evans."

"Tell me Sharps, you aim on talking me to death or fighting?" Corey smiles easily at Sharps.

"You ready to die Stallings?"

"I heard all you Sharps stink. I reckon whoever said it was right." Corey rests his big hands on the horn of his saddle. "Cause I can smell the stench of you from way over here."

"Let's stop the palavering and get to it. Get down off that horse, Corey." Travis Pike swings a leg over his horse's rump and steps to the ground.

Ben Stallings watches helplessly as the three men dismount. They sit gathered around Ben's wagon, wanting to ride forward to help their brother, but the patriarch of the Stallings holds them back.

"This is Corey's fight, we'll wait." Ben holds up his big hand. He shakes his huge head in disbelief. He remembers as kids, these same men, who were fixing to shoot it out, swam and played in the Arkansas River. How did it ever come to this?

"There's two of them, Pa." Caleb kicks his horse forward.

"You heed my words boy, we'll wait."

A younger man kicks his horse forward beside Caleb. "You aim on getting Corey killed, Pa?"

"Hush your mouth, Lambert Stallings." Caleb points his finger at the boy. "You're just sixteen so don't you be questioning Pa's judgment."

Ben watches closely as Corey eases slowly from his horse. He questions himself, by holding the others back, is he intentionally trying to get Corey killed? No, he knows better. Somewhere behind them, Levi Pike and his sons have followed all this way. He could sense all morning that someone was watching them. If he lets the boys charge across the river to help Corey, the feud could possibly rekindle. Levi Pike said he wouldn't interfere, but he is still a father. If he sends the boys to help, it would look like they were ganging up on Travis.

No, Corey is on his own, this time. As he watches the fight unfold, Ben wonders if he judged his son fair. Corey didn't start this fight and maybe the rest wasn't his fault either.

Not a word is spoken as Corey drops the bay's reins to the ground and stares at the two men in front of him. They came to fight, here on the banks of the Red. He already knows someone will not leave the riverbank alive.

Suddenly, without warning, Travis and Manny reach for their guns and open fire quickly. Too quick, both shots throw up sand five feet in front of Corey. Turning sideways, Corey lays his long-barreled pistol across his left arm and aims at Travis. Lead whistles around him and throws up more sand as both men empty their pistols before Corey hears them snapping on empty cylinders. The distance is too far for accurate pistol shooting with any speed. The roar of the huge pistol breaks the stillness as Corey fires, throwing Travis backward onto the sandy riverbank, dead before he hit the ground, a hole dead center through his heart. Corey turns the pistol quickly on Sharps and takes careful aim again.

Flinging his pistol from him, Sharps falls to his knees, holding one hand in front of him. "Please Stallings, please don't kill me, I'm unarmed."

The pistol sight looks right into the eyes of the kneeling man. Falling forward with a whimper of fear, Sharps covers his head with his trembling hands.

Corey studies the shaking figure on the ground and mounts the bay, riding past him, down the road. The big man never looks back to see if anyone is following, or down at the cowardly form of Manny Sharps, groveling in the sand on the banks of the Red. Corey Stallings lets the tension ease from his body as he rides west, the pistol still warm and smoking in his hand. He hates the killing. He knows, behind him in the wagon, Sarah would see her dead brother and blame him for it. Holstering the pistol, Corey fishes in his pocket and pulls out makings. He doesn't smoke much but he needs one today.

Only Ben notices the riders emerge from the timber as they pass the body of Travis Pike and the cringing Manny Sharps. He looks back several times as Levi Pike crosses the river to claim the body of his son Travis. Maybe this would be the last killing, but Ben Stallings isn't sure. He asked Sarah if she wanted him to stop, but she didn't answer, nor did she look down. Tears stream down her face as the wagon passes the body of her brother. She loved Travis, but she knows he brought this on himself. Her eyes are on the broad back of Corey as he rides ahead with his head high, shoulders straight, tall in the saddle, and proud.

Manny Sharps raises his head as the wagons roll past him. Shaking his fists at the retreating wagons, he picks up his pistol and reloads.

"You're a stinking coward Manny." Nate Pike glares down at Sharps as the Pikes ride up.

"We saw it all."

"Maybe I am, but I'm alive," Sharps bares his teeth like a cornered coyote. "My gun was empty. He had me cold."

"Are cowards ever alive?"

Manny Sharps looks up, into the cold, hard, accusing eyes of Levi Pike. "He would have killed me for sure, Uncle Levi."

They hear the slap clear to the wagons as Levi leans from his saddle and knocks Sharps back to the ground. "Don't you ever call me uncle or come around my place again, never, or I'll shoot you like I would a rabid skunk."

Trembling with sorrow and pain, Levi Pike stares after the wagons and the retreating Stallings. He can see Corey Stallings further ahead shaking his head as he leans over his son Travis. This time, Stallings didn't start the fight, his own son did.

CHAPTER 3

The wagons travel for fifteen long, hot days, through the flat, untamed grasslands, and then push on into the cooler hill country of north Texas. Corey and Caleb rein in their horses, studying the beat down grass where a herd of mustangs passed by as they mingled with a few buffalo. They see them stampede and disappear over the nearest rise with their tails straight in the air.

"If it's mustangs Pa's after, looks like we came to the right country." Caleb slouches in the saddle with his leg hooked around the horn.

Corey only nods as his eyes busily scan a long, low, flat-topped hill in the distance. A flash from the hill catches his sharp eyes.

Caleb notices his brother's attention locks on a distant hill. He squints as he tries to see what is catching Corey's interest.

The wagons are coming into view, stirring up thick dust under their large, iron-rimmed wheels. Three long legged geldings, tied behind the first wagon, plod along, kicking up their own dust as they walk, adding to the powder choking air. Several other horses are loose herded by Lambert and Colby Stallings. Another long legged bay, this one a stallion, is tied behind the second wagon.

"Well, one thing's for sure, he came equipped with the horses to run them mustangs down with." Caleb nods toward the remuda the younger boys are herding. "Along with that bay stallion, we should be able to build up a fair size ranch in no time."

Corey acknowledges his brother's comment with a nod as he continues to study the small hill.

"What you looking at Corey?" Caleb questions his brother as he straightens in the saddle and removes his leg from the horn. Whatever moved up there now has Caleb's curiosity aroused. "Sure ain't what these Texans call hills. Our mountains back home make these sandpiles look like gopher mounds."

"Somebody up there is looking us over real good."

"You see 'em yet?" Caleb focuses on the far hill.

"Nope, just a flash, but they're up there all right." Corey looks to where the wagons approach. Nudging his gelding lightly, he walks the horse over to where Ben pulls to a stop.

"We got trouble boy?" Ben asks easily.

"You see the flash?" Corey looks to where the boys are bringing the horses along slowly.

Ben never looks up toward the hill. He only nods his head. "I seen it, way back yonder. I figured that's why you pulled up and waited."

"What you figure?" Caleb speaks up, looking over at Sarah, who sits quietly beside Ben. "Outlaws or Indians?"

"It's hard to say, it could be Mexicans, Indians, who knows."

"We making camp for the night, Papa Ben?" Sarah looks over at Corey and smiles slightly.

"We'll do that, gal." Ben twists his great head and laughs. "Down there along the creek. The stock needs rest and I'm hungry for some of your good cooking." Ben acts nonchalant since he doesn't want to unnecessarily scare the women by worrying. Driving the wagons into a stand of blackjack and post-oak trees, Ben orders them to hobble and turn the remuda loose to graze along the creek bottom. Hobbled horses cannot run far, even if someone stampedes the herd during the night.

"What we doing all this work fer, Lambert?" Colby Stallings stammers the words out. Colby is next to the youngest of the boys and the smallest. Rheumatic fever, when the lad was six, left him with a bad stutter and weak-minded. All the Stallings look over the youngster like sitting hens. Even the Pikes disregarded him as a harmless idiot in the feud, a defenseless Stallings, unworthy of their attention.

Lambert smiles at his brother. "Well, for one thing, papa said so, and because horses with hobbles on, sure can't run off."

"Why would they run off, Lambert?" Colby shakes his head. "They ain't never run before."

"Now Colby, you go eat. Miss Sarah and Judith have supper ready and you know sis don't like us to be late."

Lambert watches as his brother ambles toward the fire. Easy going and slow, Colby would do what anyone asks of him, which caused Lambert many a fight, plus many a black eye, back in Arkansas. Lambert was always protecting his older brother from bullies and pranksters.

The night passes quietly as the brothers take turns, standing night watch over the camp and horses. Nothing stirs out in the darkness, only the sounds of bullfrogs, crickets, and the usual noise of night critters. Occasionally, a lone coyote howls, causing another coyote to return his mournful call and answer him back. Sometimes several make a racket, if they smell rabbit, as they try to scare him into the waiting pack's jaws.

Corey has every horse saddled and ready as Ben ordered, just for insurance in case the horses are needed quickly, in the middle of the night. Trying to saddle a plunging horse in the dark and half asleep, can be an interesting experience, to say the least.

An hour before daylight, Corey orders the boys to herd the loose horses in closer to the wagons where they are easier to watch over.

"You still s'pecting trouble, Corey? It's been quiet all night." Caleb studies the dark gloom and murky fog that settled along the creek bank. The early morning mist seems to have soaked into every pore of his body, chilling him to the bone.

"Yep brother, it's way too quiet."

"You sure someone's out there?"

"No, I ain't sure, but a little caution won't hurt any if I happen to be wrong."

"That's a fact for sure." Caleb waves his arms around, trying to get his circulation moving so he can warm up.

"Caleb, why don't you have the boys grab their rifles, and the girls, then crawl under the wagons, behind some boxes. Get them plenty of cover." Corey whispers quietly.

"Okay, Corey. I'll get to it." Caleb doesn't argue with his younger brother. Back in Arkansas, many times, Corey smelled trouble long before anything happened.

They come in as the eastern sun comes up, twenty-five riders, all wearing huge sombreros and carrying rifles across their big horn Mexican saddles. Walking their horses slowly toward the camp, they pull up quickly when Corey steps from the trees with a pistol held in each hand.

"That'll be far enough. Hold right where you are." Corey cocks both pistols, the sound carries loudly across the space separating the men. He isn't sure they will understand him, but he knows they'd understand the sound of the hammers being pulled back.

"Por favor, señor." The tall man out front of the group smiles widely, holding out his hands. "Why you pull the pistolo on us? It is so unfriendly of you."

Corey looks the speaker in the eye. "What do you want?"

"Perhaps some coffee?" The man looks around the camp, spotting the three long legged thoroughbred geldings, tied beside the wagon. "Perhaps more?"

"No coffee, no nothing." Corey takes another step forward. "Now, git."

The tall, scar-faced speaker, looks to where the Stallings' saddled horses are picketed. Five horses stand hipshot. Only the approaching riders arouse them enough to prick their ears in the rider's direction.

Still smiling, the man returns his attention to where the tall white man stands, his pistols unwavering. "Señor, señor, you are on our land, and yet you ask us to leave."

"Ain't asking you Mex, I'm telling you, and this sure ain't your land."

"You gringos ride in here and claim the land that has been in our family for centuries?" The tall Mexican spits. "Why you do this thing?"

"I doubt it's been in your family at all," Corey smiles. "I'm telling you only once, we've got legal title to this land and we plan to stay, now git."

The scar faced one shrugs his lean shoulders, "Señor, there are twenty five of us, against five of you."

"Yep, you got me there for a fact, but there's fixing to be only twenty four of you. Last chance Mex, if you ain't moving the next time I blink, you're a dead man."

Looking hard into the tall man's cold eyes, then into the mouth of the huge pistols, the Mexican smiles, and with a flip of his hat, he turns his horse back the way he came.

Corey quickly calls to Samuel and Lambert. "Follow them a ways and make sure they leave."

Ben watches as his two younger sons ride off to the west. "You should have sent Caleb with them."

"No, Pa. It could be a trick. There could be more of them hiding, waiting on us to ride out." Corey watches as Samuel and Lambert disappear. "We need you and Caleb here."

It is close to sundown when the two youngsters ride back into camp. Ben has been pacing and fretting, worrying more with every passing hour, they were away. Walking quickly to where the boys dismount, he pats each one on the back, relieved they are back safe. Losing so many sons in the feud, makes him even more protective of the ones he has left.

Corey walks to where they stand. "How far did you follow them?"

"S'pect about twelve or fifteen miles." Samuel loosens his cinch and strips the saddle and wet blankets from the tired bay's sweaty back.

"Did they know or suspect you were following?"

"They knew," Lambert nods. "They watched us coming from the ridges."

"What'd they do?"

"Nothing; nary a thing, just turned and rode off," Samuel shrugs. "Then we followed them further."

"You boys took a terrible chance," Ben wipes the sweat from his hat. "A terrible chance."

"Corey wanted them watched." Samuel looks over at his older brother. "Wouldn't want to disappoint him, now would we."

Corey catches the antagonism in Samuel's words, but chooses to ignore them. "Keep your eyes peeled, they'll be back."

"Is this land really theirs, Pa?" Lambert speaks up.

"Could have been once, don't know." Ben replaces his hat, and pulls a rolled up leather skin from his shirt. "It's ours now, the deed says so. Boys we're here to stay and we're not leaving."

The next two days pass slowly, under the wagon's squeaking wheels. Corey rides point, far ahead of the huge wagons, checking out every small hill that is big enough to hide the Mexicans. Overhead, almost a mile ahead, several buzzards circle lazily, floating gracefully on the air. Corey has been watching them for over an hour, his sharp eyes scanning the tall grass and thickets as the wagons move slowly toward where they circle. Kicking his horse into a short lope, he rides ahead, turning off, down into a small ravine.

Reining the tall bay in hard, just as the horse smells something in the grass and spooks sideways, Corey looks down at the remains of what was a man. Surveying the surrounding prairie for several minutes, making sure no enemy lurks nearby, he quiets the animal, dismounting slowly, kneeling beside the dead body.

"You poor devil." Corey cuts his words off as Caleb and Samuel ride up. "Somebody really done a job on you."

"What happened?" Caleb stares down at the body as Samuel covers his mouth and nose to keep out the stench.

"Don't know, but someone really cut this poor soul up, something awful." Corey takes in the knife marks and burns on the naked torso. "Samuel, ride back and get a couple shovels. Caleb you keep the wagons moving. Don't stop or come near here, there's no need for the women-folk to see or hear about this. You hear me, Samuel? Go get some shovels."

"I ain't deaf, you know." Samuel spins his horse and rides toward the wagons, lashing his horse hard, something he rarely does.

"What's the burr under his blanket lately?" Caleb stares at his younger brother. "I've never seen him so out of sorts."

"I reckon he figures I'm the reason we left Arkansas in such a hurry." Corey shrugs. "You know he had a sweetheart, Miss Nita Fay Lowe, back there."

"Nita Fay Lowe? Why, she was as ugly as a board fence!" Caleb's jaw falls open. "He's mad over her? Shucks, if it were me, I'd thank you and still be running from Arkansas."

"Well, ain't you ever heard brother, love's blind?"

"I did, I heard exactly that, and now I believe it for a bona fide fact." Caleb shakes his head. "Nita Fay Lowe, I'll be dogged. Really, he should be thanking you, probably will too, when he wakes up and gets his head on straight."

"You best be getting along. We don't want to upset the womenfolk."

"How long you figure he's been dead." Caleb steps up lightly, on his gelding.

"Yesterday, in this heat I reckon, no more."

"You figure it was those same Mex's what done him in?"

"Looks that way, the ground is tore up, there had to be at least twenty or more horses." Corey studies the hoof prints of many horse's hooves in the soft dirt. "It was them, leastways that's the way I figure it. Indians don't brand a man."

"Brand?"

"Look at his arms." Corey points to a big H burned into the dead man's left arm and more on his chest and stomach.

"I'll be jiggered," Caleb spits and turns away. "Who'd do a thing like that?"

Four days later, Ben Stallings pulls his wagon to a stop and looks across the Brazos River. Tall trees line the sloping banks of the fair size river. Grass and smaller trees and shrubs take over the land across the flats, before finally turning into a never-ending sea of grass. Pointing his huge fingers across the river, he clucks to the team and eases into the water.

The map is accurate and they are home. As far as the eye can see, this land belongs to the Stallings. No other human laid a plow to it or cut a tree from it. No living soul laid claim to it except the wild things that belong there. The crossing is marked on the map, almost dead center in the middle of the map.

"Right there, in that small canyon, is where we'll build our house, right in the middle of those large oaks and pecan trees." The big man gestures with his chin. "We'll put our corrals and barns there, where the canyon cliffs will protect them from the strong winds that'll come this winter. We're close to the river for water and timber to build, all the comforts of home."

"How far do we own, Pa?" Lambert kneels and scoops up some of the sandy earth.

"The man said we couldn't ride across our land in two days. That's pretty big I'd say."

Lambert looks out across the sea of tall grass. "Well, how do we know when we get off our land?"

"Lambert," Ben breathes deeply and smiles, "I s'pect long before you get that far, you'll be getting hungry and come home."

Lambert doesn't like the answer, but he knows there is no use asking any more questions. Tossing the sand from his clenched hand, he nods and smiles up at Judith and Sarah. Jerking the hat from his curly dark head, he bows deeply to the giggling women. "Reckon we're home, ladies."

"Lambert Stallings, you're such a romantic," Judith laughs.

"Where's the mustangs, Pa?" Samuel Stallings looks the surrounding grasslands over from the seat of the second wagon. Samuel is the horseman of the family. Men actually saw him roll and light a cigarette on the back of a bucking horse. Some declared he could ride greased lightning. Course now, he didn't let Ben see him smoking at his young age of nineteen. Yep, many a local lost their money betting on a bad horse instead of a slender slip of a boy.

"Don't know for sure, Samuel. I reckon as soon as our buildings are finished, we'll take us a look." Ben steps down from the wagon, causing the box to groan under his weight.

"Reckon it'd be alright if I took a quick look-see?" Samuel is horse crazy and itching to start looking for all the mustangs he heard about. They saw a few small herds mixed in with buffalo as they traveled west, but there was supposed to be thousands of the wild horses on these prairies.

Ben looks over at his sons and nods. "Tell you what, we'll take the day off and rest like the good book says. Tomorrow we'll start building, but first, you unharness the teams, then water and stake them out on some good grass."

With a yell of delight, Samuel and Lambert dance around the wagons. Finished with their chores, Samuel saddles the horses and the boys light out. They race their long legged geldings across the flats of what would later become known as Brazos Flats, Texas. Corey watches as his two younger brothers slowly fade from sight. How long has it been since he was as carefree as they are? Maybe out here, in this wild expanse of land, just maybe, he would be able to relax and forget.

Judith watches her brothers race off as she pours feed to the lone milk cow Ben kept. Sitting down to milk, she looks up smiling. "This is a wild country, Corey. I hope they survive to manhood."

Looking down at her, he nods. "They'll be fine out here, Sis. They'll have plenty of room to spread their wings."

"I hope so."

"Is there something bothering you Judith?" Corey kneels beside the cow.

"No, but this is such a huge land, and we're out here alone."

"You scared, kid?"

"Not really Corey, not when you and papa are near, but we are kinda outnumbered with no one to help us, if we need it."

"That's true enough, but we've got one another, so don't worry."

"I'm not really, except," she doesn't finish.

"Except what?"

"It's just, we've lost so many and mama too. I miss them, don't you?"

Corey stands and looks down at her upturned face. Flipping her nose, he nods and starts off. "Yes, I do."

Ben Stallings is a man of his word. Daybreak finds the men cutting timber for their log house and barns that they snaked up from the river bottoms. For two long weeks, the boys fret and work over the big ranch house that will house all of them over the coming winter. Now, only the roof shingles are lacking. They lay out the area for the bunkhouse for the men to build the coming spring. Right now, they need corrals and a barn for their saddles and hay. Both Samuel and Lambert are itching to be in pursuit of the plentiful horse herds they spotted on their first day in this country. However, Ben is adamant, they will build the house, barns, and corrals before the horse hunting starts in earnest.

"Horses ain't gonna do us any good if we can't hold them."

"Pa, what we gonna do with these horses when we catch 'em?" Lambert stands propped up on a double bit axe.

"Drive 'em into town and sell 'em. Settlers coming west are gonna need well broke horses." Ben turns his attention to the posthole he is digging. "Even the army will look for good sound animals for their horse soldiers."

"I would like to be a soldier someday," Colby, pipes up from where he just snaked a heavy log into the yard.

"Colby you better stay here with us. The Injuns are liable to eat you," Lambert laughs.

"I like Indians. They are nice to me, 'sides, they don't eat people." Colby smiles in his innocent way.

"What I seen of the mustangs, they're pretty small, maybe good for riding, but I don't know about pulling a heavy wagon or plow." Samuel stands up a stout cedar pole in the finished hole.

Ben steps off another eight feet and hands Lambert the posthole diggers. The land here is mostly deep sand and easy to dig. "There'll be enough big horses to fit the bill."

Colby stays busy snaking logs from the draws where the cedars grow tall and straight, perfect for corral posts and gates, not like the squat cedars of Arkansas. Further, down in the river bottoms, Caleb's shirt is drenched in sweat from swinging the razor sharp axe all morning. Only Corey is absent from the hard labor of corral building. Ben agreed Corey would stay away from the ranch work. It is more important for him to keep a sharp eye out for intruders.

The Mexicans are out there somewhere. Corey and Ben both know they'll be back in time. Out here alone, without neighbors and only five grown men for protection, the Mexicans will think the ranch is an easy target. The dead man, and the way he died, was on the men's minds. They aren't about to let down their guard for a moment. The work on the ranch buildings will continue without Corey. Someone must keep watch and he is the best one for the job.

Smoke drifts from the large cabin as Judith and Sarah prepare supper for the hardworking men. Everything, except for the men's bunkhouse, is finished. The new logs to build the house and corrals still ooze sap and have the lingering smell of fresh cut wood.

Corey stands alongside the new corral fence, unsaddling a worn out gelding, when Colby runs up, trying to speak. Pulling at Corey's sleeve, he stutters, trying hard to get out the words.

Taking his younger brother gently by the arm, Corey leans over him and talks quietly to the young man. Only around Colby, would Corey show any softness. He has always doted over the boy. Corey remembers his mother, and in many ways, Colby reminds him of her. Gentleness glows from the boy's face, the same gentleness she had. He cannot clearly remember Colby when he was young, before the fever, but he does remember her. Both of them were so much alike.

"Now Colby, calm down, brother and tell me what's the matter."

Unable to speak, the boy points toward the big bend of the river that leads to the Brazos River crossing. Corey's eyes narrow as he looks into the western sun and spots a lone rider coming into view. Corey sends Colby to run to the house to warn the others. Checking the priming on his long rifle, he steps away from his horse to meet the newcomer.

As the rider moves up, out of the river and approaches him, Corey doesn't recognize the man, but he knows the type of man he is. The pack animal, loaded with furs and the animal skin cap atop the man's head, gives him away. He knows either a mountain man or a fur trader is riding slowly toward him. The man's rifle lay slackly across the pommel of his saddle. The man's sleepy but sharp eyes take in the new buildings and corrals. He then focuses on the tall man standing by the corrals, waiting with a rifle held in the crook of his arm. Pulling the bony horse in, the rider looks down at Corey, and waits before stepping down.

Corey looks the old hunter over, studying the road up from the crossing.

"I'm alone boy, if that's what you're wondering."

"Who are you?" Corey has heard many tales of these hard, crusty old men, from hunters back in Arkansas. He is fully aware they can be as dangerous as a bull with a bellyache. His dark eyes don't blink as he studies the trader. He knows the man is watching him just as close.

"Micah Halleck, fur trader." The trader looks into Corey's cold eyes and knows the big man before him is a hard case, if he ever seen one. One that wouldn't shrink from his obligations if he had to kill. Something about the dark eyes, not arrogance exactly, but a self-assuredness, confident in his own abilities, a man that would not back up from hardship. Yes, he knows a few men like this one, not many but a few.

Mountain men, Indian fighters, they have a no-nonsense way about them, and he knows this one is cut from the same cloth. Men like these would as soon shoot you as squash a bug.

"Get down, Mister Halleck. Have some coffee with us." Corey relaxes, letting the rifle hang loosely in his big hands.

"Well, thank you kindly." Micah looks the ranch yard over carefully, then steps down easily for a man his age. "Last time I was through here, this place was only coyote dens and buffalo wallows."

"Name's Corey Stallings, from Arkansas," Corey introduces himself, but the man notices he doesn't offer his hand. "Pa bought this land from some feller back East. Now we own it."

"You people work fast." Micah looks around at all the work that has been done. "Yep, mighty fast."

Ben Stallings, followed by the rest of the menfolk, walks from the house, toward the corrals where the two men stand talking. After introductions all around, they all troop toward the cabin. Micah's eyes narrow, as he steps through the door and spots Sarah and Judith.

"Something wrong, Mister Halleck?" Ben notices the curious look of the trader.

"Nope, not a thing," Micah shakes his shaggy head. "I'm just surprised to see a white woman way out here. Ain't seen one in quite a long spell."

"These are my daughters, Sarah and Judith."

Micah removes his foxtail cap and bows deeply, gallantly to the women, causing them to grin. "Ladies, Micah Halleck at your service."

Both girls laugh, and Judith asks the trader to sit, while Sarah places a steaming cup of coffee in front of him. "Leastways we have a gentleman with us now." Sarah looks shyly at Corey.

Supper finishes and the men pull up seats outside the cabin, beneath the limbs of a huge ageless oak tree. The home site for the house was chosen especially because of the shade the old tree would offer on hot summer days. Ben positioned the house to face due east, with the tree shading the yard.

Micah pulls out his old pipe and produces a foul smelling mixture of some kind, causing Colby to wrinkle his nose and back away quickly. "Don't blame you, lad." Micah laughs. Already, he notices the boy is slow. "Been out of real smoking tobacco nigh on two years now, and I hanker for a good smoke most every day."

"What is it?" Samuel asks curiously.

"Anything I can mix up, from tree bark to, well you probably don't want to know all of it."

Ben smiles knowingly. Not a big smoker himself, he still enjoys his pipe from time to time. "Well Micah, we just may be able to slake that thirst for you. Colby go fetch my tobacco pouch."

The old fur trader's eyes light up, like a pine knot on a hot fire, when he lays his eyes on the pouch. As Ben hands it over, he takes a long deep sniff of the tobacco inside, and closing his eyes, smiles contently.

"This old man thanks you, sir." He nods at Ben. "It's almost like Christmas."

"You trade with the Indians, Mister Halleck?" Corey asks as the old man taps tobacco into his pipe. "I noticed your horse was loaded with pelts when you rode in."

"I do," Micah puffs contently. "Comanche, Kiowa, and if you don't mind, just call me Micah."

"Wow, you ain't scared?" Lambert is infatuated with the man. "I heard they scalp people."

"Nah, I don't fear the red man, just the Mexicans scare me." Micah inhales. "Can't trust them cutthroats, leastways that is since old Santa Annie started running things again down there in Mexico."

Corey straightens up at the mention of the Mexicans. "Mexicans, are there many of them around?"

"Plenty down south. They're alright though, it's the ones out here you need to be careful of."

"Why's that?" Ben leans forward. "Are they different?"

"Yes, sir. Very different." Micah shakes his long hair as he nods. "As different as daylight and dark."

"How so?"

"Most of them out here are renegades from the Mexican army, mean plumb to the bone, tough as whip leather, they are." Micah lights his pipe again. "Slice your throat just for pure enjoyment."

"Why?" Lambert asks curiously.

"Nothing to lose as they can't go back home, old Santa Anna would string 'em up or shoot 'em." Micah puffs on his pipe contently. "They're dangerous boy. Comancheros, they call themselves, real bad men."

"Reckon we met up with some of them renegades of yours a few days back." Caleb speaks up.

"You did? You folks have trouble with 'em?"

"We were fixing to, until Corey sent them packing." Lambert looks across at his brother proudly.

The old hunter turns his eyes on Corey. "You don't say. You put the run on them? Tell me, what happened?"

"Nothing much, Corey told them to ride out and they rode." Ben speaks up.

"They skedaddled just like that?"

"Just like that," Ben affirms. "Don't reckon they had the guts to face his pistols."

"How many you figure there was of them?" The hunter is curious, the pipe all but forgotten.

"We counted twenty five riders," Corey answers. "Could have been more out of sight of us, but I don't think so."

"Were they all wearing big sombreros? Micah inhales, "The one doing the talking was he a tall, dark-skinned feller with a long scar down his left cheek?"

"Most were wearing them big round hats, and the one doing the talking did carry a scar," Ben acknowledges. "You know him?"

Micah nodded "I do, for a fact, saved his life once. He's called Santiago Manuel Hernandez."

Lambert's eyes grow wide. "You saved his life, wow."

"Yep, south of here a ways, horse drug him pert near to death. I got him loose from his stirrup and patched him up. Took some doing, almost a week, when his men found us."

"I'll bet he was sure glad you came along." Samuel speaks for the first time. His own horse had fallen with him once as he was running a cow across a wash. Lying on his side, he couldn't tell if his foot was hung in the stirrup or not. If he let the horse get to his feet, he could have spooked. Sometimes a young horse sees something dragging from him and starts sidestepping, then gets scared and runs off. The rider lying on the ground, with his foot hung in the stirrup, has no way of controlling the animal. Samuel saw a man drug to death once. He was afraid to let the horse up, so he lay there, holding the horse down until Lambert finally came along, looking for him. Yep, he knew exactly how the man felt.

"I reckon he was at that." Micah remembers. "He was hurting pretty bad."

"Reward you, did he?" Ben asks.

Micah grins, pulling up his buckskin shirtsleeve. "He did. His men held me down while he branded me. That, my friends, was my reward."

Corey sits straight up, looking at the H burned into the traders arm, exactly like the one on the dead man back down the trail. "That's all the reward you got for saving his life?"

"Yep, said all I had to do was show this brand and nobody in Texas would bother me again. Kinda like a free pass to travel anywhere I wanted."

"And the Indians, Micah?" Ben is curious, as he has never heard of such a thing. "Do they honor the man's brand?"

"Now, I don't know so much about them and the free pass stuff, but I get along with them since they trust me." Micah puffs happily. "Course now, I've been out here in this country quite a spell, and traded many a time with them and even their fathers."

Corey and Caleb both stare at the brand on the man. "Bet that hurt like the dickens." Lambert pipes up again.

Ignoring the statement, Halleck becomes curious as Corey and Caleb stare at his arm. "Say, you men act like you never seen a brand before. You know something I don't?"

"Yes, sir. We know something." Caleb clears his throat. "We found that same brand on a dead man, couple months back."

"Dead man, where?" Micah sits straight up with his eyes wide open.

"It was east of here, fifty, sixty miles or so." Corey watches as Micah's facial expression changes.

"This dead man, can you describe him?" The voice is barely audible. "Can you tell me what he looked like?"

"Maybe, but he was messed up. Young man he was, maybe twenty five or so, slight of build, medium height."

"And his hair, what color was it?"

Caleb shrugs. "Can't say for sure, he was burned; it may have been brown."

"His eyes, what color were they?"

Corey drops his eyes. He feels Micah is connected with the dead man somehow. Looking up, he looks into the anxious eyes. "I don't know Micah. They had been shot out of his head. I'm sorry."

Everyone watches as Micah drops his head then stands and walks off toward the river. Lambert rises to follow, but Ben waves him back to his seat. "Let him be boy, he's ailing. Maybe this dead man was his kin or something."

"I should have kept my mouth shut." Caleb watches Micah as he walks off.

Ben shakes his head as he watches Micah walk out of sight. "It don't matter much. It'd come out sooner or later."

CHAPTER 4

Thetrap men were busy and the corrals were already full of fighting, kicking mustangs of every description. Traps were set along well-used trails, leading to watering holes. The horses they caught, now fill the corrals, keeping the wildest in the fenced canyons.

Samuel was right, most of the horses were too small to make good working stock. Ben culled all but the biggest and blemish free animals, turning the others back out on the open range. Keeping only the stallions and the larger mares, large enough to work harness. At Ben's insistence, Lambert counts the remaining horses in the canyons and corrals. All total, there are fifty seven head ready to geld, break to saddle or wagon, and head east, to the first town they come to. It was a fight to bring the wild horses from the canyon traps to the corrals. After snubbing each mustang between two powerful geldings, the mustangs are at least broke to lead when they reach the ranch.

After returning from the river, where he walked alone, Halleck asks for a pencil and paper. He sketches out a rough map of the grasslands and settlements to the east and south. Few words were spoken by the trader and the dead man was not mentioned. Halleck only asks where the grave is. Unfamiliar with the country, Corey and Caleb could only give the old hunter a few landmarks in the grave's vicinity that they remember. Halleck warns the Stallings to watch out for Hernandez and his men, or the Indians that frequent the land. The old trader thanks them, saddles his horse, and rides away quietly, without a backward glance.

Corey watches curiously as the old trader crosses the river and disappears into the ample growth of mesquite trees. Shrugging his shoulders absently, he pulls his pistols and checks the priming on each. A practice of pure habit, but it is one habit that keeps him alive.

Manny Sharps, with his two cousins following, ride into the sleepy town of Red Bluff, just as the sun begins to set. This is where he was told to wait. The town is a staging point for all travelers heading for the Texas frontier. Red Bluff is also wide open for the frontier characters unwanted in other larger towns. The newer and larger town of Jacksboro is only a few miles distant, but Sharps was instructed to go to Red Bluff and wait.

Corey Stallings ruined him in Arkansas. He was an outcast, branded a coward by his Uncle Pike. Now, Stallings and his family will pay. Sharps knows Ben Stallings left Arkansas with a small fortune from the sale of his farm and cattle. Manny Sharps wants that money, but he wants Corey Stallings worse. Plus, there is one other thing; Sarah Pike, now Stallings. He has been in love with her since they were children. Now he will have her too, even though they are cousins, she will be his. Sharps smiles evilly, Levi Pike will know his daughter is the woman of Manny Sharps.

Sharps has been in touch with a man that knows Texas. Slocum is his name, an outcast that knows where to find the men Sharps needs to get his revenge. Men, he was told, lived by bloodshed and violence, exactly the men he wants. Word was sent for him to wait in the town of Red Bluff until he is contacted. Sharps hates taking orders or waiting on anybody, but this time he has no choice; he needs help. This is not Arkansas and he is completely lost in the huge land of grass and mesquite trees.

The small cantina sits back on a dark street on the Mexican side of town. Sharps with his cousins, Lon and Rafe, sit in the back of the room eating tortillas, beans, and downing the fiery Mexican drink Tequila, like it was water. Invisible from the front of the room, their sharp eyes take in everything happening inside the little cantina. From the Mexican girl, dancing and swirling, and the three-piece band, to the dark skinned vaqueros, standing belly up to the bar.

Occasionally, dark eyes shift their way, curious why gringos would be here in a drab little cantina, instead of across town whooping it up in the bigger saloons of the whites. No eyes linger long on the three gringos. They are all vicious looking men. Tall, redheaded Manny Sharps, is even more of an imposing figure. Three revolvers, two in holsters and one in a shoulder rig, hang from the man. A huge bowie knife hangs from his gun belt. The Mexicans have seen his type before, a pistolero, looking for trouble, a born killer, vicious as a loafer wolf. Manny lets his cold eyes drift slowly over the crowd, then resumes eating.

The bitterness from being branded a coward by his Uncle Levi, rankles him, even here in this remote little place where he is not known. He knows the people inside the cantina are watching. Did they know about him? A bully with a hair-trigger temper, when he was up against lesser men, tonight Manny is on the prod. The tequila is warming his insides, igniting the hate, giving him the bottle nerve that would make the natural killer in him start to come forth. Tonight he feels it, the meanness. Tonight he will show everyone he is no coward.

Lon and Rafe know the moodiness of their cousin. They know the Tequila is bringing his hard personality to the surface. Both grin at each other, they have seen the same thing happen in other towns. Both men are cut from the same mold as Sharps, meaner than a wild boar. Why their uncle Levi Pike labeled him a coward, they didn't know. They heard rumors of what happened, but to them, words are cheap and mostly lies. They have never seen the cowardly side of Manny. They have seen the mean side, many times, and from the looks of him, they are fixing to see it again.

Snaking his long arm out, Sharps pulls the beautiful dancer into his lap as she passes, holding her around the waist with one arm and forcing a kiss from her. Screaming, the woman tears from his grasp, the knife in her hand dripping blood. Sharps looks down at the blood running from the long cut on his arm. Standing slowly, he pulls his revolver as two vaqueros step between him and the girl.

The pistol's roar cannot drown out the cussing and hysterical laughing of Sharps, as he empties one pistol, then pulls another. He keeps firing at the two men and girl, who collapse dead to the floor. Grabbing Manny's gun arm, Rafe pushes him through the door and out into the night air while Lon covers their retreat.

Slinging his arm loose, Sharps fires one last round through the cantina's door before stumbling off, down the dusty street, to the white side of town. Lon studies the street. Somewhere, there is a lawman of some sort, but here in Mexican town, he doubts anyone will even bother to investigate the shooting. Most figure it was just some Mexicans getting liquored up and fighting. Still, he keeps watching their backs as Sharps staggers unsteadily in the middle of the broad street toward a large, well-lit saloon.

Lon turns his head as Rafe falls in beside him. "Old Manny is a caution, ain't he though?"

"Yeah Rafe, he's a real caution alright." Lon shakes his blond curly head. "Trouble is, one of these days he's gonna get us hung, sure as shooting."

"Shucks Lonnie, they were just Mexicans for Pete's sake," Rafe grins widely.

"Yes, sir. Old Manny showed them greasers alright."

"Defenseless Mexicans, brother Rafe," Sometimes Lon can't understand his brother.

"They had guns, didn't they? And the girl, she done up and cut Cousin Manny with a knife."

Sharps enters the huge saloon and weaves his way through the crowd to again take a seat in the rear. Ordering whiskey, the three men study the large assortment of men occupying the room. They have no idea who they are waiting for, only that he is supposed to find them.

"We could be here a month, waiting for a man we don't even know," Lon grumbles. He wants to pull out, with the shooting and all. This waiting around, like sitting ducks, makes him nervous. "If whoever this character is, comes at all."

"Cousin Emmett says we should wait here, until a man named Josh Slocum finds us so we're waiting." Sharps stares across the table at Lon. "He'll come. I promised him good money to join us here. We need him and his men."

Rafe slowly straightens in his chair and drops his eyes. "Manny, there's a badge studying us from the end of the bar."

"So?"

"A Mexican just came in, spoke to the lawman, nodded at us, then ducked back out the door."

"We ain't done nothing, just defended ourselves."

"Well, maybe so, but here he comes."

Sharp's whiskey sodden eyes find the tall man wearing a town constable's badge on his shirt, making his way to their table. Stopping in front of them, only an arm's reach away, the lawman stares down at Sharps.

"Can we help you, Marshall?" Sharps grins drunkenly.

"You men do some shooting over on the Mexican side of town tonight?" The man is indeed tall, an inch or two over six feet. A handlebar mustache covers his mouth and lips. The eyes are icy, cold as frost on a window.

"Self-defense Marshall, purely self-defense." Sharps shows the man his slashed arm. "Dang woman tried to cut my arm off."

"That's up to the judge; hand over your guns." The hard voice makes Sharps sober up some, as he studies the constable. The man's hand is poised above his pistol butt.

"I told you it was self-defense."

"You're under arrest, now hand them over."

Lon moans under his breath. He cusses himself, knowing they should have ridden on. Now the fat is in the fire. If Manny kills a lawman, they'll hang for sure, that is, providing they don't get killed in the process.

Sharps stands unsteadily to his feet. "Nope, ain't gonna do that. We'll turn ourselves in at sunup, then we'll go see your judge."

The cocking of shotgun hammers sounds like thunder echoing across the barroom. All three men turn as the saloon becomes deathly silent. Their eyes focus on the huge mouths of two sawed-off shotguns, pointing directly at their midsections. The deputies holding the guns are a rough looking pair and a blind man can tell they aren't bluffing. At ten feet, they know, their shotguns could tear a man in two.

Sharps pales slightly, and grins as he eases his pistols out, butt first. "Sure didn't know you were serious Sheriff, sorry."

The tall man never blinks as he points with his finger toward the door.

Lon only shakes his head in disgust as he hands over his pistol. "Yep, and the hanging could be more serious than you thought too, Cousin Manny." He whispers as he follows Sharps and Rafe through the swinging doors and into the street.

Josh Slocum stands slouching against the bar as the men pass. He was about to approach Sharps when the constable stepped between them. About to pull his own pistol and intercede, he slowly lets his hand relax as he heard the shotguns being cocked behind him. Slowly he turns back to the bar. No man in his right mind argues with a full load of double-ought buckshot; he will wait.

From what he heard, Manny Sharps has the money he was promised, but to buck a ten gauge shotgun, no thanks. Not even Josh Slocum is that tough, to shoot a lawman in the back to free a man. In Texas, it isn't a good idea, if he is to live a long prosperous life.

Stepping out into the cool air, Slocum watches as the constable herds the three cousins down the street to the jail. Watching, as the lawman, his deputies, and their prisoners, disappear into the small building, he stands across the street and waits. He needs to meet with the constable alone because a man doesn't want witnesses around when he is being bribed. Finally, the two deputies leave the jail, with only a backward wave, as they wander up the street and pass out of sight.

Slipping quickly to the oak door, Slocum raps lightly, waiting. From inside, he hears the rustling of a chair, followed by floorboards squeaking, as boots approach the doorway.

"Who is it?" A hard voice from inside the adobe building growls.

"Josh Slocum, you know me, Andy." The heavy door squeaks harshly as it opens, and Slocum finds himself looking into the barrel of a shotgun, cocked and pointing right at his midsection.

"What can I do for you, Mister Slocum?"

Slocum knows Constable Andy Enloe alright, very well, too well some would say. On several different occasions, Slocum has been locked in this jail and managed to talk his way out of trouble. Months earlier, he was one of Enloe's deputies, at least until he gunned down an unarmed suspect and Enloe fired him, immediately advising him to leave town at once, if not sooner.

"Like to talk to you Andy, that's all." Slocum grins in his lopsided way.

"Thought I told you to get out of Red Bluff."

"You did Andy, and I did leave." Slocum smiles friendly like. "You didn't say how long to stay out."

"Talk!" Enloe frowns coldly.

"Let's go inside Andy, out of sight and hearing."

"You try anything funny Slocum and I'll blow you into next week."

"I ain't about to buck that scattergun, Andy. You know I ain't the heroic type."

Enloe backs into the office, the shotgun never wavers from Slocum.

Sharps' eyes settle, focusing on the man. He heard the constable call the man Slocum and figures this is the Josh Slocum he has been waiting for.

Enloe kicks the door shut with his toe, not taking his eyes from Slocum. "Now, what do you want?"

"Them." Slocum nods his ruddy face over at the two cells where the cousins sit.

"They're prisoners." Enloe eyes Slocum warily. "Will be, at least until Judge Teel hears their story in the morning, then we'll hang 'em."

"I've got fifty dollars apiece for their bail, that is, if you'd be willing to turn 'em out, on my word that they'll show for the trial."

"On your word, Slocum?" Enloe scowls. "Last time I took your word, you shot down an unarmed man, right where you're standing."

"That was just a misunderstanding, you know that."

"Just like this is a misunderstanding, huh Slocum?"

"They're not gonna do anything to them for killing a Mexican, 'cept maybe fine them." The heavy man looks over at the cells again. "You might as well have the money as that worthless judge."

"They killed Maria, Slocum. You do remember Maria, don't you?"

Slocum frowns, yeah, he remembers Maria, Enloe's dancing woman, a lady of beauty who the constable was very jealous of. Of all the people in Red Bluff, why did Sharps have to kill Maria, why her? "I remember her, she was a wonderful lady." Slocum knows, no matter what the judge says, Enloe would never permit these men to leave town alive. "Tell me, which one of them done the shooting?"

Enloe turns his head slightly to nod at Sharps, averting his attention for only a fraction of a second and that is the last thing he remembers. Sharps never sees the heavyset man draw his weapon or even move. Only the pistol cracking on the constable's head and his tall frame crashing onto the wood floor break the stillness. All three men are on their feet instantly, as Slocum takes the keys from the desk and opens the doors.

"You men get your horses and get back here quick." Slocum bends down over Enloe.

"He dead?" Sharps peers over his shoulder.

"No, just knocked cold."

Sharps courage returns and he steps forward now that the constable is disarmed. "I'll finish him."

"Leave him be." Slocum pitches money onto the desk. "Get your horse."

"You're paying out good money to an unconscious man?" Sharps can't believe his eyes.

"I am, now let's move." Slocum pushes Sharps and the others toward the door, wanting to be gone from Red Bluff long before Enloe wakes up.

"Craziest thing I ever saw." Sharps stops and stares at Slocum for several seconds as he buckles on his gun belt.

"He was once a friend of mine." Slocum starts for the door. "I might want to come back to Red Bluff again someday."

Sharps grins viciously. "I'd kill him myself."

Slocum only nods toward the door. "Yeah, I figure you would, now let's move."

They ride through the night, distancing themselves from the town of Red Bluff. Sharps pulls his blowing gelding in behind Slocum as the sun starts to appear in the east. Dismounting, he studies their back trail as the cousins start putting together the makings for a fire. Slocum squats and smooths over a sandy piece of ground, free from any grass.

"You boys pay attention now, we're right here." Slocum points to the ground, using a sharpened stick to trace out a makeshift map. "I'm going after the help I told your cousin about. We'll meet right about here." Slocum stabs the ground.

"How we gonna know we're at the right place?" Sharps scratches his head. "We ain't from these parts."

"You'll know, just stay west until you cross the river, then turn a little north and you'll see the twin buttes. That's where I'll find you." Slocum tosses the stick into the flames.

"How many of them dang Mexicans you bringing back with you?" Rafe sets a blackened coffeepot on the flames.

"Don't know. Normally Hernandez carries twenty or so with him, why?"

"I hate them little brown devils," Rafe swears. "They killed our pa at Goliad, during the war."

Sharps watches, as Rafe glares at Slocum, pushing the coffeepot closer to the flames. "Can you trust them?"

Slocum stands, looking down at Sharps. "Reckon so, at least as much as I can trust you."

"Alright."

Picking up the trailing reins of his horse, Slocum mounts. "It'll take you two days to get there. I wouldn't be late if I were you."

"We won't."

"Good, Hernandez gets a little nervous if he has to wait."

"I said we'd be there." Sharps throws a rough look Slocum's way as the man kicks his horse into a lope to the south.

"You see that you are."

Rafe watches as the man and horse disappear into the vast grasslands. "I don't trust that man, nary one bit."

"Me either, but we need him for now," Sharps adds. "Later, we can dissolve our partnership."

"Can't trust anybody that sides with a Mexican." Sharps kicks dirt over the fire, causing Rafe to leap back as the hot ashes cover him.

"You gone crazy, Manny? You done kicked dirt in our coffee."

"We're riding." Sharps walks to where his horse stands hipshot, his head hanging down. "Now!"

Lon has a bad feeling in his gut as Sharps starts back east, the same direction they just rode in from. What is his cousin up to now? They were heading in the wrong direction to meet with Slocum.

"Where are you heading now, Manny?" Rafe is scratching his head in confusion.

"Red Bluff."

Lon looks over sharply. "Manny, have you gone crazy? That constable will be waiting on us, sure as shooting."

"Good, that's exactly what I want him to do." Sharps grins wickedly. "Constable Enloe ain't running me out of town, no sir!"

"You are crazy." Rafe grins from ear to ear. "We gonna kill that badge toter back there, are we?" Lon shakes his head in disbelief.

"You heard Slocum, we need to head west. This feller Hernandez wants us there on time."

"We need supplies before we head west into a land we know nothing about." Sharps shrugs his shoulders. "You remember, we were gonna get some before we rode out of Red Bluff."

"I remember." Lon shakes his head.

"Good, we'll get our supplies and settle the score with Constable Enloe at the same time."

The three ride warily to the east, watching for any sign of a posse. All three expect Enloe to come charging over the hill, right at them at any moment. He looks like a hard case lawman to them, a man that would not allow anyone to escape or put a blemish on his record. So far, they guessed wrong. There isn't a sign of anyone following them.

Red Bluff is ghostly quiet, as Sharps rides ahead of the other two, down a back alley leading behind the general store. Tying their horses, the three men slip quietly in the back door. Only one elderly clerk works behind the counter, as the three cousins push through a curtain from the back. The store man stiffens as Sharps presses his bowie knife against his throat.

"We've come for some supplies, mister." Sharps jerks the clerk to his feet. "Keep shut and get what I tell you."

Supplies pile up on the counter, as the old man hurries to get whatever the three men order. Sharps takes a double-barreled, twelve gauge, from the gun rack and he examines it. Smiling, he slips two shells in the tubes of the barrel and several in his pocket.

"What you gonna do with that, Manny?" Rafe is curious.

"You'll see, now sack the stuff up and let's get."

"You boys are just asking for trouble. Constable Enloe is nobody to mess with," the old clerk warns them as he retreats behind the counter.

"Where is your constable, old man?"

"Reckon he's over at the jail, but he'll be after you quick enough."

Sharps move closer to the clerk. "After you tell him, is that it?"

Watching the bowie knife reappear in the redhead's hand, the old man shakes his head. "I won't tell anyone, mister. You take the stuff, and welcome to it."

"I thought so."

Lon hears the gasp of the clerk, as the knife plunges into his chest.

"You won't now, for sure."

"Dang Manny, you didn't have to kill the old man." Lon is about ready to split from Sharps, whether Rafe goes or not. Enough is enough.

Outside in the alley, the three men lead their horses behind the small adobe jailhouse and tie them securely. Rafe is grinning as usual. Anything his hero Manny wants is fine with him. Lon, on the other hand, worries. He knows Cousin Manny as usual, is just asking for unneeded trouble. The sun is shining brightly as they gather in the alley.

"You two go around to the front and call him outside." Sharps checks the shotgun and points to the front. "Get him outta that jail and keep his attention.

Lon doesn't like it, but he knows the volatile temper of his cousin, and isn't about to refuse. Enloe surely wouldn't be stupid enough to walk empty-handed out in the street, and Lon remembers the sawed-off shotguns from the night before, all too well.

Walking up the small alleyway, between the two buildings, Lon checks the street. Seeing nothing, he steps out, walking to the front of the jail.

"You in the jail, Constable Enloe? Bring yourself out here, now."

Rafe and Lon stand side by side in front of the jail as the door opens wide and the tall constable steps out onto the sidewalk. The grey eyes are like razors as they stare at the two men.

Recognizing his escaped prisoners, Enloe reaches for his pistol as Sharps steps in behind him.

"Now I wouldn't do that, Constable Enloe."

Turning slowly, Enloe's eyes widen as he looks into the barrels of the shotgun. Raising his hands slowly, he looks into the leering face of Sharps.

"Now that's better, Constable. You remember when you had one of these pointed at my belly yesterday?"

"I remember."

"Well, you should have used it when you had the chance," Sharps grins wider. "Now it's my turn."

The heavy roar of the shotgun, as both barrels go off, bring several shopkeepers and onlookers, rushing into the street. Calmly reloading, Sharps waves the gun at several people near the sidewalk. "You people need a new constable, I believe," Sharps laughs aloud. "I'd appoint myself, but I can't stay, you understand, business elsewhere is calling."

"Let's git out of here Manny, now." Lon steps forward. "My name's Manny Sharps. The next time I'm here, you people remember that." Sharps laughs again wildly, "Manny Sharps!"

Rafe is smiling and strutting like a barnyard rooster as he leads their horses around from the alley. Mounting casually, the three men ride slowly, out of Red Bluff. Sharps stops briefly in front of the saloon, staring at the swinging doors. Lon is beside himself, as he knows his cousin is fixing to go inside and get drunk again. He is just about to kick his horse on down the street when Sharps pulls the trigger on both barrels again, and grins as the two swinging doors are blown from their hinges. Laughing, he tosses the shotgun through the saloon window and leads Rafe and Lon out of town.

"Told you boys, didn't I? It don't pay to mess with Manny Sharps."

Lon looks back and watches as the two deputies, from last night, run up the street, with several townspeople chasing behind them. Lashing his horse cruelly, he doesn't wait to see if Sharps and Rafe are following. Riding up beside him, Sharps hollers over the drumming of the hooves. "What's your hurry, Cousin?"

"You see all those armed men coming after us?" Lon never slows his horse.

"Storekeepers and drunks are nothing much to worry about," Sharps sneers.

Lon only shakes his head. Manny Sharps is either a fool or downright stupid. Any man armed with a sawed-off shotgun is definitely something to worry about. Red Bluff is many miles behind them before their horses are pulled down to a slow walk.

CHAPTER 5

Ben looks across the table where Colby is sitting quietly, eyeing his full breakfast plate. With an enormous appetite for one so small, normally, he is the first one to start eating and the last to finish. This morning he hasn't touched a biscuit or the thick brown gravy the girls prepared.

"What's ailing you lad?"

Colby sits holding his hand against his left jaw. "My mouth hurts Pa, something awful."

Ben stands up, walks around the table, and kneels down beside the boy. Removing the small brown hand, he studies the slightly swollen face and slowly opens the lad's mouth.

"You got yourself a bad tooth, I reckon." Ben pats the boy, moving back to his chair. "Your sister will pack it with cherry and birch. We'll see if that helps."

"Yes, sir." The big eyes look hopefully at his sister. "I hurt something awful."

"I know you do, Colby." Judith walks over to the medicine cabinet. "I'll fix it."

Ben studies the boy a minute, then looks around the table. "This being the Sabbath, we'll take the day off like the good book says."

"Amen." Samuel speaks up, between mouthfuls of food. "I'll drink to that."

"What's ailing you, Samuel?" Corey eyes his brother. He knows

Samuel loves working with the wild horses and rarely misses a day. "You got a bad tooth too?"

"Big brother, you try topping out ten head of broncs a day and then ask me that." Samuel shakes his head. "After riding them mustangs, a man is lucky to have any teeth left in his head at all."

Corey notices Samuel has been gimping around for the last week. He has ridden rough horses, all of his young years, but he has never run into horses as mean and downright ornery as these mustangs. He swears they could jump through themselves, then double back on their tracks and snap a kink right through a rider's back. To top that, if they manage to buck a man off, it's a footrace to the nearest fence, because they'll take a hunk out of a man's backside. He thinks the mustang's name is wrong. They should have been called devil horses. He hasn't started one horse yet that hasn't fought him tooth and nail to the very end. To top that, he doesn't think they'd be worth a plug nickel after they are gentle, if you can gentle them. Even after he rides them down, a rider still can't trust the little horses. They are mean ones for sure.

Most of the horses Ben wants to break and get ready to sell are at least four or five years old. Never touched by a rope or a man's hand, they only know to fight and they will buck, kick, and bite. He has never seen an alligator, but Samuel heard about them by men from the Louisiana Bayous. He figures they don't have anything on these mustangs when it comes to teeth and temper. No, sir, they could out bite anything he has ever heard of.

Samuel looks sourly over at Corey then shovels another fork full into his mouth. It is Samuel's job to ride the rough edges off the wild ones, then Caleb and Lambert put the miles on them so they will be gentle enough to sell. The mustangs are a hardy breed, with plenty of wind and endurance. The boys find, the easiest way to keep them ridden down, after Samuel has them somewhat gentle, is to lope each horse around a large oval track, knee deep in sand. It's a little like cheating the horses, but to ride them across the flats would take a half day riding on each bronc to tire them. They have too many horses that need riding to settle them down. They just don't have the time or inclination. Even the track is a rough ride as the mustangs buck at least halfway around, the first time.

Bored in the ranch house, Judith rides the gentler ones, helping the boys get them ready to sell. Ben warns Samuel several times not to let her on anything that will buck a lick. When asking Sarah if she wants to ride, she declines in a good-natured way, declaring she is a lady and ladies have their own work.

"Samuel, you rest a day or two." Ben interrupts the argument that is fixing to take place between Corey and Samuel. "Have Caleb rub some of old Doc Bailey's horse liniment on your back."

"Yes, sir."

Looking back at Colby, with a father's concern, he smiles. He knows Colby loves to fish more than anything. "Lambert, you and Colby catch some grasshoppers, dig some worms, and fetch us a mess of fish for supper. That is, as soon as Judith puts some fixing on that tooth."

A toothache out here is serious. Ben has seen grown men develop an infection and die, back in Arkansas where there are doctors. Knowing how Colby likes to fish, he hopes the river would take his young son's mind off the hurting tooth. The lad has always been sickly, even after the bad fever and sickness finally left him, which made Ben naturally protective of him.

"Can we go to the big hole, upriver?" Colby brightens up a little. "That's where the big cats are."

Looking over to where Corey is finishing his coffee, Ben waits for an answer. Corey is the outrider of the outfit. His judgment in matters like this is the final say. Corey sets his coffee cup down and looks at the two expectant faces. The big hole the boys refer to is a deep hole of water in the river that holds the best fishing they have found since coming here. Caleb stumbled on it accidentally, or he should say Caleb fell into it by accident. He rode his horse into the river for a drink. The sandy bottom gave way, causing both horse and rider to disappear beneath the water. At first only Caleb's hat floated to the surface, then finally Caleb came up splashing and gasping.

Staring openmouthed, in disbelief, Lambert quickly roped Caleb's horse, catching him around the neck and dragging him back to shore. Lambert still laughs and tells when Caleb sputtered to the surface, his only concern was his old, beat-up hat.

Looking over at Colby, Corey nods, as he too is concerned about the swollen face. "I reckon it'll be alright, just stay alert and be home before dark."

Judith doctors Colby's tooth as best she can. Still, it throbs a little, but the fun of fishing helps diminish some of the pain. Packing the tooth with crushed birch bark, laudanum, and coal oil relieves the steady ache, at least enough for Colby to forget the tooth for the time being. The boys pack their lunch and saddle two gentle, saddle broke mustangs. Waving their hats, they disappear across the flats in a puff of dust, hurrying toward the river to the deep fishing spot. They are eager to get to the fish they know are just waiting to jump on their hooks.

Corey watches them disappear, then swings his saddle on the back of a pinto stallion he has been riding. The mustang is a black and white studhorse, a real beauty. Normally, he would not ride a paint horse, as they stand out like a bright fire, easy to spot. This one though, is special, with a small head and beautiful arched neck, tapering into a short, powerful back and stout clean legs. Yes, he is a thing of beauty. Corey knows he would bring a good price back in the settlements and that's why he is putting so much riding on this particular horse.

Stepping up, onto the paint, he walks a few steps and kicks him into a slow, ground-eating lope, to the south. The old-timers would say the horse could lope in the shade of a small tree all day and never tire himself or his rider. Corey believed them, the horse is a pleasure to ride. Today, he will search the vast grasslands to the south, toward the sandhills looming in the distance. Corey is always looking for signs of intruders, and at the same time, searching for small horse herds. He likes being out alone, away from his brothers and Pa, but mainly Samuel and Ben Stallings, away from their accusing eyes. Yes, he has killed, but so did the Pikes and he would do it again, if needed. Was he a killer? No. He asked himself the same question before; he didn't think so. Did he like killing? No, the men he killed attacked him first, forcing him to defend himself.

Tying their horses in the shade on the riverbank, Lambert cuts two willow poles while Colby retrieves their fishing lines out of his saddle-bags. Propping their rifles against a dead log, the boys plant themselves on the sandy bank, out of the sun and bait their hooks. A dry, hollowed out vine, notched on both ends, tied to their lines, floats lazily on the smooth surface of the river, acting as their bobbers.

Colby laughs in glee as his pole bends nearly double, as a big catfish swallows his hook and worm, almost as soon as it hits the water. Lambert smiles, as Colby manages to land the big fish and put it on a rope stringer. Quickly pulling another wriggling worm from the rusty tin can, Colby is back fishing, as he temporarily forgets his toothache.

The morning passes quickly as the boys sit fishing, enjoying the peacefulness of the slow moving river. They are so quiet, that a small fox creeps down to the river to drink, completely unaware of their presence. Only the current's silent ripple, against the sandy bank, breaks the serene quiet river. Colby quietly watches his line as another fish pulls the bobber under the water.

"You alright, Colby?" Lambert notices his brother's face is swelling more, and he hasn't said a word for a while. The youth looks over at his younger brother.

"No, my tooth is hurting again, something awful."

"Here." Lambert pulls out a paper that Judith gave him and unrolls it. Wetting the folded leaves, inside the paper, he packs Corey's sore tooth and waits for the effect of the birch leaves and laudanum to kill the pain. "How's that?"

Colby only nods his head and leans back, against the dead log, absorbing the warm sunshine and the quiet solitude of the morning. Laying his willow pole aside, he places the wet cloth Lambert gave him against his face. Lambert stands and starts gathering their fishing gear, dumping what is left of the bait into the river. He knows he better get Colby home before the toothache worsens. Turning, he straightens slowly, staring straight into the faces of several mounted Indians, who sit their horses quietly, studying the two youngsters.

Seeing Lambert standing still and not moving, Colby turns to see what he is staring at. Standing slowly, Colby calmly starts toward the Indians, smiling as he approaches them, despite his swollen face and toothache. Lambert doesn't know whether Colby has lost what sense he has left or is putting on a show of bravado in front of the warriors.

Looking to where their rifles rest, he knows he can never reach them. Stepping up, alongside Colby, he puts on a show of cheerfulness, like his brother. In Arkansas, they lived close to some Cherokees and he heard an Indian could smell fear on a man. He also knows they respect a brave man and loathe a coward. Maybe Colby, in his slow way, knows this too.

A broad, chunky warrior, slips from his horse and steps in front of the two youngsters, looking them over closely. Touching Colby's swollen face, he says something to a warrior behind him. Colby winces a little at the pressure on his jaw, but he doesn't pull back or cry out. The warrior studies Colby for several minutes, his face holding an awed expression, almost like fear.

Stepping back, away from the warrior, Colby retreats to the river and pulls the rope holding several catfish they caught, out of the water, and brings them to the warrior. The older warrior looks at the fish Colby offers and nods slowly as he looks deeply into Colby's unflinching eyes for several more minutes. Turning to the warrior behind him, he utters something Lambert cannot understand.

Fearing for his brother, Lambert steps in front of Colby. "He's been sick with fever and it made him slow."

The broad warrior nods again, taking the fish from Colby's outstretched hand. Lambert can't tell if the warrior understands his words.

The leader motions to the warrior behind him, who steps forward and looks closely at Colby as the broad warrior speaks again. "Chief Cayuse says you are brave young warriors, and yes, he sees the other one's mind has gone far," the warrior touches his own head. "He also has a bad tooth."

Lambert is surprised when the warrior speaks to him in English. "I was just fixing to take him home."

"My chief asks that you come with us to our village."

"He needs doctoring," Lambert argues. "He's in pain and I must take him home."

"You will come with us, now." The warrior's face hardens. "My chief orders this."

Lambert is shocked when his rifle and Colby's are handed back to them after they mount their horses. The big warrior, the other warrior called Cayuse, gruffly mumbles something and leads them away at a trot to the west.

"Why do you give us back our rifles?" Lambert looks over where the warrior rides alongside him.

"These warriors are Kiowa, they fear the touched one." The warrior again touches his forehead. "To harm one such as he or take from him, would bring much bad luck on our village."

"But the rifles?"

"You cannot fight all of us." The warrior shrugs. "My chief believes the boy is touched by the great spirits. To harm him would bring the wrath of our grandfathers down on all of us, but you young one, are not protected."

"How far is your village?" Lambert looks over at Colby. "My brother is hurting bad."

"Not far."

"What are you called?" Lambert looks again at the warrior. There is something different about him. He is not the same as the Kiowa.

"The Kiowa gave me the name Kianta Hoye. It means two tongues in your language."

"Because you can speak our language too?"

"Yes, my mother gave me the name Jose Palane."

"Your mother was Kiowa?" Lambert is shocked. "You have white blood too?"

"No, I am half Kiowa, half Mexican," Palane answers. "Some call me half-breed. My mother was Mexican."

"Why are you here with the Kiowa?"

Palane nod and shrugs again. "My father and the Kiowa people captured my mother many years ago. Then I came along. Both my father and mother are dead now."

"How did you learn to speak English, if your mother was Mexican?"

"My mother was Mexican, of Spanish blood and born into an aristocratic family. She could speak many languages."

"She taught you?"

"Yes."

"When we do not return, our pa and brothers will come for us, sure as shooting."

"You're from the house back in the canyons across the flats." Palane looks questioningly at Lambert. "We watched as you rode out this morning. Another one rides a loud colored, black and white pinto, off to the south."

"That was my brother, Corey." Lambert puts on a show of bravado. "It don't pay to fool with Corey".

"You are few in numbers, five men and two women."

Lambert realizes the warrior knows their strength exactly. The ranch has been scouted out, yet the Kiowa haven't attacked or tried to raid the horse herd. "There are more of us coming," he lies.

"My chief has discussed this. We do not think so," Palane laughs. "No, it is just you five against all of us."

"What are you going to do?" Lambert worries now. Would they attack the ranch?

"We go to our village, that is all for now." Palane kicks his horse and lopes ahead.

The Kiowa encampment spreads along the banks of the Brazos River at least twenty miles west of the ranch. It has been a hard, painful ride for Colby. Lambert has thoughts of shooting the warrior Palane called Cayuse, grabbing Colby and making a run for it. His finger almost encloses the trigger of his rifle when the half-breed speaks up, from behind him.

"You would be foolish to do such a thing. Both you and your brother would die." Then, Palane kicks his horse forward, into a trot, never looking back to see if the white still gripped the trigger of his rifle.

Lambert relaxes; yes, it would be foolish. He doesn't even see the warrior circle around behind him. He could try to run, but Colby is in so much pain, running a horse would only cause more pain. He looks around at the Kiowa and their horses, but they are well mounted on fleet-looking horses. Lambert doubts the small mustangs they are riding can outrun the Kiowa's long legged horses. No, Lambert knows, even with the warriors leaving them loose and presumably ignoring them, there is no way they can escape so they must wait. Colby's well-being was entrusted to him. He has no choice but to follow the warriors to their village.

Riding out of the river bottoms, Lambert sees the Kiowa village appear before them. Up and down the river, reaching far downstream, most of the village is back in the shade of the trees, hidden from sight. Horses graze everywhere. Lambert figures they number in the hundreds. Mares, colts, and stallions, are all together feeding quietly on the deep grass growing abundantly along the riverbanks.

Lambert sees hundreds of lodges with their smoke fires burning, stand pointing skywards, proudly adorned with all kinds of symbols and paintings. Horses are tethered outside each lodge in case they need them in a hurry. Lambert eyes the horses, all are long of limb for speed and deep chested for endurance, exactly like the ones that encircled him and Colby. These Kiowa people definitely know a good horse. He knows Samuel's mouth would be watering if he saw them. Women, children, and old people, gather about, watching curiously, as they ride at a walk through the village.

Cayuse stops in front of a skin covered lodge with buffalo skulls painted all over it, and speaks something to Palane. Lambert shrugs loose from his captors as he is pulled roughly from his horse. None lay a hand on Colby as they are in awe of him or afraid. Lambert doesn't know which, but they seem more afraid.

"We take young one inside. Our medicine man Grey Owl, will fix tooth of touched one." Palane motions for Colby to follow him. Lambert starts after them but two young warriors block his path. Seeing the futility of arguing with the determined warriors, he leads his and Colby's horses to some trees and unsaddles them. After rubbing the sweaty horses dry with grass, he leads them down to the river for water. Several hours pass and dark is coming on when Colby emerges from the lodge, smiling down at Lambert. The swelling has gone down noticeably and the youngster appears free of pain.

Lambert looks up at his grinning brother. "They fix your tooth?"

"It don't hurt a lick now, Lambert." Colby looks back at the old man, standing in front of the lodge. "He fixed it good, real good."

"That's fine, Colby, mighty fine." Lambert is amazed. He has no idea what the old medicine man did, but if Colby's tooth no longer hurts, he is thankful.

"I gave him my best skinning knife. Was that alright, Lambert?" Colby stares down quietly at his brother.

Lambert nods. "Yes, Colby, it was alright; you did fine."

Cayuse and Palane walk over to where the boys spread out their horse blankets and reclining comfortably against their saddles. Standing up, as the two warriors approach, Lambert waits.

"The old medicine man says the Touched One has no more pain in mouth." Palane translates the chief's words.

"It is true; I wish to thank your medicine man." Lambert looks down at Colby. "My brother Colby, he is special to all of us. My father will pay you well for helping him."

"My chief will speak with your chief. We will go there with the coming sun, after the young one has rested."

Lambert only nods. Could it be an ambush, a trap of some kind? He remembers Micah Halleck, the old fur trader, saying these Kiowa and the Comanche are a warlike people, always raiding and stealing horses. Why did they help Colby, and why do they want to speak with his father? Halleck's final words of warning, before departing the ranch, was to trust neither Indian nor white man out here, and to trust Mexicans least of all.

Palane grins. "I know what you are thinking; it is not a trap. If we wanted, we could attack your village without warning. My Chief Cayuse only wishes to speak with your chief."

Lambert realizes what the Kiowa says is the truth. With so many warriors, they could overrun the ranch if they wanted to. The Kiowa helped Colby and for what reason, he doesn't know, but they have. Still, uncertain of their motives, he nods. "My chief is my father. He will repay you for your kindness to his son."

"Rest, the women will bring food, but he is not to eat anything except soup for several days." Palane doesn't speak to Colby, only to Lambert. "We will leave before the sun comes again. Rest well and be ready."

Ben paces the long front porch of the ranch house, his eyes looking to the west every few seconds, searching the far-reaching horizon. As supper time approaches, and the boys have not returned, he begins to worry. When Corey rides in at sundown and finds the boys have not come home, he switches his saddle to a fresh mount, riding out without a word to anyone. Ben knows where he is heading. Caleb volunteered earlier to go look for the youngsters, but Ben knows Caleb isn't near the tracker Corey is, so they wait for his return. If Corey needs to track the youngsters, Ben doesn't want any tracks erased.

The deep fishing hole is only a couple miles from the ranch. Ben knows by now, Corey should have reached the river and be on his way back home, providing nothing is wrong. Finally, after straining his ears for hours, but was actually only a few minutes, Ben hears the distant hoofbeats of a single horse, coming at a hard lope toward the ranch. Rushing out to meet the rider, as the blowing gelding slides to a stop, Ben looks west and then at Corey.

"Indians took them, Pa." Corey loosens his cinch strap to let the horse blow.

"Indians?" Ben's eyes question his son. "Are they?"

"No." Corey knows what Ben is about to ask. "They were taken alive; looks like the Indians probably surprised them while they were fishing."

"Why?" Ben wipes his huge hand over his face. "My boys, why?"

"I'll get 'em back, Pa." Corey can feel the old man's pain. "Come sun up, I'll be on their trail."

Caleb and Samuel stand by, stunned, listening to the conversation. "I'll be going with you." Caleb speaks up.

Corey nods, retreating to the corral to take care of his horse. Cussing himself, for letting the boys go off so far away from the ranch alone, he loosens the cinch strap and pulls the saddle from the sweaty back, and curries the mustang. Staring off into the western sunset, he wishes he knew more about the Indians out here. He also wishes Micah Halleck was still here to tell him what to expect from them, and how to get the boys back.

"It's not your fault, Corey." The soft, feminine voice of Sarah, jerks him from his deep thoughts. "You couldn't have known."

Turning, he looks down, into the green eyes of the young woman, wife of his dead brother Eli. He is surprised, as she barely ever speaks to him or acknowledges his presence. He killed her brothers and several more of her kinsmen so he figures she hates him, and justly so.

"I shouldn't have let them go." Corey turns his broad back to her and resumes currying the horse. Caught up in the hatred and bloodshed of the feud, he never had time for women. He was never the woman's man Eli was.

Sensing his nervousness, whenever she is near, Sarah steps around in front of him. She is surprised, as she knows he is a big man, but this is the closest she has ever been to him. Dark skin, like his father, she sees the resemblance in the two. His huge hands, strong shoulders, and back show his massive strength, as did the iron will, shining forth from his dark eyes, eyes as cold and hard as a deep well. She shudders slightly, whether from his huge stature or cold demeanor, she doesn't know. So soon after Eli's death, she is ashamed to admit she is attracted to him. Is it his animal maleness or is it knowing he is a killer, maybe that is what excites her.

"You couldn't have known," Sarah whispers almost inaudibly. She knows the Pikes and even his own family blamed him unjustly for many killings back in Arkansas. "This time, it is not your fault."

"It is my fault. I should not have let them go so far from the ranch alone." Turning the gelding loose, into the corral, he slaps him on the hip and stalks away from the girl.

"Corey." He turns slowly toward her. "Don't blame yourself for my brothers; I don't."

Nodding, he starts toward the barn, walking away from her, then stops and turns around. "Thank you Miss Sarah. That means a great deal to me."

Returning to the house, Corey refuses supper and starts filling sacks with blankets, spare cooking utensils and anything else he can think of to try to trade for Colby and Lambert's release.

Sipping down a hot cup of coffee, Sarah sits before him. Corey stops what he is doing and stares solemnly into the hot coals in the fireplace. Samuel sits in the far corner, cleaning his weapons, his eyes studying Corey closely.

"You reckon they'll trade Colby and Lambert back to us?" Caleb asks from where he is watching curiously, as the packs are loaded.

"I can only try. We're too few to take them back by force." Corey shrugs. "They'd kill the boys before we get anywhere near them."

"What if they just kill you and keep the stuff you're packing?" Samuel speaks up. "What then?"

"Well then brother, I reckon I'll just be dead." Corey looks hard at his younger brother. "Then you can try."

"What about the army?" Judith speaks up.

"There's no army out here, Sis." Caleb shakes his head. "In this, as most things, we are on our own."

Ben Stallings stands up, looking around the room and shakes his head. "We'll get them back. Of that, I have faith."

Corey looks over at his pa. The past few years have aged him. His hair is mostly grey now, the shoulders slightly stooped. Losing so many sons and their mother has affected his health, turned him old.

Judith turns the coal, oil lamps down, as the men retreat to the front porch and sit down. A coyote calls from somewhere in the darkness, then another answers, a nightly, spine-chilling routine on the prairie. Quietness settles along the porch as each man keeps his thoughts to himself. The uncertainty of the coming day weighs heavily on their minds. Again, the lonely cry of a hunting coyote comes from the darkness.

Corey rolls a smoke and settles back, against the log wall of the house. Blowing smoke upward, he feels as helpless as the rabbit that now flees for his life from the hungry pack of coyotes. He wishes again, Micah Halleck were here to tell him what to do. Fighting the Pikes is one thing, fighting an enemy he knows nothing about, is entirely different. He feels almost helpless.

He doesn't even know for sure which tribe has taken the boys. Tomorrow, all he could do is pick up their tracks and follow them, hoping to overtake the warriors before they discover him. Flipping the butt away in frustration, Corey leans back, against the log wall and stares off into the darkness. Tomorrow, there is always tomorrow.

CHAPTER 6

Corey's sixth sense wakes him in the early morning darkness of the cabin. He feels something is wrong and whatever it is, it pulls him from a troublesome sleep. Slipping quietly into his clothes and boots, he buckles on his gun belt. Unbarring the door, he eases it open a few inches, waiting and listening, before stepping cautiously into the early morning dawn. The sun is trying to break the eastern sky, but it is still gloomy and dark outside.

The shadows along the riverbank are black as coal. He cannot see anything, but he senses something or someone is out there. He can feel it.

His dark eyes pass back and forth between the corrals and the river.

"What is it?" Ben steps quietly behind Corey.

"Don't know, but there's something out there, for sure." Corey strains his ears and eyes, trying to see into the darkness.

"I feel it too, you hear that?"

"What?"

"Nothing," Ben whispers. "No frogs, no horses moving around, nothing, nary a sound, that's what I mean."

"I know, Pa."

Ben reaches above the doorframe, takes down his long rifle, and buckles on his pistol. "What do you think? What should we do, Corey?"

"Wake the others and fort up. I'll have a quick look see." Corey starts forward.

"You be careful out there, boy." Ben places his hand on Corey's shoulder as he walks away. Ben shakes his head sadly, as Corey disappears into the dark shadows of the house. This morning is the same, as Corey goes forth, putting his life on the line for his family. He always accuses Corey of being cold blooded, a killer. Who made him this way, Ben Stallings, Levi Pike, the feud? They were all to blame. Corey was just a kid when the fighting began. It has molded him, made him stronger and maybe colder than the others. Ben has always relied on Corey when trouble starts, Corey does most of the fighting, always protecting the family. How many other family members would be lying dead, back in Arkansas, if Corey hadn't been there, standing between them and the Pikes? Ben shakes his massive head. Why was he so rough on the boy, when in his heart, he knows Corey isn't altogether to blame for all the bloodshed.

Slipping silently as a ghost, across the yard to the corrals and barn, Corey feels the hairs on his neck stand up. The early morning is so eerie and quiet, a feeling he has never experienced before. Barely able to see the corralled horse silhouettes, he can tell by their actions, they are sensing something too. His boots don't make a sound on the sandy ground as he eases along the corral fence, cautiously feeling out every step he makes. He remembers Micah Halleck telling him how Indians normally attack in the early morning hours or during a new moon.

Corey stands still as there is no doubt in his mind, something or somebody is out there. He can barely make out the horses, but they are directing all their attention toward the river. Their ears all perk up, pointing due west, toward the heavy timbered bottom where their house logs were taken. Something or someone is down there and whoever it is, remains hidden.

Kneeling down, beside the corral, he waits as the sun is slowly showing itself in the east. Indians, Corey cusses under his breath when he is finally able to make out the line of horses waiting near the woods. Still too dark to make out their individual faces, he can tell each horse is carrying a rider.

Retracing his steps, silently back to the house, Corey finds the others waiting for him on the porch. Ushering them all back inside, he finds the house shutters closed and every weapon they own is lying across the kitchen table. Samuel is already on the roof in the small log enclosure.

"What'd you find out there?" Caleb speaks as he opens a firing port in the heavy shutters.

"Indians, lots of them, enough to go around."

"What kind?" Corey shakes his head. "It's still too dark to tell, even if I knew my Indians, which I don't."

"Probably Comanche, the kind Mister Halleck said to watch out for." Judith speaks up.

Sarah pales slightly, moving closer to Corey. Closing the porthole, Corey pats her hand softly, trying to reassure the girl. "It'll be alright, Sarah. We've got a good strong place to hold them off."

Nodding, she tries to put on a brave front. "I know it's just that I've heard about Indian raids back home. With the boys held captive and all, are you sure they're alright?"

"For now they are." Corey tries to reassure the frightened girl. "I think maybe I seen 'em out there."

"We've got six rifles in here, gal. They won't attack us yet." Ben fought Indians most of his life, back east. He knows an Indian would not waste his life foolishly, attacking a fortified position because there is no glory in it. No, he doesn't figure they will attack, not right now.

Palane studies the dark house. His sharp eyes saw the tall figure slip like a shadow across the yard, back to the house. The whites are alert and they will not be surprised. Always before, in their raiding, they attacked with the early morning light, always surprising the white people who lay asleep inside their walls. Riding forward alone, he stops his horse thirty feet from the ranch house. He smiles slightly, the house is dark as night but he knows several eyes are on him, wondering what he wants.

The warrior sits immobile, his dark eyes watching intently as two men step through the door. Big, powerful men, he can tell they are father and son, almost spitting images of each other. He can also tell the men are fighters, not afraid and cowering, like some he has seen. These men carry their shoulders straight, their chins stuck out, proud men, men that would be dangerous adversaries if it comes to a fight.

Ben and Corey study the warrior, sitting straight as an arrow, astride a long-legged bay horse. Arrogance or maybe haughtiness emits from the warrior. Breechcloth, leggings, and leather moccasins are all that adorn the warrior's body. Strong arms and a heavily muscled chest, match the man's well-proportioned body. A short bow, with a quiver of arrows is strapped to the man's back. The warrior's dark eyes focus on the two men, unblinking, curious.

The jingling sound of small bells, attached to the warrior's armband, ring out, as he raises his arm and points at the line of warriors near the tree line.

Turning in unison, their eyes take in Lambert and Colby, sitting their horses beside a warrior attired in a long bonnet of feathers hanging down his back. Ben starts forward, but Corey places his hand on his father's arm.

"We have brought the Touched One and the other young one back to you safely." Palane studies the two men. "Our healer fixed the Touched One's tooth."

Corey is curious, why would the warriors help his brothers? What did they want? "We thank you for bringing our brothers home safely and for doctoring the sick one."

"Our Chief Cayuse will speak with your chief." Palane studies the faces of the two whites closely. He can see rifle barrels protruding from the white man's house, their barrels aimed straight at him, but he says nothing, nor does he let it show.

Ben steps forward. "You have brought my sons home safely. We are indebted to you. You're chief is welcome to my home."

The ranch house yard is full of horses and mounted warriors. Lambert and Colby are pulled into the strong embrace of their father as they dismount. Palane introduces Cayuse to the two whites, following the men to the front porch to find seats.

Corey has Caleb and the women, stay inside, out of sight. The warriors seem friendly enough, but Micah warned them not to trust anybody, Indians, whites, or Mexicans. Only Chief Cayuse and Palane dismount and the rest sit stoically on their horses, not moving, their faces blank with no visible expression showing.

"I wish to thank the Kiowa and their great Chief Cayuse for helping my sons and bringing them home safely." Ben speaks, as Corey stands back, listening, amazed. His father seems at home, conversing with the Kiowa.

"We could not do otherwise. The spirit people would be mad at the Kiowa if the one with the faraway mind was not helped." Palane translates the words of Cayuse. Corey knows the warrior speaks the truth. Even back east, the tribes of every nation treat a person whose mind they thought had gone far with much respect. Many a trapper pretended to be mad, to escape death when capture was imminent.

Lambert steps beside Samuel, seeing the confused look on his brother's face, "They call Colby the Touched One because he's slow."

"Why?" Samuel, who just descended from the roof, still does not understand. "Why would they call him that?"

Lambert shrugs. "They mean no disrespect, quite the contrary. They hold Colby in high esteem because he is slow. They think the Great Spirit looks over him."

Samuel nods slowly, beginning to comprehend their meaning. "I see."

Palane stares hard at Ben. "My chief wishes to know why you are here, why you chase our horses, and how long your people will remain here."

Ben studies Cayuse for several seconds before answering. He knows he is on shaky ground here and thinks out his answer carefully. "We come here from the east. My people bought this land from the big chief in Austin." Ben watches the Kiowa's face closely. "The horses are just running free, so we take what we need to work the land."

"How can the white chief, in this far away place, sell this land? It is ours."

"I thought the land of the Kiowa lies to the north in the Indian badlands, or out on the Llano Estacado."

Palane interprets. "This land has always belonged to the Kiowa and Comanche. You will pay us if you wish to live here."

Ben nodded politely. "What does the Kiowa want for this land?"

"We wish only to pass through this land in peace and speak with the young one, to see if he is okay, no more." Palane nods at Colby as the two whites look at each other in confusion. "In return, my chief gives you his word to watch over the Touched One."

"Then we have an agreement. You are welcome on this land anytime you wish to cross." Ben looks at Cayuse. "Also, you can see Colby anytime you want. Now, we would like to pay you for taking care of my son and healing his tooth."

"Whiskey, we like whiskey," Palane speaks up.

Corey shakes his head. "No whiskey. We have no whiskey."

"Cayuse has not asked for much, just whiskey." Palane speaks softly. "You give whiskey, make chief happy."

"We have no whiskey. We do not drink."

"Maybe, white man lies."

"I do not lie." Corey holds up his hand, walking toward the corral, leaving Ben to talk with the Kiowa.

Ben speaks to Lambert, who disappears inside the house. "We do not have whiskey, but my son will bring coffee and biscuits."

Palane nods. "This is good; my chief will eat with his new friends." Corey halters the pinto stud, stroking him softly on the neck, before taking him from the corral. Leading the prancing stallion toward the house, he hears the murmurs of approval from the mounted warriors, as he leads the Pinto by them. Stopping in front of the porch, Corey turns the horse slowly in circles, first one way then the other. Making a hackamore out of the lead rope he had on the horse, Corey nods at Samuel.

"Samuel, show these gentlemen how this horse handles."

"Yes, sir, your honor."

Palane does not completely understand the words of sarcasm, but he does understand the tone. He knows these two brothers are not on the best of terms. He watches closely as Samuel takes the lead from the bigger man, and swings easily upon the broad back.

Slowly at first, he loosens him up by walking the stallion around the yard. Samuel then works the horse into figure eights, rollbacks, circles, lead changes, and finally kicks the horse into a hard run from the yard. Almost reaching the corrals, he spins the Pinto and brings him charging straight back at Palane, bringing the stallion to a sliding stop, almost on top of the unmoving warrior.

Unruffled at the near collision, Palane nods his head and looks hard at Samuel as he strokes the animal's fine neck. "You ride well for a white man."

"That I do." Samuel stares hard at Palane. He seems to challenge the warrior. "Better than most."

Wanting to change the subject, before they say anything else, Corey steps forward and takes the blowing stallion's lead rope. "This is a great horse, a horse for a great chief to ride. We wish you to have him for what you have done for the young one." Corey hands the halter rope to Cayuse.

A slow smile spreads on the chief's face as he steps from the porch, accepting the lead rope. His hands stroke the fine neck as he nods his head in approval.

"The horse is much better than whiskey, huh Palane?" Lambert grins at the half-breed.

Palane only nods. "Cayuse like whiskey, but him like horse more maybe."

Corey watches as the last of the warriors disappear into the west. Naturally suspicious, he doesn't believe the Kiowa came to the ranch, just to ask permission to cross their land in peace. No, there is more. With their great numbers, these warlike people don't have to ask anyone's permission to ride where they want. Whatever they are after, he doesn't know. Maybe they just want to check out the whites, anyway, they fixed Colby's bad tooth and he is thankful. Something nags at him. There is definitely some other reason the Kiowa helped the boys and brought them home safely.

Quickly saddling a dun gelding, he leaves the yard at a lope to follow the hard riding Kiowa. It could be as they said, but he follows them until they are well away from the ranch, just to be sure. Ten miles pass and the warriors are still heading due west. Corey is about to turn for home when he sees a lone warrior ride from behind a mesquite thicket and head his way. Quickly unsnapping the pistol straps on his revolvers, Corey nudges his horse forward, all the while studying the oncoming rider. He recognizes the man and the sound of the bells. He is the same warrior who was translating back at the ranch. Corey studies the surrounding grasslands for any more approaching horsemen. Reining in with less than ten steps separating them, the two men study each other.

"You follow Kiowa, why?" Palane speaks first. "Maybe, white man, you no trust Indian?"

"Maybe."

"Kiowa no lie. Chief Cayuse come see white man village earlier. Then we find the Touched One on way home and take him back to village. We fix him."

"Like I said before, for that, I thank you." Corey sits his saddle slackly, his big hands resting on his saddle horn.

Palane looks far off, across the grassy plains. "We have watched you since you came here. If we wanted to harm your people, they would all be dead."

"You might find we Stallings don't die easy, my friend." Corey smiles slightly.

"This is foolish talk between friends. I go, white man. Maybe we meet again."

Corey nods his head and turns his horse, pointing him back to the east and home. He is still suspicious why the Kiowa came, but being suspicious is just his natural disposition. He has always been distrustful of anything or anyone he didn't fully understand. Many times in the past, it paid off for him.

"White man!" Corey stops his horse as the warrior calls out and turns back to where Palane still sits. "Maybe you should worry about the Mexicans. The brown men watch you."

Corey waits until the warrior turns his horse and rides out of sight. Puzzled, Corey turns his gelding back to the ranch and wonders why the Kiowa told him the Mexicans are watching the ranch? Why was he so interested in the welfare of whites? This is a big land. Yes, the Mexicans could be watching the ranch, but as of yet, he hasn't seen any signs of them while riding the range, none at all.

CHAPTER 7

Dust and sand clods fly everywhere around the cedar corral as the roan mustang, Samuel is topping out, bucks and bellows, back and forth across the sandy ground. Ben, Colby, and Lambert watch, perched in safety on the top rail. Caleb stands near the gate, ready to come to Samuel's aide, if needed.

Several times, the roan has thrown himself sideways, landing on his side, trying to pin Samuel under him. Finally, in disgust, Samuel holds the roan down, while Lambert hog-ties him where he can't get to his feet. Covering his eyes with a blanket, they leave him lying where he is, for a couple hours. A horse that can't see, or get to his feet, is a scared horse, and Samuel is hoping the roan will be too scared to throw himself again. Most times it worked. Sometimes, with a hardheaded horse, or one that is loco, it fails and you have to do it all over again.

"I think you should just turn him back out on the range." Ben hollers from his perch on the fence. "Before he kills you or breaks your neck."

"No, sir." Samuel jerks the rope from the horse's front legs. "He's a red roan and I ain't never seen one that was easy to break. Plus, I've never seen one that, when broke, wasn't a top grade horse. Most are tough as nails."

Letting the roan back to his feet, Samuel steps smoothly back into the saddle. He can feel the power of the animal as he leaves the ground. This time the roan stays on his feet, not trying to get down, but he bucks and bawls. Ben swears later, you could hear the horse bellowing all the way back to Arkansas. Finally, sweaty and blowing, the roan stands spraddle legged, in the center of the corral. It has been a tail twister of a ride, but the roan horse finally figured out he was fighting a losing battle.

Samuel lets him blow a while, then touches him lightly with his off spur. Not wanting to give up, the horse crow hops a few more times, but the fight has gone from him. Oh, there will be days, he'll put on a little show, but not like today.

Samuel nods knowingly, plow reining the tired roan around the corral. It has been a fight, but treated gently and trained with a soft touch, now he should make a good horse. Samuel smiles, the roan has a Roman nose, which just adds to his character, but he has never seen a Roman-nosed horse yet, that wouldn't buck a lick.

As the horse is led from the corral, Ben laughs. "He's a tough 'un Samuel, but then, so are you. Your nose is bleeding."

"He'll be a good horse in time, Pa, but for now, I better ride him myself." Samuel wipes the blood from his face. "If he dumps someone, he'll go sour again, then we'll have this same fight again."

"Sounds like a good idea to me." Lambert laughs, wanting no part of the roan. "Brother Samuel, you can have my part of them kind all to yourself, cause I sure ain't selfish, not one bit."

"I want to ride the next one." Colby jumps down from the corral. "It's my turn."

"Now Colby, you know your job is to ride the ones in the other corral." Ben looks over at his slender son.

"They're broke already." Colby squares his shoulders. "I want to ride one of these."

"Which one you want cut out brother?" Samuel reaches for his lariat. Colby has pestered him for days to ride and Samuel figures to let him get it out of his system, even if it means he might get thrown a few times. Maybe a few good jolts on the ground, might change his mind.

"That little horse over there." Colby points at a small buckskin gelding, standing in the catch corral. "I'll break him for Miss Sarah."

Samuel smiles knowingly. "Alright Colby." He knows Colby is sweet on her. Shoot, he reckoned they all were, with the possible exception of Corey, who never thought of anyone, only the ranch and killing.

Samuel eases the gate open and steps through, playing out his loop slowly, as he moves toward the milling horses. Whirling the loop once, he lets it fly backhanded, watching it settle perfectly over the gelding's head.

Not familiar with the bite of a rope, the little gelding flies straight into the air, pawing and running backward. Samuel fights to stay on his feet as the buckskin pulls him, sliding around the corral. Lambert opens the gate into the larger corral and lets the horse out. Reaching the snubbing post, Samuel dallies and starts working the fighting gelding closer, inch by inch, to the post, taking up the slack in the lariat as the horse pitches and lunges.

Lambert ropes a hind leg on the buckskin, stretching him out to the corral. Standing, spread out on three legs, the horse can't kick, bite, or paw, while the boys saddle him.

Samuel looks over to where Colby waits. The buckskin is ready. The saddle is cinched down and a blindfold now covers the bronc's eyes. Ben sits atop the cedar rail, saying nothing. Colby, as a child was sickly. He always knew the lad was babied too much, but he can't help it. Concern shows in his face, concern of a loving father. Ben knows Colby wants to show he is a man and he wants the others to respect him as a man. He wants to do a man's work. Colby has ways like his mother, gentle and easy going. He reminds Ben of her, more so than even Judith, who favored her mother as well.

"You sure you want to ride him, brother?" Samuel gives Colby another chance to back out.

Samuel knows, watching a bucking horse pitch from the ground is one thing. However, walking toward a bad horse, about to step on board, makes a man wonder if he has the nerve. Many men found their chili come up, when they started to climb on a loco bronc, one about to explode. It is definitely dangerous work. When that old ground comes a meeting you, it is mighty unpleasant. Any horse can be rode and any rider can be thrown, but for either to happen, a man has to get in the saddle, and some men just don't have the grit.

Colby never says a word, as he eases up beside the buckskin. Samuel grabs a fistful of ear and twists it, as his brother steps nimbly into the saddle. He has to admit, as he pulls the blindfold and turns the horse loose, Colby shows guts. He doesn't seem afraid in the least. Now, if he could loosen up and keep both feet firmly in the stirrups.

The buckskin stands for a few seconds, blinking. Reaching around, he tries to take a bite out of Colby's leg. The hard toe of the youngster's boot finds the soft, tender muzzle of the horse and the wreck is on. For a small horse, Samuel has to admit, the little buckskin could sure get in the air. Colby rides him four good jumps before being launched several feet in the air.

Landing flat on his back, Colby turns over, crawling several feet, trying to get his breath back. The corral floor is sandy and broke up from the many horses passing through, but landing flat on his back still knocked the air out of him. He can hear Colby gasping for air. Rolling to his knees, as Samuel catches the buckskin again, Colby stands slowly to his feet and retrieves his hat. Spitting dirt from his mouth, he starts unsteadily over to where the horse stands.

"You want me to ride him, Colby?" Samuel looks closely at his brother. "You done took the edge off him."

Shaking his head, Colby pulls his hat down hard and waits for Samuel to ear the horse down. "No, I ain't took anything off him, but I will this time."

Ben wants to interfere, but he doesn't want to embarrass his young son. Some things a man just has to do, and getting on this horse is Colbys.

"Get you a hand full of that hame strap and hang to him, brother." Samuel nods at the leather strap around the swells of the saddle. "And watch his ears."

"Ride him Colby," Lambert hollers as the buckskin bucks around the corral.

Corey rides up and sits outside the corral watching, as Colby flies through the air for the fourth time. Shaken and covered with dirt, Colby picks himself up from the ground and kicks a dirt clod disgustedly. Colby is sore and give out, plus he has a bloody nose, but the buckskin is tiring as well.

"Why don't you let him rest tonight, then we'll finish him tomorrow." Samuel is holding the lead rope of the gelding.

"You get back on him, Colby lad. Show us you can ride him," Corey yells encouragement.

Shaking his head, Colby hitches up his pants and starts for the buckskin again. "I'll ride him this time."

"Well little brother, I'll say one thing, you're a glutton for punishment, but you sure got sand." Samuel takes a good hold on the buckskin again as Colby stiffly climbs aboard. "He's tired, so just stay with him a couple more jumps."

Corey watches with a hard-set to his jaw, as the buckskin squats down and erupts again, reversing himself and bucking back down alongside the corral fence. The little horse has some real tricks in his bag, but he is tiring. On the other hand, so is Colby. Corey is proud of the youngster. Very few men would have the nerve to keep getting back up on the little mustang.

Twice more, Colby hits the ground a rolling, but finally the horse gives out and starts walking around the corral with his head down. The youngster won, and has a grin on his tired and bloody face to prove it. Corey nods to him, riding on to the house. Tomorrow morning, he doubts the boy would be able to get out of bed by himself, but for today, he was proud. He has earned his respect and that's what a man needs more than anything.

Breakfast is a noisy jumble of dishes and hungry men, eating their fill. Ben sits sipping coffee, his eyes roving over his five sons. He is proud of each of them, all different, but all Stallings men.

His mind also wanders back over the fine sons he has lost. Looking across at Sarah, he remembers Eli. Tall and arrow straight, Eli was his third son, born in the middle of a hard snowstorm. Ben's horses were all out in the pasture. He was forced to walk eight miles downriver for the doctor, a walk he never forgot. Snowflakes the size of walnuts, blew sideways in the wind, almost freezing him solid. Several wolves shadowed him all the way into town, almost to the doctor's house. No, that was one night he never forgot, but when the wail of Eli's small voice pierced the cabin, it was all worth it.

Shaking his thoughts loose and back from the past, Ben looks about the warm room. "We got ourselves forty well-broke horses in the corrals, all branded and ready to go." Ben cleared his throat. "We need to take them into the nearest town which I figure will be Jacksboro."

"That's the closest big settlement alright." Corey rode the trail into the small town of Red Bluff only last month for supplies. "Shouldn't take over a week to get there and back, it's just a few miles past Red Bluff."

"Good," Ben nods. "You'll leave at first light."

"Who's going, Pa?" Colby stares expectantly across the table.

Ben studies the boy and looks over at Corey. "Reckon three riders should be enough, don't you?"

"The horses are trail broke good enough, they should follow along easily. Three should do it."

"Then you Corey, Samuel, and Colby will take them into town." Ben smiles when Colby lets out a yell.

Corey looks across at Ben then over at Colby. Well, the boy proved himself a man yesterday. It's time for him to take his rightful place as a Stallings.

Early the next morning, Corey stands by his saddled gelding and waits until Ben shakes hands with Samuel and Colby, then walks over to him. Looking about the homestead, they had built from the wilderness, Corey nods. The family has been here less than a year, but they have prospered. He has finally been able to relax and enjoy living.

"If I were you Pa, I'd keep the boys close, just in case." Corey doesn't offer to shake his father's hand, nor did Ben expect him to.

Ben looks into his son's eyes. "You expect trouble?"

Corey lets his eyes wander, far out toward the small hills. "Yes, sir, trouble is always just over the hill. I would stay alert."

"You want us to fort up until you get back, is that it?" Ben looks over to where the girls are standing.

"Yes, sir, I do," Corey follows his father's stare. "Just to be on the safe side."

"Alright Corey, we'll stay in close. You all have a safe trip."

Corey's eyes linger on Sarah for several seconds. Then he tips his hat to her, before turning toward the corrals.

The old bell mare leads the small band of horses quietly along the same trail she followed on many occasions as a young mare on her way to the Brazos River crossing. She was the lead mare in one of the bands of horses they captured, and Samuel insisted they keep her to lead the horses to town. It has been a good decision. She's old, but trail wise and a good traveler. They should make good time if the weather holds. The horses are fresh and so far, they are traveling along behind the old mare quietly. Fall is in the air and it's nippy as they cross the river Corey thinks is the Trinity. Unfamiliar with the country, he can't be sure. He meant to ask in Red Bluff on his last trip, but had forgotten.

By the map Micah made him, Corey remembers he is another two days from Red Bluff, which lay to the east and south where they make night camp. A small canyon with only one exit is a natural holding pen to let the horses rest and graze for the night. A slow running stream divides the canyon, giving the horses a good place to water. Corey has camp set up, a fire started, and four sage hens that he was able to shoot, roasting over it, as the final rays of the sun start to hide in the west.

"Samuel, you take first watch holding the horses in the canyon, then wake me at midnight." Corey rolls himself a smoke and leans back against his saddle.

Nodding, Samuel checks his rifle priming and pistol, and retreats away from the glow of the fire. "Corey, how come you never let me watch over the horses?" Colby stammers, looking over to his brother.

Corey raises an eyebrow and smiles, "Never, because little brother, we need you to be alert while we're a riding, not half asleep like me and Samuel."

"Yes, sir."

"Now you get some sleep." Corey leans back further on his bedroll and looks up at the vast Texas sky. Stars sparkle by the millions. Flipping away his smoke, he closes his eyes and thinks of Sarah, of the look she gave him as he rode out. Her face is the last thing he remembers, before falling into a deep sleep.

Jacksboro is still wrapped in sleep as Corey leads the horses into the empty corrals near the edge of the little town. Dismounting and slapping the dust from his coat, the big man checks his pistols and strolls slowly toward an adjoining building with a lettered billboard sign reading, Stewart's Livery.

The big double doors stand open, welcoming the first bright rays of sunlight to ward off the morning chill. A heavyset man in overalls sits, pulling on his boots, watching them approach.

"Morning gents."

Corey nods as he smells the aroma of brewing coffee. "Coffee smells good."

"You boys help yourself." The big man nods at the woodstove. "Cups are there on the shelf."

Corey nods again as he pours three cups of the dark liquid. "Much obliged."

Pulling a strap over his shoulder, the liveryman stares out at the corral. "Good-looking bunch of broom tails."

"Yep."

"Where you get 'em?"

"West of here, a hundred miles or so."

"Heard there was a family of men moved in over on the Brazos River running horses." The big man nods. "Would that be you?"

"Probably." Corey tips the metal cup, eyeing the fat man over the rim. "Name's Stallings."

"Yeah, Micah said you would be in sooner or later, providing you survived that is." The liveryman nods. "My name's Stewart, Hiram; Stewart at your service."

"Well, Mister Stewart, we survived so far."

"Yes, I see you did at that." The big man pours himself some coffee. "He said to thank you for burying the boy."

"Who was he, the boy I mean?" Samuel speaks up.

"Sorta like Micah's adopted son." Stewart blows on his steaming cup. "Micah set a store by that boy, yes sir, quite a store."

"Adopted?" Corey is curious.

Stewart nods slowly. "Yep, few years back, Micah found him captive in an Apache village and bought him. The boy's been with him ever since; named him, Alonzo."

"Then the ones that killed him knew who he was?"

"If it was Hernandez and his cutthroats, yes, they knew the boy, for sure." Stewart spits. "Micah saved that Mexican's skin once. Yeah, I'd say he knew the boy, real well."

"Why would they kill him?" Samuel is curious.

Stewart spits. "They're a bunch of killers and renegades. People like that, they don't need a reason. Just for pure cussed meanness I'd say. They're a bad lot to mix with, that's why."

"Where's Micah now?"

"He was over at the saloon last night getting drunk." Stewart shrugs. "Can't say for sure where he is this morning."

"Well, Mister Stewart, we got forty two head of horses to sell. You interested in buying?"

"Might be," the man looks over at the corral. "You only got thirty two head to sell."

"No, sir, there's forty two out there in that corral."

Stewart nods agreement. "Yes, Mister Stallings, there is, but you see I figure you're fixing to get a visit from Ira Randle. He runs this one-horse town. I'll guarantee you, he or one of his henchmen watched them horses come into my corral."

"So?"

"Well, you see, Mister Randle takes twenty five percent off the top of every transaction that goes on in his town."

"Twenty five percent, you mean ten of my horses?"

"Exactly." Stewart looks away embarrassed. "I'm sorry, but that's the way it is."

"Mister, I've got forty two head of well-broke horses for sale, not thirty two. Are you buying?"

"I ain't bucking Randle or that crazy killer Clint Tabor, he has working for him."

"We got one of them kind ourselves, Mister Stewart." Samuel mumbles off to the side. "I'll talk to this Mister Randle. Now, are you buying?" Corey glares at Samuel.

"You're gonna buck Randle and his killers?" The big man looks across at Samuel, curious of what the boy had said, turning back to Corey. "Okay, Mister Stallings, you do the troubleshooting and I'll buy 'em all. How much?"

"How much you offering?"

"Twenty-five a head, for the lot."

Samuel shakes his head. "Forty."

"Thirty."

"Thirty-five." Samuel spits back.

"Thirty, and you're handling Randle."

"I told you, I'll take care of this Randle feller." Corey looks over at Colby. "What you think, Colby?"

"Sell 'em. We got plenty more just like them at the ranch." Colby grins.

Corey looks over at Colby and smiles. "Alright Mister Stewart, it's a deal."

"Good, and like I said, you take care of Randle and his men, cause here his bullyboys come." Stewart looks toward the corral. "I'll pay you just as soon as you settle with them, providing you're still around."

Corey already spotted the three men, walking slowly past the corral. He also notices their eyes, taking in the horses standing in the enclosure.

Samuel laughs. "Don't worry yourself, Mister Stewart, he'll be around."

"I hope so boy, I truly hope so." Stewart retreats several steps backward as the men approach and stand looking Corey up and down. "But, I doubt it."

CHAPTER 8

Manny Sharps, along with Rafe and Lon, sit quietly behind a small, brushy knoll as Corey and his brothers pass with the remuda of horses heading toward the east.

"There's only three of them." Rafe looks across to where Manny waits, studying the passing horses. "Let's take them now."

Manny's eyes smolder as he looks down on the big frame of Corey Stallings. His trigger finger curls automatically around the trigger as he sights down the long barrel at Corey's broad back.

"What you waiting on Manny, for Pete's sake, shoot him and be done with it." Rafe is shaking with anticipation.

Shaking his head, Sharps lowers the weapon. "No, we'll take the ranch first, then be waiting for him when he returns."

"Are you crazy or what?" Rafe raises his own rifle, only to have Sharps bat it away.

Sharps dark blue eyes, glitter, as they study the man who humiliated him. "I don't want him to die quick like, no sir." Manny spits. "There's plenty of time. I want Corey Stallings to know what I done to him and his family."

"Crap Manny, shoot him now, whilst we got the chance." Rafe is beside himself as he watches Stallings and the herd moving away.

"No, Cousin Rafe." Sharps smiles, reminding Lon of a lobo wolf. "We'll take the ranch first." Sharps rests the rifle across his lap, looking over at his cousins. He knows Rafe could never understand there was more to killing and revenge than just shooting a man. A bullet was too quick. No, sir, Stallings would suffer first. Only then will he die.

Watching the trail dust settle, after the horses pass, Sharps walks to where his horse is tied, and tightens his cinch strap. Stepping lightly into the saddle, he looks at his two cousins and grins.

"Come on, you boys cheer up. Let's go meet Slocum and that bunch of Mexicans he's supposed to be bringing in."

"You should have finished it, now." Rafe isn't about to let it go.

"Now, I tell you!" Whirling his horse, Sharps points east. "There they go, Cousin Rafe. Even you could find their trail. Go get him if you want him that bad."

"Alone?"

"Me and Lon are headed for them mesas over yonder." Sharps kicks his horse. "If you don't get yourself killed, meet us there."

Shaking his head in disgust, Rafe reluctantly follows along behind Sharps and his brother. He has known Manny Sharps all his life, but he would never understand him. The man hungers for revenge against Stallings, but refuses to shoot him. In his own way, Rafe is a killer, the same as Sharps, but he isn't near the gun hand Sharps is. All of his victims were helpless or had their back turned. He knows Corey Stallings will be neither.

Slocum scans the horizon, watching the three riders head in his direction. He knows it is Sharps and his cousins, but he never throws caution to the wind. He has ridden the shady side of the law all his life, living by his wits, staying just one jump ahead of a hangman's noose and he intends to stay that way. He wonders what has taken them so long to get here. Hernandez has been chomping at the bit all day. In his line of work, he knows death is only a bullet, knife, or rope away, but a rope, choking him to death, always horrified him. Why, he doesn't know, dying was dying.

Hernandez and his riders are lined up, just below the swells of a small knoll, waiting for Slocum to wave them forward.

Sharps is well aware they are being watched from the knoll, but he isn't prepared for all the riders that suddenly appear. Rifles point from every horse, as he recognizes Slocum and rides calmly up to him.

"Mister Sharps," Slocum smiles easily.

"Slocum."

"Glad you could finally make it." Slocum turns to Hernandez. "This is Señor Santiago Hernandez and his men."

Sharps nods as he takes in the cold, hooded eyes, of the Mexican. Slocum has told him a few things about the renegade Mexican, but the cruel emotional eyes of the man tell even more. Here in front of him, is a killer, a man deadlier than a rattlesnake, a man that kills with no compulsion. Sharps can sense it without even knowing or speaking to the man.

"Señor Hernandez claims all this land is his." Slocum looks over at the scar-faced man. "It seems his family owned it before the revolution, before the gringos took over."

"Far as I'm concerned, he can have it." Sharps, eyes the man. "All I want is Corey Stallings and his bunch."

"And you need my help, is this right, señor?"

"I do."

"Tell me, Señor Sharps, what do me and my men get for helping you kill these people?" Hernandez calmly looks into Sharps' eyes.

Sharps shrugs, "Everything. All I want is the redheaded woman, and to see the rest dead."

The Mexican knows nothing of the money Ben Stallings has at the ranch and Sharps isn't about to tell him. He has seen the women, traveling with the wagons on his first encounter with Stallings and both are beautiful.

"There is another woman."

"She is yours, if you want her."

"Everything else is ours, guns, horses, everything?"

"Everything!" Sharps looks over at Slocum.

Slocum smiles. "Sounds like a good set-up to me, Santiago."

The cold, dark eyes of Hernandez studies Sharps for several seconds, then he grins broadly. To rid the whites of the country he claims as his own is reason enough to throw in with these gringos. "This is good Señor Sharps. Si, we will be compadres."

Slocum sits silently watching as Sharps deals with Hernandez. He says nothing. He already made his own private deal with Manny Sharps. He hasn't known Sharps but a short time, but he doesn't trust the man. He also heard the man is a coward, but back in Red Bluff, he proved he was a killer just the same. Would he try to double cross Hernandez? Others have tried, but now they are in their graves. Hernandez and Slocum have been partners in crime for many years, since the revolution, since the coming of the whites. Slocum knows who he would side with if Sharps tries any funny business. Hernandez is an evil man, but it has been a profitable relationship between the two men and Slocum can see no reason to change sides.

Lon watches Slocum from where he sits his horse, wondering what the man will do when he finds out Manny killed Constable Enloe?

Ben Stallings has an uneasy feeling since Corey departed. He followed his son's advice and forted up inside the heavy walls of the ranch house. Only one man at a time is permitted outside the house to feed and take care of the horses. Haying the mustangs in the corrals, and milking their one cow, is all the work around the ranch that is being done. Ben allows no one to ride out from the ranch and none venture far from the safety of the house. Two lookouts are posted atop the shingle roof at all times. From there, they can see anyone approaching for miles.

"This is crazy," Lambert protests to Sarah, who stands beside him on the roof. "Pa's gone loco or lost his nerve. Ain't nothing out there, nothing."

"Papa Ben is not loco, and he sure ain't afraid. If Corey said we need to be careful, then we should be careful."

"Are you sweet on Corey or what?" Lambert grins over at the redhead. "Sure sounds like it to me."

"Lambert, you know I'm married." Sarah's green eyes flash hard at the boy.

"Nope, not anymore you're not; Eli's dead."

"My Eli is dead, but he's still my husband, and he always will be," Sarah frowns.

"Sorry Sarah, I didn't mean that. It's just being cooped up like this is wearing on my nerves."

"I know," Sarah smiles at him. "Corey will be back soon."

"I hope." Lambert looks over at the girl then over her shoulder. "I feel safer when he's around and I think you do too."

Sarah starts to reply, but instead points off to the east, her eyes wide. "Lambert, look yonder!"

Many horsemen, strung out in a straight line, are approaching the ranch at a slow walk. Hollering down from the roof, Lambert and Sarah quickly climb down the ladder and meet Ben, coming from the inside of the house.

"Riders, Pa, lots of them."

"Take the ladder inside after I get on top." Ben starts up on the roof. "Caleb's inside, pay heed to him, shoot straight, and shoot to kill."

A solid, thick, square box structure has been erected atop the roof, out of oak logs. Mere bullets could never penetrate the heavy walls. Two good men with rifles would have a clear field of fire in every direction, and could pick off a lot of attackers. Small portholes for firing were cut in each side. Ben quickly notes the supplies of water, food, bullets, and powder as he slips slowly over the walls. A hundred yards out, the riders pull to a halt and sit quietly, surveying the ranch house. Their sharp eyes find the man on the roof quickly. Sharps, kicks his horse and walks another thirty yards forward. Ben recognizes Manny Sharps immediately, and he figures the dark skinned Mexican, sitting in the rear, is the same man they encountered on their way here.

"That's far enough, Manny Sharps."

"That be you up there Ben Stallings?" Sharps laughs.

"You know it's me. Speak your piece, then ride out." Ben has his sights dead center of Sharps' chest.

Sharps, pushes back his hat and sits looking toward the house. "Now Ben, that sure ain't neighborly of you, at all."

"We ain't neighbors."

"We were once, before you Stallings started killing us Pikes."

"I'll ask you for the last time, what do you want?" Ben despises the voice of Sharps, his red hair, everything about the man.

"You got something that belongs to me, and I come for it," Sharps grins.

"And what would that be?"

"My cousin Sarah; send her out and we'll ride on." Sharps omits wanting the money. From where he sits, he knows the Mexican can hear his words and he doesn't want Hernandez knowing about the money. Why share when he could have it all. To him, the Mexicans were nothing but simple minded fools. They'd settle for the horses and saddles.

"Hogwash." The rifle belches smoke and lead, sending Sharps' hat flying into the air, and Sharps races back, out of rifle range.

Santiago Hernandez watches as Sharps face turns from a smile of smugness and contempt to a sickened paleness as he retreats toward them. The gringo is a coward. Hernandez can smell it on him.

"Well, señor, it seems the coyotes have turned into wolves with fangs," Hernandez laughs as Sharps composes himself. "What do we do now?"

"Attack; spread your men around the house."

"No, señor. I do not think I will do this." Hernandez clicks his tongue. "My men, they would be killed maybe."

"They're getting paid to take their chances," Sharps looks behind him at the waiting Mexicans.

"Perhaps we will be paid, but we have seen nothing yet, señor." Hernandez looks toward the house. "I think maybe you should lead us."

Sharps, looks into the Mexican's ugly eyes and over at Rafe and Lon. He knows Hernandez isn't asking. He is telling him to go first. To refuse could start a shooting, right here. Nodding, he slips from his horse and starts forward. Following what cover they can find, the three, work their way toward the corral.

"You are sending them to their death, my friend." Slocum watches the three men as he speaks to Hernandez.

"Si, thank your lucky saints I ain't sending you with them." Hernandez hisses. "You tie me up with a coward."

Slocum remains quiet. No man dares cross Hernandez when he is mad. The slightest nod and he knows he could be a dead man, or sent to follow Sharps.

"Sharps," Slocum cusses the name. Why did he ever get himself involved with this man?

Another shot rings out from the roof and Rafe falls forward, with a bullet through his chest.

"I told you, Manny. We should have killed Stallings back there when we had the chance," Rafe sputters, as life ebbs from him.

Lon looks into the unseeing eyes of his dead brother.

So far, only a couple shots have been fired from inside the house. Sharps knows the mountain men inside. They will not waste powder and lead firing blindly into the fading light. He can hear the Mexicans behind him, their boots making soft noises in the deep sand as they edge forward, waiting for Hernandez to give them orders to attack. Lon lays his brother softly onto the ground and starts toward the corrals.

"Be careful, Cousin, that's Ben Stallings up there and he can shoot."

"Maybe they're low on powder or something." Lon looks back to where Sharps waits. Shaking his head, Sharps starts forward. "No such luck, they be mountain folk. When they shoot, they normally hit something. Their kind don't waste powder and shot."

Suddenly, from the rear, the screaming yells of the Mexicans sound, as they charge across the open ground toward the house. The first volley from the house windows and roof take two Mexicans out of the fight. Again, as the bullets from the attackers sink harmlessly into the log walls, the window slits explode powder and lead and this time, another man goes down.

Hernandez screams something in Spanish that Sharps cannot understand, and what is left of the men, start a slow retreat from the deadly rifle fire of the defenders. Sharps nods to Lon and they follow the retreating Mexicans.

Ben takes careful aim, on what he thinks is a man's leg, and pulls the trigger. Smiling with satisfaction, as a scream comes from the underbrush surrounding the corral, he reloads his long rifle and waits.

Hernandez is in a fit. Three of his men lay scattered about the front yard near the ranch house and one has a broken leg where a bullet has shattered the bone. All of this happened in less than a few minutes. He knows further frontal attacks on the house will result in the death of more of his men. Pacing back and forth, he glares at Sharps as he walks over to him.

"You told me, señor, this place had no defenders, that it would be easy."

"I was wrong. Someone must have warned them we were coming."

"I have lost four men." Hernandez looks at both Slocum and Sharps.

Slocum steps forward, his hand extended. "You have only lost three Santiago, my friend."

Pulling his pistol, Hernandez shoots the wounded man through the head. "Four señor, do you call me a liar?"

"No, of course not," Slocum speaks hoarsely. He knows, the way Hernandez is shaking in rage, death is only a breath away. He is at the mercy of a madman if Hernandez goes berserk.

For some reason, Sharps does not fear the Mexican as he does Corey Stallings. He knows few men can draw and fire as fast as he can. Looking calmly into Hernandez's face, Sharps readies himself, in case the Mexican turns on him.

Hernandez sees the look of contempt on the gringo's face when he turns. Perhaps he was wrong about this one being a coward. "What would you have us do now, Señor Sharps?" Hernandez holsters his pistol.

"Well, we can't attack them across this much open ground, that's for sure." Sharps' eyes survey the flat ground, leading to the ranch house and the dead bodies. No, he doesn't want to try a frontal attack again.

Suddenly, his eyes focus on the spring wagon, sitting alone near the corrals. Slocum sees the interest Sharps takes in the wagon and grins broadly.

"We'll burn them out," Slocum laughs.

"It'll be full dark soon. Me and Lon will go after it, as soon as it's too dark to shoot." Sharps looks over at Hernandez. "Have your men drag up some dead limbs from the river."

Ben Stallings relaxes against the wall of his little fort and sips on the hot cup of coffee Lambert brought him as night falls. Suddenly, his ears tense. Something is near the corrals. His eyes strain in the dark gloom of evening, trying to see whatever is out there.

He can hear the squeak of the wagon as it is being moved from where it sits. Sighting by sound only, Ben fires a round in the direction of the noise.

"You missed, old man," Sharps laughs.

Lon hastily fires back at the roof, bringing several answering shots from the house. "Don't fire you fool; gives away our position," Sharps scolds his cousin.

"Sorry Manny, but he killed Rafe."

Sharps leans hard into the wagon, pushing it away from the corral. "I know Cousin Lon, I know, and I promise we'll get him, just don't give our position away."

"No, I'll get him." Lon's face is set. "I'll have his liver for killing poor old Rafe."

"You're welcome to it."

"You hear that old man?" Lon hunkers down, behind the wagon and bellows toward the house. "I aim to have your liver over a fire tomorrow."

The only answer is the smack of lead as it tears into the oak-sided bed of the wagon.

"They aim to burn us out, Pa." Caleb climbs up the replaced ladder and is looking out across the flats where the Mexicans loaded the wagon with dead grass and dead limbs. A fire glows beside the wagon, just out of rifle range, letting them see what is happening. "What'll we do?"

"Fight boy, fight." Ben listens to the laughter of the Mexicans from his high perch on the roof.

Again, near the corrals, Manny Sharps' voice penetrates the night. "Ben, why don't you be sensible and give us Sarah."

Only quiet comes from the dark walls of the house. "You still up on the roof, old man?" Lon's voice cuts the night.

"I'm here; you boys come on in," Ben answers, sending a round over Lon's head. "We'll greet you real nice."

"You old devil," Lon hollers out. "I'll see you in hell before this is over."

"You'll get there first, Lon Sharps." Caleb hollers from the roof.

"Last chance Ben Stallings, before we burn you like rats in a cellar," Sharps calls once again. "You ever see anyone burn, Ben? Smells, something awful."

"You'll burn in hell yourself, Manny Sharps," Ben calls back. "Corey will be after you."

"We already took care of that killer son of yours," Sharps laughs. "He's a dead man. Leading them horses like they were, him and the others didn't know what hit 'em."

Ben stiffens, did he hear right? Is Corey, Samuel, and Colby already dead? "You're a liar Sharps. You ain't got the guts to face Corey alone."

"We had help, old man, lots of it." Sharps is hoping his lies will scare the defenders into giving up.

"You gonna burn the women, Manny Sharps?" Caleb calls from the house.

"We are, if you don't surrender real quick like."

"Come and get us." The loud boom of Ben's heavy rifle resounds across the flats.

A blaze slowly catches, as hot coals from the campfire are dumped onto the dead brush in the wagon. From his position on the roof, Ben can see figures walking around the wagon, silhouettes from the fire's light. Quickly climbing down from the roof, he and Caleb slip through the front door, barring it behind them.

CHAPTER 9

Corey watches as three men walk slowly past the corrals, toward the livery stable, their boots kicking up small puffs of dust from the dry, powdery street. Handing his coffee cup to Samuel, he points toward the building and the corrals. The fat stable man stands big-eyed, fidgeting from one foot to another, his hands opening and closing nervously, wishing he was anyplace but where he is.

"You boys wait in there." Corey jerks his head at Samuel and Colby. "You, Mister Stewart, wait here with me, so you can introduce me to these fine gentlemen." Corey sees the stable man start to turn away.

"Mister Stallings, you said you'd handle Mister Randle," the fat man whines.

"I aim to, but we need introducing," Corey smiles coldly. "Man can't talk to another man unless they've been properly introduced, now can they?"

Frowning, Stewart nods toward the oncoming men. "I reckon not; that's Clint Tabor, Bill Nunley, and Red Collins coming this way."

"No Randle?"

"No, sir, but these three will probably be enough to keep you busy." Stewart steps sideways, two steps. "You watch that crazy Clint Tabor, the small man in the middle, he's plain loco and sneaky. Those other two ain't much better, but Tabor's the worst of the lot."

Walking up, the three men stop ten steps away from Corey. The shorter of the men, motion at the corral where the horses mill, then cuts his eyes hard on the liveryman. "Well, Mister Stewart, I see you've acquired some good-looking horses since last night."

"Yes, sir, Mister Tabor," Stewart stutters. "They belong to this gentleman here."

"Do they now? And just who is this gentleman with the horses?" The little man is bowlegged and fidgety with a continual twitch to the left side of his face, making him seem like a coiled spring, ready to snap. A riding crop hangs from his left hand, which he slaps against his leg nervously. "I didn't catch it."

"I didn't give it, but the name's Corey Stallings."

Tabor smiles wickedly, looking over at the horses again. "Well, Mister Corey Stallings, we charge ten percent sales tax on every animal that goes through our town, whether you sell them or not."

"Your town, Tabor?"

Tabor glances at the squirming Stewart. "I see you know my name. No, actually it's Mister Randle's town, but he expects his tax money, so just how many head you got in there?"

Corey studies the three men for several seconds before answering. He wants to gauge them, to figure in his mind, which is the most dangerous of the three. Finally, he chooses Tabor as his first target. After that, it probably wouldn't matter who is second, providing he is still standing.

"Well, Mister Tabor, I've changed my mind. We're riding on through to the next town, if that's acceptable to you?"

Tabor grins coldly. He thinks he can feel the man backing down, scared. "You can ride out if you want, but you still owe Mister Randle, his tax money for using his corrals."

"I done paid Stewart here for the use of his corrals."

"Not enough, now pay up, pronto." Tabor drops his hand to cover his pistol grip.

"I hate to disappoint this Mister Randle, whoever he may be, but you ain't cutting my herd, and I don't plan to pay your tax money." Corey's thumbs hook his gun belt.

Tabor lashes down with the quirt, against his leather chaps. "Didn't Stewart tell you, you ain't got no choice in the matter, mister? Now, we're taking either the horses or your money. Which will it be?"

Corey stands calmly, studying the small man before him. "Neither one, little man."

"Last chance Stallings. Mister Randle is a reasonable man, but if you don't pay, how can we expect to collect from the other sellers that come through?" Tabor squares his shoulders, jutting out his jaw. "Personally, I'd just as soon collect out of your hide."

"I'd say that's your problem, Mister Tabor." Corey purposely pushes Tabor, his fighting blood is up. He wants to fight. He feels the taste come up in his throat, the taste of death.

"Red, count them nags, then cut our part out." Tabor keeps his eyes on Corey.

"You touch that gate mister and you're a dead man." Corey catches a glimpse of Tabor's gun hand, as it streaks for the pistol. Two shots ring out, almost at the same time. Corey feels the slap at his side, turning him slightly sideways as hot lead tears a chunk from his heavy pistol belt, taking hide with it. Tabor sinks slowly to the ground, a surprised look on his face, as another shot rings out behind Corey, sending the one called Red, rolling backward. Turning, as the last of Randle's men slowly backs off, his hands raise away from his pistol, Corey sees Samuel holding a smoking pistol in his hand.

"Thanks Samuel." Corey nods, pulling the trigger, putting a slug through the last man's chest. "That was mighty close."

Samuel stares as the man slowly collapses with a groan. "You didn't have to do that, he was backing out."

"Maybe, I see it different. If it had of been me, he would have done the same." Corey eyes the dead man, retreating to a water trough and sits down.

"Pa's right about you being a killer."

"Maybe he is Samuel, maybe he is."

"Are you hit hard?" Samuel keeps his pistol cocked and ready as several men appear from inside the saloon. None offer to come across the street. Seeing Samuel's drawn pistol, most retreat inside.

"I've had worse."

"Your side looks nasty to me."

"It'll be sore a few days I s'pect." Corey looks over to where Stewart waits nervously. "You go over to that saloon and tell Mister Randle I want to see him."

"He won't come himself." Stewart is sweating profusely, scared plumb near half out of his wits. Stewart is no fighter, a gentle man. He hates violence of any kind.

"You tell him he better not make me come over there." Corey looks down at his blood-soaked shirt. "I ain't in the mood, and you tell him not to send any more of his bullyboys."

"Yes, sir, I'll tell him." Stewart retreats from the cold stare of Corey and hurries toward the saloon. The wound isn't serious unless blood poisoning sets in, but it's going to be uncomfortable to sit a horse for a few days or wear a pistol belt. The skin was clipped deep as the bullet almost cut Corey's belt in two.

Packing the wound with some folded clothes, to stem the blood flow, Samuel steps back, pulling his pistol as Stewart and another man walk toward them.

"You'll be sore as heck for a few days, but I reckon you'll live." Samuel doesn't take his eyes off the oncoming men.

"Thank ye kindly." Corey stands up slowly, looking down at Samuel's pistol. "You've been practicing some with that thing?"

"Some, but you ain't, he almost got you." Samuel looks down at Tabor. "He was fast, real fast."

The man walking beside the liveryman is tall, almost as tall as Corey, but not nearly as heavy built. Corey can see he isn't armed unless he carries a hidden gun or shoulder holster under his suit coat. He can also tell by the man's steady stride and set face, he isn't scared. To the contrary, he walks like a man in control, sure of himself.

Corey can feel it as he had seen the type before. Arrogant and cocky, here is a very dangerous and shrewd man. The tall man, stops several feet from where Corey and Samuel are standing, silently watching him.

"I understand you want to see me." Randle looks down at the body of Tabor and over at Corey's side. "It seems you've already met Mister Tabor."

"I met him. The man died doing your bidding, Randle." Corey nods. "You should have taught him better."

The tall man nods. "That's what he's paid for, but you're the one that is supposed to be lying there, not him."

"Sorry to disappoint you." Corey frowns, nodding to Tabor's lifeless body. "Hope you pay good; seems to be dangerous work."

"Stewart says your name is Stallings. You asked me here, now what can I do for you, Mister Stallings?" The man is definitely sure of himself.

"Just this, Mister Randle, I'll be bringing horses into Jacksboro from time to time. The next time you sic your bullyboys on me, I'll be coming after you, and only you. Guns, knives, or bare fists, it'll be your choice, and we can finish it right now, if you're a mind to."

"This is my town, was before you came and it will be after you're long gone." Randle steps closer to Corey. "Sell your horses and don't come back."

"Randle you don't hear so good, but you listen again; I'll be back." Corey grabs Randle's shirt, almost lifting him from the ground. "Don't ever cross me or my family again, or the people I do business with in this town."

As Randle's shirt is released, he starts to say something, but changes his mind, turning back to the saloon. Corey knows he hasn't seen the last of the man or his hired killers. Nothing has changed, only Tabor and the other two are dead. The next time he comes there will be someone else to replace them. The man has been warned so the choice is his.

"You gonna be alright, Mister Stewart?" Corey looks at the sweating liveryman. "I mean, after we leave?"

"I'll be fine. He'll probably send one of his bullyboys around to collect his so called tax money, but you don't chop down your money tree." Stewart shrugs.

"He's been warned to leave you alone." Corey watches the back of the retreating Randle. "He will, I think."

"Not Randle, he'll send his men as soon as you have gone."

"Well then, if he does, I'll just have to retrieve your money when I return, won't I, Mister Stewart?" Corey looks over at the saloon as Randle passes through the swinging doors without as much as a backward glance. "You got a sheriff in this town to report this to."

Stewart smiles, looking down. "Yes, sir, Mister Tabor here was."

"Well then, I figure he knows what happened."

Samuel steps closer as Colby walks from the livery. "You got a sawbones in this town, Mister Stewart?"

"Doc Wheeler, he's better with a horse or mule, but he's pretty good at fixing gunshot wounds."

"He'll do. Brother Corey here has been described as being more mule headed than any man in Arkansas." Samuel looks to where Corey is trying to stand.

"Take your brother over to that small building." Stewart points to a small house across the street. "When you get back, I'll have your money ready."

Corey looks up at Samuel. "You've growed up some, Samuel."

"Yeah, I started to act like you."

"Thanks for saving my bacon. That one might have gotten me, for sure." Corey nods down at the man, Samuel shot.

"He would have for a fact; let's go," Samuel answers, following Corey and Colby over to the building Stewart pointed out.

Corey smiles, as his younger brother has grown at least a foot in the last few minutes.

Micah Halleck stands waiting in front of the livery stable as the Stallings return from the doctor's office. The heavy smell of liquor emanates from his buckskins, but his sharp eyes tell a different story. Today, he is cold sober, the first in many. The death of Alonzo saddened the old hunter. The boy meant a great deal to him. Now, someone will pay.

Shaking hands with Halleck, Corey sits down on some feed sacks and leans back against the building. His side is neatly bandaged, but it starts to throb, causing a momentary weakness to come over him.

"Watched it from the saloon, I did," Halleck nods. "Y'all did a bang up job on them boys, and old Randle is fit to be tied."

"Weren't none of our choosing," Samuel speaks up.

Micah looks up at the boy. "No, it weren't lad, but when a snake needs stomping, you stomp him fast and you stomp him hard."

"Well, brother Corey sure stomped the last one, yes sir." Samuel stares at the old trapper.

"He done right boy. Out here, you don't give a skunk a second chance to spray you. Kill him and don't look back."

"We're sorry to learn the dead man was your boy, Micah," Corey changes the subject.

"He weren't my blood, mind you," Micah drops his eyes. "I thought of him as if he were."

"Anyway, we're sorry."

"He's dead and gone now, and I thank you for putting him under. Now let's talk no more of him, ever."

Nodding, Corey knows exactly how the old man feels. Every time he lost a brother, he just wanted to forget. Sometimes forgetting comes hard, especially in the dark of night, alone, lying flat on your back, looking up at the stars. A man can almost see their sad faces looking down at him. It's unsettling when the faces are your kin and seem almost real.

"Where you bound for now, Mister Halleck?" Colby kneels beside the old hunter.

"Reckon with you boys. That is, if you got room for a useless old man." Halleck nods his head.

Corey looks over at Micah and sees a deep look of sadness in the old hunter's face. "You're welcome, Micah."

"When you fellers pulling out?"

"Just as soon as we get our money," Corey looks over where Stewart sits. "The quicker, the better."

"No," Samuel speaks up. "We'll leave at first light. You need some rest, brother."

Corey is shocked. This is the first time in many a day, Samuel referred to him as brother.

"Morning it is then. Let's get our money and find us a good meal to sit down to."

The meal is found, and it, along with a good night's sleep, is exactly what the doctor ordered. Corey's side is stiff and sore, but he feels strong and is eager to return to the ranch. The doctor checks the wound for infection and replaces the bandage with a fresh one, placing a bottle of evil smelling medicine in Corey's hand moments before they ride out of Jacksboro.

Samuel leads the small column west, out of town, with Micah bringing up the rear. Two packhorses, heavily loaded with supplies, are led by Colby. Corey looks at the wide shoulders of Samuel, sitting ramrod, straight, surveying everything they pass. Yes, his brother has matured; he had become a man.

Even considering Corey's sore side, they are making better time going home than they did pushing the herd of horses to Jacksboro. Micah keeps riding to the top of the small knolls, they pass, sitting a few minutes then returning to the column. Finally, Corey pulls up, waiting for the old hunter to catch up.

"You worried about something, Micah?"

"Nope, just making sure we don't have nothing to worry about."

"Mexicans?"

"Anybody," a stream of tobacco leaves Micah's mouth, "Injuns, whites, Mexicans, don't matter. Out here, they're all dangerous as a hydrophobic skunk."

"We didn't have a lick of trouble coming in," Samuel shrugs.

"Naturally, they don't want horses, too much work, besides they can get plenty of them. No, sir, they'd rather wait and collect the money them horses brought."

Corey nods, he knows the old man is right. "Reckon I need to ride point from here on in."

"The ranch is another good two days ride from here. If it were me, I'd ride on ahead and check things out," Micah spits again. "That is, providing you feel up to it. I'll keep a close watch out for this bunch. You just make sure the trail is safe."

"Don't know Micah, I hate to leave the boys alone." Corey searches the surrounding brush and flatlands. "If something should happen to them, it would kill pa, for sure."

"Suit yourself, just giving an old man's advice."

"You're fidgeting about something. Tell me, what is it?"

"Just this, Hernandez would never let you get through with that herd unless he had something else planned for you or the ranch." Micah stares hard down the trail. "Somewhere ahead, he'll be waiting for you. I just figure you rather run into it alone, without the boys in the line of fire."

"You got yourself a strong hunch then?"

"Believe so. I'd go if I were you; now, tonight."

Corey studies on the idea for several minutes, rolling it around in his head, and rides up to where Samuel is leading the way. "I'm gonna ride ahead and check on the ranch. You follow along slow and pay attention to what Micah tells you."

"We got trouble, Corey?"

Corey looks back to where Micah slouches in his saddle. "The old man thinks so, and he's survived out here many a year. He knows these people and this land better than we do."

"We'll keep a close look out, and ride along slow," Samuel nods. "Good luck, brother."

Corey looks over at Samuel. "Thank you, brother."

"Why don't we all just hurry home, instead of just you Corey?" Colby was listening to the conversation.

"Because, little brother, I can make better time alone and make a lot less racket going in, that's why." Corey smiles and slaps the brim of Colby's battered old hat. "Now Samuel, you're in charge, but listen to the old man and keep a sharp watch."

"I'll do it; see you tomorrow."

"Ride slow and keep your eyes on the ridges," Corey nods.

"How's the side?"

"Well, thank ye for asking. It's sore as the dickens, but I'll live." Corey kicks his gelding into a lope and rides out.

"They got our wagon really burning hot, Pa." Lambert turns to where Ben sits at the long table, seemingly unconcerned, drinking his coffee. Setting down his coffee, Ben picks up his rifle and eases over to the window facing the corrals, where he can see the wagon.

Men are seen pushing and shoving on the blazing pile of brush with long poles as the wagon starts to roll slowly down the slight grade toward the house. Three shots ring out from the house, causing the attackers to drop their poles and retreat, but it's too late, the damage has been done. The wagon is coming straight at the porch, sheets of flame leaping high into the dark night.

The sickening thud of the wagon sounds as it crashes heavily into the timbers that hold up the front porch. Flames lick hungrily up the walls of the log house as the thin shakes on the roof catch and start to burn like paper.

The raspy voice of Manny Sharps calls through the blaze. "Give it up Stallings and come on out before you burn to death. We'll treat the ladies real nice."

"What we gonna do, Pa?" Judith is terrified as the smoke starts to fill the room. "It's getting so hot."

"Caleb, check the rear boy, see if we can get clear."

Caleb slowly pushes open the thick shutter, only to be met with several rifle slugs, thudding into the oak wood. Closing the shutter, Caleb shakes his head. The whole front of the cabin is ablaze with flames roaring onto the roof.

"Surrender! Dang your hide, Ben Stallings, surrender and come out. We won't harm you. You have my word."

"Your word, Manny Sharps, you rat." Caleb fires through the smoke and flames. "Rot in hell."

Smoke fills the room as Ben pulls the buffalo robe from the small trapdoor leading down to the root cellar, below the house.

"The fire will come down there, Pa, we'll be roasted." Caleb frowns as he watches Ben pulling open the door. "We can't survive down there."

"Maybe it will, but if we surrender to that devil, he'll have Judith and Sarah, and then shoot us down."

"Leastways the women will live," Caleb argues.

"With that scum, that ain't living boy." Ben looks at the girls. "What do y'all want to do?"

Judith walks calmly over to the black hole and starts to descend. Sarah follows, then the men. Standing in the door, Caleb fires one last round through the blaze and nods as he hears a scream, out in the yard. Ben is the last to climb down the steep ladder, dragging buffalo robes over the trapdoor behind him as best he can, to conceal the passageway.

Two large barrels of water sit against the dugout wall of the cellar. Ben cusses his failure to have the boys put more down in the cellar. Soaking several blankets, Ben places them over the women's heads, where they sit crouched under a heavy oak table. Lambert wraps himself in a wet blanket, crawling under a shelf that is laden with can goods and vegetables. Ben looks at the smoke seeping through the floor and crawls under another table.

Manny Sharps cusses as he watches the roof of the cabin burn, then collapse into a pile of flames. He knows no one inside the cabin could survive the inferno. He has lost both Sarah and the money. Why was

Ben Stallings so hardheaded? Cussing again in a fit of rage, he kicks the ground, walking forward, as close to the house as the heat will permit.

Hernandez stands beside Slocum, staring at the burning cabin. "It seems, señor, we have nothing to show for my dead men except a burned cabin."

"You still have the horses and saddles." Slocum knows, as he says it, his words mean nothing.

"Horses and saddles? These things we already have, señor."

Retreating to where the others wait, Sharps notices the cold hardness of the Mexican's set jaw. The men backing Hernandez, stand poised, like a pack of wolves, ready to pounce. They lost brothers and cousins in the attack on the ranch. If they had women or something to show for their losses, it would be different, but to come away empty-handed, with nothing, their tempers flare as they glare toward the three white men.

"Saddle up, we ride." Hernandez whirls on his heels.

"Wait, let's see in the morning if there's anything left."

"Señor Sharps, anything in that fire is useless; we go." Hernandez glares at Sharps and Slocum. "Now!"

Slocum grabs Sharps arm and pushes him backward, away from the Mexican leader. "He'll kill you right here, Sharps, don't argue."

"I ain't going nowhere," Lon steps forward into the glare of the fire's light. "I'll have Ben Stallings liver before I leave this place."

Only the hiss of a knife and the unbelieving look on Lon's face as he stares down at the knife projecting from his chest, break the silence outside the burning cabin.

Sharps watches, as Hernandez walks over, pulling the knife from his cousin's body as he collapses.

Hernandez slowly wipes the bloody blade on the dying man's shirt, before looking up at Sharps. "Do you wish to join your friend, señor?"

Sharps' hand drops slightly toward his pistol, before Slocum grabs him. He watches his stomach contracting as Hernandez is handed the red-hot branding iron and walks over to Lon.

Corey can see the spiraling smoke plumes as he rides at a hard lope toward the ranch. Throwing caution to the wind, he whips the tired gelding hard as he rides rashly into the yard, sliding to a stop in front of the burning cabin. The walls are smoldering, but they still stand. The bullet riddled logs, attest to the hot fight that was waged.

His eyes widen as he recognizes the body of Lon tied upside down to the corral. What has happened here? Why is Lon Sharps in these parts and who killed him? Why did they rope him upside down to the corral fence? It couldn't have been Ben or Caleb. Dismounting, he looks carefully through the empty windows of the cabin. The bodies, he expected to find, are nowhere to be seen. Where is everybody? Where are the women? Have they been captured? Were they taken captive? Thousands of questions flow through his mind as his eyes search the rubble pile and still smoking ranch house.

The signs of the fight are plain to see, but there are no bodies anywhere in sight, although plenty of other signs are strewn about the front yard. Corey reads the signs quickly. The burned wagon he sees, is the way the fire started. Only the frame and iron rims of the wagon are left where it collided with the front porch. Three blood trails and boot scrapes, show where bodies were dragged back, out of rifle range.

There has been a battle, at least until the burning wagon ran into the house. The timbers of the cabin were still green, so the walls haven't been burned, only singed black on the outside. The roof, on the other hand, with the thin shakes, burned hotly and collapsed into the cabin's rooms. Most of the furniture burned to ashes. Little is still intact, but the wood floor only burned on the outside, hardly penetrating the green planking. Corey reasons, there wasn't enough dry wood to get the fire hot enough to keep the house burning.

Corey, in his shock, temporarily forgot about the root cellar and trapdoor. Kicking the burned oak door open, he walks to the trap and pulls the smoking buffalo rug away from the opening. The iron ring is hot to the touch so Corey uses the fire poker to lift the door. Luckily he did, as two rifles explode from the cellar, just as the trap falls backward on the floor.

"Hey down there, hold your fire. It's me, Corey."

"Corey boy, my God, we could have killed you, son." Ben is the first out of the cellar. His hair and face are black from smoke, but he has survived as well as all the others. For the first time in his life, Corey feels Ben Stallings is glad to see him.

Caleb clasps Corey's hand and wrings it, then Lambert grabs him with a bear hug. Next, Judith hugs and kisses him. Caleb's eyes drop to the floor as he watches Sarah walk to where Corey waits, standing on her tiptoes, kissing him. He watches her eyes and face as she reluctantly releases her hold on him. Her look of admiration speaks volumes.

"What a mess," Judith surveys the aftermath of the fire, almost in tears. "All our hard work, gone."

Ben shakes his head. "No matter, we're all alive, that's what counts."

Lambert stumbles in from the corrals as the others leave the burned cabin. His face is white as a sheet. He can only shake his head and point.

"It's Lon Sharps."

"I know Lambert, he's dead." Corey already saw the body when he rode in.

"They branded him all over, Pa. They burned him bad." Lambert retreats behind the house, out of sight and sound.

In his haste to find his family, Corey didn't walk near enough to see the branding and mutilation that was done to Lon Sharps.

"It was that no-account Manny Sharps and his cousins, that brought them here." Caleb looks toward the corrals. "They deserve whatever they get."

"It was the Mexican Hernandez alright, but why would he brand Lon Sharps, who apparently was riding with him and his men?" Corey shakes his head. "Don't make sense."

Ben runs his fingers through his graying head. "We killed several of them Mexicans. They probably figured this was an easy layout. When they rode out empty-handed, they probably took it out on the boy."

"Boy, he weren't no boy, Pa." Caleb shakes his head, looking toward Ben. "He was worse than them Pikes we left back in Arkansas."

"What about Manny Sharps and Rafe?" Corey is stumped.

Lambert comes walking back to the front of the cabin in time to catch Corey's last question. "Don't know about Manny, but old Rafe is behind the corrals, deader than a doornail. They didn't brand him, though."

"Reckon he was the one we hit last night, right at dark." Ben grins. "Heard one of them hollering for revenge."

Corey stiffens; in the excitement, he forgot about his brothers. "Pa, you, Lambert, and the girl's fort up again, behind the walls, while me and Caleb go after Samuel and Colby."

"Where they at?" Ben looks out across the grassland. He too has forgotten about his other sons.

"Shouldn't be too far, but that may be why the Mexicans pulled out. Maybe they're planning on waiting on me and the boys to come back from Jacksboro."

"Ride, I don't think they'll come back here." Ben looks around the ruins of the house. "There's nothing left here for them."

"We should be back before sundown. Stay close, in case you have to go back down in the cellar. They can't get to you down there."

The corrals stand empty, but several loose mustangs graze nearby in the open rangeland. Corey shakes out his loop and rides quietly toward the grazing animals. The horses have become accustomed to the smell of humans, so they don't panic and run when Corey rides in among them. A quick spurt of his horse and a couple swings of the loop, and Corey has Caleb a mount.

Saddling the animal quickly, Corey and Caleb ride out of the ranch yard at a high lope. Corey's horse is used up, but he doesn't want to waste the time to catch a fresh one. His horse will just have to last until they find the boys and Micah Halleck.

Corey doesn't figure them to be far from the ranch, maybe ten or twelve miles at most. This part of Texas is flat, but the deep sand is as hard on a horse as mountain trails are, maybe even worse. Studying the vast grasslands, Corey rides on, cautiously. He doesn't want to run unexpectedly into the Mexicans or Manny Sharps.

"Listen." Caleb looks over at Corey, pulling in harshly on his mustang. "I hear gunfire."

Corey cocks his head. In the distance, he can faintly hear the boom of a heavy caliber rifle. They had hardly come five miles from the ranch, but on the flats, the sound of gunfire carries several miles.

"That sounds like one of them heavy caliber buffalo guns," Caleb voices.

Corey nods agreement. "Micah carries one of them."

Kicking their horses, they let them run all out, toward the sounds of the fight. Riding up the side of a small mesa, they make a running dismount and fall to their stomachs, surveying the scene in front of them. Samuel and Micah Halleck are pinned down in a buffalo wallow, surrounded by Mexicans. Three saddled horses and the two pack animals, lay dead around the wallow, giving them plenty of protection from the incoming rifle fire.

Corey can't see Colby, but figures, Samuel would have him in the bottom of the wallow, out of harm's way. Two rifles speak in unison, every time a target presents itself. Corey grins, Hernandez and his men have run themselves into a Texas tornado for sure. He can make out at least three dead men, lying on the ground where they fell in front of the dead horse barricade.

From their little fortress, Samuel and Micah are giving a good account of themselves, as the Mexicans are learning. After losing several men, none of the attackers seem inclined to rise and charge the wallow again.

Looking over where Caleb dismounted beside him, Corey smiles coldly. "You reckon Samuel would mind if we helped him out a little?"

"Doubt it; this is probably the first time he ever took a shot at anything except squirrels and bears." Caleb grins, checking his priming.

Corey remembers he forgot to mention Samuel shot the one called Red, back in Jacksboro. He was as cool as a cucumber afterward, no shakes, jitters, or nothing.

"Yeah, probably is." Corey figures if Samuel wants it told, he'd tell it himself, providing, of course, Colby or Micah don't spill the beans first.

Crawling forward along the ground, to a more advantageous spot, the two position themselves on the lip of the mesa. Mexicans lay scattered about, taking cover behind every available mesquite or swell around the wallow. They never figured on two sharpshooters getting behind them, making them clear targets.

"Well, brother, it's kind of like a turkey shoot." Corey sights along his rifle barrel. "Don't miss or you're out of the winnings."

Caleb scowls, "ain't aiming to, brother. I'm sick and tired of these Mexicans shooting at us. Now it's my turn."

Corey's long rifle roars and a Mexican rolls over on his back, his face turns up to the hot sun. Caleb's rifle spits fire and another Mexican pitches sideways. Corey gets in one more shot before the attacking Mexicans locate the shooters and begin returning their fire as they retreat toward their horses. Two more Mexicans have gone down under the sharpshooting from both sides as they stand up and try to run. Only a cloud of dust presents itself, as Hernandez and his men ride out of sight in a hard run.

Mounting their horses, Corey and Caleb ride down to the wallow as Samuel and Micah stand up.

"Where's Colby?" Corey looks around for the boy as he dismounts in front of Samuel.

"They got him at first light this morning." Samuel looks into the cold eyes of his brother. "He went to check on the horses and they took him."

"Is he dead?"

"No, he was alive when we last saw him, before they came at us."

Corey's face turns red as he glares at Samuel. "You let them cutthroats take our brother?"

"Weren't his fault at all." Micah steps closer to the enraged Corey. "If it be anybody's fault, it's mine. I should have kept the boy closer to camp this morning. They nabbed him before we knew they were anywhere close."

"Then you're sure he's still alive?" Corey's voice loses some of the hardness. "What happened then?"

"We holed up in this here buffalo wallow, killed our horses, and used them for a barricade, weren't nothing else to do." Micah shrugs. "Figured you'd be along directly."

Putting his big hand on Samuel's shoulder, Corey nods. "We'll get him back. You have my word."

"You reckon he's still alive?" Caleb speaks up from the lip of the wallow.

"Didn't see any sign of him out there, so I figure he's alive." Corey looks off in the direction the Mexicans had taken in their flight. "They probably took him with them."

"Why didn't they use him for bargaining? I heard they do that." Samuel looks over at Micah.

The old hunter rubs his jaw. "Can't say for sure, but they'll use him sooner or later I reckon."

Caleb kicks the sand with the toe of his boot. "Bargain for what, dead horses?"

Micah spits a stream of tobacco. "Money, boy, I told your brother they would be waiting for you to come back through with the money he got from them horses."

"Then why didn't they use him to get the money, Micah?" Corey is curious.

"Don't know for sure, but it does seem peculiar alright." The old man shrugs. "Could be he ain't alive. We ain't seen him since he was taken."

"He's alive," Corey growls, refusing to think differently. "If he ain't, I'll kill every Mexican in Texas."

"We done killed quite a few, brother." Caleb is making a head count of the dead bodies. "Six here and five back at the ranch."

"They attacked the ranch?" Samuel is shocked at the news.

"They did," Caleb nods.

"Pa and the rest, are they okay?"

"Little dark from the fire and smoke, but all in prime shape last we seen of them."

"Colby's alive," Corey repeats.

"I hope so Corey. I like that boy." Micah turns back toward his horse. "Old Hernandez may have different ideas about using the lad. He's lost a lot of men."

Corey, Caleb, and Samuel stand in a huddle, each buried in his own thoughts. Micah feels this is family business and he knows these are hill men who hold their families close, so he remains silent as they talk. A moan sounded from one of the downed Mexicans, drawing instant attention from the old hunter.

"You got one still alive over here, boys." Micah stands looking down at the wounded man on the ground.

Corey notices the huge amount of blood soaking the man's back as he rolls him over. "You speak English, mister?"

Nodding in pain, the man grimaces at the tall figure towering over him. "Si, señor."

"Tell me, where's my brother?"

The Mexican is young, his face smooth, unlined. Shaking his head, he looks off as Corey pulls his pistol. "Last chance, amigo. You talk, maybe you live, you don't, and you're a dead Mexican for sure."

The man's lips pull back into a snarl, his snow-white teeth exposed. Summoning up the last of his strength, he spits, as Corey pulls the trigger.

"He was game to the end. I'll say that for the youngster." Corey reloads his spent shell.

"What we gonna do, Corey?" Samuel looks over at his brother.

"I'm going after your brother. You and Caleb go back to the ranch and help Pa start rebuilding, but remember, they could be back, so stay alert and keep a guard out at all times."

"You aim to go it alone, Corey?" Caleb asks.

Nodding, Corey starts for his horse.

"I'll be going with you," Samuel speaks up.

Corey looks at his younger brother, the brother who only days before saved his life, also the brother that resented him for all the killings back in Arkansas.

"Alright Samuel, but it's liable to be bloody."

"I'm going."

"Reckon I'll be trailing with you, boys." The hard voice of Micah leaves little to argue about.

"I ain't holding you responsible, Micah." Corey looks over, into the set face of the old hunter. "This could be a long trail."

"No matter, I'm going," Micah shrugs, looking down at the dead body. Frowning, he kneels down, examining the body closely. "Well, I'll be jiggered."

"Micah, do you know him?"

"I did once, before you put that ounce of lead through his brain." Micah spits and stands up. "I'd say Mister Stallings; you have a real problem now."

"What might that be, besides Colby that is?" Corey shrugs unconcerned.

"This young feller is the brother of Don Ricardo Luis Sebastian de Lorenzo."

"Pretty long name, is that supposed to impress me?" Corey looks down at the body.

"It should, providing you have half a brain like I figure you do."

"Who is he Micah?" Samuel steps forward.

Micah nods. "Don Ricardo is second in command to Santa Annie, down in Mexico. You might say, he's the brawn behind the brains."

"And?" Corey asks impatiently. He's in a hurry to be on the trail of Colby and whoever has him. "What's he supposed to mean to us."

"In all of Mexico, Don Ricardo is the one man I don't want any trouble with, period."

"What, does he have a bunch of men following him too, or all the Mexican Army?" Samuel speaks up again.

"Neither, he don't need them." Micah looks over at Corey. "He rides alone."

"Okay Micah, speak clearer." Corey is itching to ride.

"Simply this; he's a mean man to tangle with. Dang near as big as you are, maybe bigger and he's pure coiled up rattler and grizzly bear when riled."

"And you figure this is gonna rile him?"

"You betcha it will, quicker than a hornet's nest." Micah climbs on Caleb's horse. "Them Lorenzos set quite a store by their relatives, and this young man was the youngest of his brothers."

"You think he'll be coming?"

"You can set your timepiece by it. Soon as he finds out about the boy, look out." Micah looks over at Corey. "He's killed more men in, ah, shall we say, disagreements over other men's wives and his own precious pride, than I care to count, and that's not including the enemies of Santa Anna."

"Seriously Micah, how many will he bring with him?" Samuel picks his hat from the ground, knocking the dirt from it.

"He'll come with a few men to pass safely through Apache country, but when he comes for you, he'll be alone." Micah turns his horse, tossing another word over his shoulder. "Listen to me, Corey Stallings, he'll come for you, I guarantee, and he's a wampus wildcat in a scrap. If you don't get a choice and you have to fight him, watch for the twitch in his left eye. I've heard Hernandez say every time old Lorenzo decides to draw his pistol, his left eye will twitch for some reason. He's one Mexican that may be arrogant and vain, but he is a bona fide killer and a very dangerous man."

Samuel pulls on his hat and looks about. "Micah, how's he gonna know who killed his brother, way out here and all?"

Pulling his horse in, Micah swivels in the saddle, causing it to squeak. "I'll guarantee Hernandez has already got a man in the saddle heading for the Don."

"Why would he go to the trouble?" Now Samuel is curious.

"Because, young Samuel," Micah smiles, "Hernandez knows Lorenzo is well aware his brother rides with him and his Comancheros. He sure doesn't want the Don down on him for not informing him of his brother's, shall we say, demise."

"How long you figure it'll take for him to get way up here?" Corey looks at Micah.

The old hunter shrugs, "Hard to say, the boy's dead, sure ain't no hurry now. A month, two, who knows, but he'll come, that's for sure. You can bet your boots on it."

Corey looks over where Caleb is preparing to head for the ranch. "We'll swing back by here and pick up our supplies on the way in Caleb. You stay close to the ranch."

"I'll do that." With a nod, Caleb turns and walks away. "Good luck, boys."

There are only the two horses left alive, the ones Corey and Caleb rode. Micah and Samuel killed theirs for a barricade and Hernandez took the extra horses of his dead riders with him. Corey, with Samuel and Micah following, trail off to the southeast and into the deeper stretches of the vast grasslands of central Texas. Samuel holds onto Corey's stirrup and trots effortlessly alongside the horse.

"Maybe we'll run across some of our horses pretty quick." Corey looks down at his brother. "Hernandez and his bunch turned them loose before they rode out. Could be, they'll head this way to their old range."

"Is Sarah and Judith alright?" Samuel looks up into Corey's face. Corey nods slightly. "They're fine."

CHAPTER 10

Earlier in the day, before Corey and Caleb intervened in the fight, Manny Sharps lay beside Slocum, hidden from the deadly rifle fire from the buffalo wallow below. A look of pure hatred covers his haggard face. Everything went wrong, everything he planned. Now, Rafe and Lon are both dead and he has neither Sarah, nor the money. Somewhere behind, he knows Corey Stallings will follow. He knows the man and he is like a bulldog. Once he takes hold, he will never let go.

At first light, they managed to capture the younger Stallings' brother, the one he remembered was a little addled in the head. He tried in vain, to talk Hernandez into using the boy to barter with the men in the wallow, to get the money, but to no avail. Finally, he gave up in disgust, as Hernandez and his men charged foolishly forward, toward the wallow and into the deadly rifle fire of the two men forted up behind their dead horses.

They were stupid, as they didn't know the fighting abilities of the men in the wallow, and that these people from the Ozarks, were all crack shots. The Mexicans lost many men, men who would still be alive, if only they had listened to him. Instead, they blame the whole fiasco on him. He has seen the mood swings of Hernandez and is amazed he is still alive.

Manny Sharps is no fool. It is just a matter of time before Hernandez blames him for the dead men and make his move to kill him. He knows the Mexican leader will have to save face with his men somehow.

Slowly, he crept toward the wallow with the others until the deadly shooting from the wallow had drawn Hernandez's attention away from him and Slocum. Motioning for the man to stop, Sharps crawled sideways to where he lies.

"I'm getting out of here Slocum, you coming?" Sharps' eyes watch the tall frame of Hernandez as he fires, then reloads his rifle, his attention riveted on the wallow.

"He'll kill us if we try to run." Slocum is undecided. He looks to where Hernandez's eyes are focused on the men in the wallow.

"If this goes sour, he'll kill us if we don't," Sharps spits. "Now, are you coming or not?"

"I'm coming." Slocum starts edging backward slowly.

Hernandez is firing round after round into the dead horses protecting the wallow, his attention drawn momentarily away from the two whites. Sharps and Slocum slowly crawl back to where two Mexicans were guarding Colby Stallings. Sharps still fosters thoughts of using the Stallings boy to barter for the money after Hernandez dies or gives up. He watched as the ones in the wallow killed their own horses and made a barricade. There is no way the Mexicans would be able to root them out without losing several men. No, Hernandez will fail, then Manny Sharps will make his move, and the boy will be his ace in the hole.

Lunging from the ground, Sharps holds his cocked rifle forward, ready to fire. It is a wasted effort because the rifle points at nothing but two dead Mexicans, lying in their own blood. Whirling, his eyes dart about furtively, his rifle swinging back and forth, trying to cover everything.

"Stallings, he's here." Sharps, in his fright, spits out the hated name, his eyes searching frantically for his enemy.

"It weren't Stallings you fool, or he would be helping the two men back there in the wallow." Slocum looks over at Sharps in disgust.

"Then who was it?"

"I don't know, but the kid's gone. Let's get out of here before Hernandez misses us."

Grabbing the reins of the closest two horses, Sharps and Slocum mount and head southwest, fleeing as fast as they can from Hernandez and from Stallings, if indeed it was him. In their haste to flee, they don't think about running off the rest of Hernandez's saddle mounts.

Sharps cusses loudly. Their plans have been thwarted, every one of them, from the girl to the money. Now, all they can do is ride hard to the southeast and try to save their own necks. Not only will Hernandez be after them, but Stallings and his family will soon learn their identity, if they didn't already know who they were.

Slocum knows the bodies of Rafe and Lon, back at the ranch, will set Corey Stallings on Sharps' trail and his name will eventually be tied in with this mess. He never met the Stallings' clan, but Sharps has told him enough for him to know they are the type of men that would stay on his trail until hell freezes over. That wasn't all; Slocum knows Hernandez will never forget they abandoned him and ran. Texas is a big land, but right now, it feels kinda small to him.

Sharps turns continually, looking behind him. "Slocum, who do you reckon killed them Mexicans and took the boy?"

"I figure it was some of that idiot boy's bunch, who else?" Slocum can see the panic in Sharps and he is sick of the man.

"No, they wouldn't have taken the boy and left the rest in the wallow. It was somebody else."

Sharps glances behind him again. "Did you notice they were killed with a knife, up close?"

"Yeah, the same way we'll go if Hernandez catches us," Slocum growls. "There's one Mex that don't forgive or forget."

"I need the boy to get the money from Corey Stallings. He's our only chance if Hernandez fails." Sharps sits astride a good stout horse and his fear starts to subside.

"Are you crazy man? We can't wait and go poking around this country. If Hernandez catches us out here, we're dead men." Slocum kicks his horse into a trot. "I'll tell you something else, he don't always brand dead men, some are still alive. Besides, we don't even know how much them horses brought."

"I ain't talking about the horse money. There's money back at the ranch and Corey will know where Ben hid it."

"You stay if you're a mind to. I'm leaving this country and fast." Slocum kicks his horse into a lope.

Frowning in disgust and disappointment, Sharps follows, knowing Slocum is right.

While in hiding, Palane smiles at Colby as he and the boy watch Slocum and Sharps ride past.

The two men disappear into the vast grasslands of Texas as they ride east.

Palane did as his chief ordered, even more. Cayuse ordered the ranch, and especially the boy, watched closely after the discovery of Hernandez and his men, scouting out the whites.

Palane was on his way to the ranch, to check on the boy as Cayuse asked, when he spotted the bright glow of the house on fire. Watching from the ridge, he saw the entire house engulfed in flames. He knew no one could live through the flames and smoke. Riding back to the east, his mind engrossed in how he was going to tell Chief Cayuse the Far Away One was dead, it didn't dawn on Palane that he was hearing gunfire far ahead.

Slipping in quietly, he watched as the Mexicans started their attack on the ones in the buffalo wallow. Palane warned the big white man from the ranch once, the Mexicans were near and watching, but he is either an arrogant man or a stupid one. Now they are caught in the buffalo wallow and they will all soon be killed. Circling, he found the two Mexicans guarding the white boy. Luckily for him, the two guard's attention was focused on the fight and not on the weak-minded one.

The two Mexicans didn't even know he was near until it was too late and his knife did its deadly work. The white boy merely sat in confusion as Palane approached him. Mounting the horse Palane had given him, Colby followed the warrior away from the noise of the fighting. He wanted to help Samuel and Micah, but all of his life, others made decisions for him. Confused, he didn't know what else to do.

Why his chief has taken such an interest in the white boy, Palane doesn't know. Sometimes a warrior's medicine dream can be tied with another. Perhaps this is the reason, whatever it is, he will do as his chief asks. The chief's interest isn't just because the boy's mind is weak. No, there is something else, some other reason the great Kiowa War Chief decided to spread his arms and look after the white one called Colby.

Palane is a member of the tribe, but he is not a relative by blood, so Cayuse does not confide in him. Only a medicine man or close relative knows the medicine dreams of another. Whatever the reason, he was ordered by his chief to watch the ranch, and look after the boy, without the whites seeing or knowing of his presence.

He saved the mindless one from harm. The boy, he will take back to Cayuse. He has done what he was told to do; it was finished.

In his old age, Micah's eyes, even now, are sharp as eagles. Out ahead of Samuel and Corey, he circles back and forth, finally figuring out the tracks of each party. Corey has heard stories of these old mountain men and their sixth sense when it comes to following a trail. He heard tales that men like Micah could track a butterfly through the air. He watches curiously as the old hunter quarters back and forth, reading what signs were left behind by the fleeing Mexicans and whites.

Finally satisfied with his findings, Micah rides where Corey and Samuel stand waiting and dismounts. "Mexicans ain't got the boy."

"Sharps?"

Micah shook his head. "Nope, near as I can figure, the two tracks leading off to the southeast are the whites."

"Well, where's Colby?"

"Hernandez and his bunch skedaddled off that away." Micah points south. "There's two other sets of tracks leading due west. I figure one of them is the boy's track."

"You sure Micah?" Corey looks over at the old hunter. "We can't afford to be wrong."

"Pretty sure. With them two Mexicans lying dead over there, I figure someone came in and killed them and it was done with a knife, right sneaky like." Micah spits. "One set of tracks was made by an injun, a horseback injun. I figure he's the one that killed them and took the lad. I'm not just blowing to hear myself talk."

"In other words, you ain't guessing?" Samuel speaks up, staring hard at Micah.

"Nope," Micah grins. "Man doesn't have to guess when he's dead certain."

Corey studies the tracks. "Well, I hope you're right."

"I'm right."

Samuel looks up at the old hunter. "Why do you call him a horse-back Indian, Micah?"

"His footprints, they dig deep into the sand on the outside, the sign of a bowlegged man, a man used to riding." Micah points out the tracks. "This one is wearing moccasins, Kiowa moccasins."

Samuel shakes his head. "Kiowa moccasins?"

"See them marks on the ground boy, them's buckskin stitches sewn around the sole of the moccasin, Kiowa decorations. All tribes decorate their footwear different."

"Tell me again," Corey heels his horse. "You said there were two white men heading east."

"That I did."

Corey knows Rafe and Lon were dead back at the ranch. Who else could be riding with Sharps? "You're plumb certain?"

Micah nods. "Way I figure it, the whites ran out on old Hernandez. No Mexican would do that, and with a fight going on like it was, Hernandez needed them. He wouldn't have let them just ride off and leave him. No, sir, it only figures, it was two white men alright."

"Let's go find Colby then."

Micah stands, looking off to the north. "No, I'll be heading south this time."

"South?" Samuel blurts out, knowing what Micah is thinking. "There's too many of them to tackle alone Micah, and we've got to go after Colby."

"Hernandez is only one man."

"But, he has men with him and you're," Samuel doesn't finish the sentence. There was no reason to remind Micah of his age.

"True, he does have men with him. I'll see you boys on the other side. Good luck to you. You shouldn't have any trouble catching up to the boy. Keep your eyes peeled." Mounting, the old hunter waves his hand, ignoring Samuel's last remark about his age.

Corey watches Micah ride off and momentarily feels guilt, but shrugging his shoulders, he turns his horse on the track of what he hopes is Colby's horse. Blood kin comes first, and he sure couldn't travel two directions at once.

"I hate leaving him alone, Corey." Samuel turns his head and watches the old hunter disappear. "He's an old man."

"His choice, Samuel." Corey looks at the retreating back. "I know it's a rough deal, but your brother comes first."

"And after that?"

"We'll see, now let's make tracks."

Palane knows he is being followed. He can tell by the flicking ears of his mustang. Someone is coming up hard behind him. The warrior motions to Colby and kicks his horse into a lope. He is still too far to the east to expect help from the Kiowa. How far the men behind are, he has no idea. A mustang can smell a man's odor or sense the presence of other horses for several miles, if the wind is right.

Soon the small hills they have been riding through kept them out of sight of the followers would play out and there would only be flat prairie land as far as the eye could see. Palane cusses himself as he had been foolish. He should have pushed the horses hard to the west instead of riding slow. Now it is too late and it will be up to the horses. If his are fresher and faster than his pursuers, he and the white boy will escape, if not, it will be a good death.

Two figures come into sight far behind them as Palane starts the horses again to the west. Colby pulls up and stares back the way they came.

"Come young one, we must hurry," Palane starts to strike Colby's horse.

"Wait Palane, it's Corey," Colby grins. "And that's Samuel walking beside him."

"It is too far to see who it is." Palane is doubtful the boy can see that far. "No man can tell at this distance."

"I can see him, it's Corey."

Palane dismounts, leading both horses into the shelter of a small ravine. He will wait to see who these men are. Perhaps the boy is gifted. Maybe his eyes are like the hawks, sharp as a knife blade. He has heard people like him sometimes are gifted with extra keen senses.

Corey takes turns with Samuel, alternating between walking and riding. Both men have run the mountains of Arkansas their entire lives.

They were used to walking, but now they are both exhausted from the long chase. The trail runs many miles before they come to where it turns due south, into a small hidden draw. Corey is about to turn the horse and follow the tracks leading into the canyon when Palane appears, with Colby following close behind.

Kicking his horse into a trot, Colby rides around Palane where his brothers wait. A grin breaks out, across his ruddy face, as he pulls up beside them and dismounts. Corey watches as Colby embraces Samuel and looks across to where Palane calmly sits his horse. The warrior rides forward to within ten feet of the whites and stops, waiting on the laughing of the reunited, happy boys, to settle down.

"Looks like we owe you, once again," Corey nods. "We thank you, my friend."

"You were warned about the brown men from the south. Why you no listen?" Palane stares over to where Corey sits his horse. "Why you leave white village unprotected?"

"We had horses to sell, and the buyers sure weren't coming to us."

"While you sell horse, Mexican warrior's attack your people, burn your village, kill your women."

Corey shakes his head. "The women are safe and our ranch can be rebuilt. The Mexicans have lost many men. They won't come back."

"They come back quick. They have many men in canyon on the plains, many men."

"Where is this canyon?"

"West, many miles, they have great village, buy stolen goods from Indians and trade them whiskey and guns."

"We thank you for helping the boy again." Corey looks to where Colby has remounted his horse and Samuel mounts behind him. "You and your people are welcome at the ranch. Come there and you will be given many presents for saving him."

"I did not do this thing for presents. You keep eye open this time white man. The Comancheros will come again, from the west; do not sleep."

Palane turns his horse and rides away, pulling up and looking back. "Maybe I come for present one day."

For three weeks, Corey hunts and searches out the surrounding area around the ranch, vigilant to every moving object. The rest of the family spends every waking moment rebuilding the burned ranch house and reinforcing it against further attack.

Corey brought in the packs from the dead horses at the wallow as soon as he returned. Now they have plenty of powder and lead from their horse selling trip to Jacksboro, so they are well supplied with ammunition. Ben learned from the last raid so he has Colby and Lambert, busy digging a tunnel under the house that can be used as a way to escape if ever needed. The only thing that saved them all from burning to death was the fact the logs of the new house were so green they couldn't get hot enough to burn. They were indeed lucky this time. It wouldn't happen again.

Several barrels full of water are already down in the root cellar. If the Indian is right and the Mexicans do return, this time they will be ready. Along with the new roof, they add a hatch from the loft so they could pass easily from the house onto the roof without going outside. A heavy rail fence, now surrounds the entire house, preventing another wagon or horseman from setting the timbers on fire.

Ben stands back, watching as the last of the wooden shakes are nailed down on the roof. Samuel smiles, tossing his hammer to the ground and scampers down the ladder to stand beside Ben.

"Well it's finished, Pa, reckon we can get back to breaking horses now." Samuel pulls a dipper from where it hangs on the porch and dips into the water bucket.

"Not until you eat young man." Judith slipped her arm around Samuel's waist, hugging him.

"Sis, you're gonna get me so fat, I won't be able to get on a horse." Samuel smiles down at her.

Judith frowns, good-naturedly at him. "Samuel Stallings, there's more to life than a bunch of old horses."

"Oh yeah, what?" He grins down at her.

After returning to the ranch, Corey wants to go after Micah, but the ranch can't spare anyone. Horses need breaking, hay must be brought in and stored for the oncoming winter, and someone has to guard the ranch. Ben and the boys have their own work to do. They need to start on a larger barn to store hay and their saddles, out of the elements. So the full responsibility for seeing to the safety of the ranch, falls on Corey's shoulders. One of the women, either Judith or Sarah, is always posted atop the roof, surveying the surrounding grassland every time the men are busy in the corrals, working with the horses.

All roundups of the wild mustangs have ceased, as the canyons still had enough of wild ones to keep the men from having to leave the ranch unguarded until these are gentled. Taking the time to round up the wild horses, would leave the ranch vulnerable to attack. All the men would be several miles out on the plains and in the canyons. Corey has counseled against leaving the ranch. The ranch and women had to be protected.

Everything settles back to normal. The corrals boil up in dust and laughter can be heard from the men as first one, then another, try their hand at the stubborn mustangs. The only blight on their happiness is the unknown fate of Micah. None talk of his departure, but it is on everyone's mind.

The fight at the buffalo wallow and Micah's departure, is almost two months past when Corey rides up to the ranch early in the afternoon with Palane riding alongside him.

Dismounting at the corral, where Samuel is topping out a rough gelding, Corey ties his horse off and gazes through the cedar poles.

Colby jumps down from the top rail and hurries to where Palane sits his horse. Reaching up, he grabs Palane's hand and shakes it. Grinning broadly, he manages to pull the warrior from his horse. Drawing out his words in an excited stammer, Colby nods and grins. "You come to visit us, Palane?"

"I come see young one is okay." Palane smiles at the likable boy. Reserved as the warrior is, he just has to grin. Colby has an infectious smile and he can't help but like the boy. "How tooth?"

Colby pulls on his lip, exposing his lower teeth. "It's fine, see."

Palane shakes his head at the excited youth. "Yes, I see young one."

"You stay and eat with us. You'll like Judith and Sarah's cooking I'll bet." Corey listens to the conversation between the two, but doesn't interrupt. He feels Palane is here on more serious business than checking on Colby. He knows the warrior will get around to whatever it is, eventually.

Samuel had another bronc gentle enough to short lope him around the larger corral.

Palane watches intently, plainly impressed with Samuel's riding. "Him ride like Kiowa, plenty good."

"He's good alright; best I've ever seen," Lambert brags on his brother. "Best anywhere."

Palane shakes his head. "Him no best; we have better at village."

"You've got a better rider in your village?" Lambert speaks up in defense of his brother, "No way."

"Yes," the warrior looks smugly at the corral, "Kiowa better rider."

"Don't think so Palane, Samuel is the best."

"Maybe we make bet; your brother against Kiowa rider." Palane nods, "If you think he is that good."

Corey grins; he knows Palane is trying to goad Lambert into betting. Well, his brother is almost a man, so he stays out of the argument.

"Okay, Mister Palane, what do you want to bet?" Lambert is hooked.

"I bet my horse." Palane looks over his shoulder. "What you bet?"

"The same; I'll bet my horse." Lambert throws out his chest.

"No, Kiowa horse is better; you must bet more." Palane is truthful as he speaks. His horse is a buffalo runner, a much better horse than Lambert's mustang.

"Ok, what do you want?"

Palane shrugs, "Me take your leather seat on horses back."

"My saddle?" Lambert looks over where his saddle rests on a tie rail. He worked almost a year to buy the saddle, and it has been hard work every day of that year. "Yes."

Corey steps forward and interrupts the betting. "You boys better wait and see what Samuel has to say about all this."

"He'll ride for the ranch," Lambert brags. "He ain't about to let the Stallings' name and his riding be put down."

"Let's have a bite to eat and we'll settle this little argument later." Corey points toward the house where Sarah is motioning for them to come for dinner.

Walking toward the house, Samuel only shrugs his shoulders as Lambert explains about the bet Palane wanted to make. He has ridden bad horses all his life, but this would be the first time he has ever wagered on the outcome of a bucking horse.

Palane follows Corey into the ranch house. This is only the second time in his life he has been in a white man's house. Looking curiously around the kitchen, where the women have a fire going under a large iron pot, he sits down in the chair Corey motions him to.

Looking over at Corey, he whispers. "I have never eaten in a white man's house, or with their strange knives."

"Well, then this will be your first." Corey shows Palane how to hold a fork.

Samuel and Lambert sit down at the table and look shrewdly over at Palane. Samuel doesn't care one way or the other, but Lambert is dead set on betting with Palane, and showing the Kiowa his brother is the best rider.

"Okay Palane, I'm gonna bet with you." Lambert nods, folding his arms on the table, "I'll even bet you two more horses, if you're willing, that is."

Corey and Ben try to change the subject. Seeing they were fighting a losing battle, they remain quiet as the subject is discussed back and forth between Lambert and Palane. Corey doesn't know why Palane is here, but he knows it isn't about riding a horse or checking on Colby. Still, he knows Indians love to wager and they would bet on anything, losing everything they owned sometimes, leastways that was the way the Cherokees were back in Arkansas.

"You in Samuel?" Lambert is chomping at the bit to bet with Palane. "Want to bet anything?"

"I'm in, but I'm making my own bet. I'm wagering three horses against three of his." Samuel nods at the warrior, who had just taken a large bite of biscuits and gravy.

Nodding his head, Palane swallows. "Me bet three horses, ten horses, it no matter, you lose."

Lambert grins, "Good, now down to the rules."

"What rules? We ride horse is all."

"There has to be rules, Palane." Samuel looks over at the warrior who has already eaten enough for two men. "You know, how many horses are we gonna ride; how long."

"You make rules, tell Palane; we ride, then take your horses our village." Palane is confident.

"You're sure a cocky injun," Lambert laughs.

"No cocky, me see him ride, me see Kiowa ride, you lose." Palane shrugs his shoulders. "You pick out good horses for Palane to trade for squaw."

"For a woman; what are you talking about for Pete's sake?"

"Palane take your horses to village," the warrior grins. "Trade them for new wife."

Corey has to hide his face in his big hands. He knows Palane is intentionally trying to goad the boys to make them lose their confidence. It's an old trick of any gambler. Scare your opponent, and the race is half over with before it starts.

"You'd trade our good horses for a woman?" Lambert is perplexed.

"You got 'em smoke maybe?" Palane asks.

Corey laughs and guides him out the front door, leaving Lambert and Samuel sitting at the table. Looking back through the open door at the table, he chuckles again as he and Palane make their way toward the corrals.

Producing a sack of tobacco and some papers, Corey rolls the warrior a smoke, then one for himself. Standing with one foot on the lower rail, Palane watches as Samuel enters the corral and starts working with a new horse.

"He is good with horse," Palane admits.

"Is that why you tried to scare the boys?" Corey watches as Samuel pulls the bronc's head around to him and mounts in one fluid motion.

Palane smiles, "Kiowa people find the fun of betting is in the talking before the actual race."

"I don't think you're gonna rattle Samuel."

"Rattle?"

"It means scare."

"We see." Palane blows out smoke. "Your woman, the dark haired one, she cooks good. Does she have husband?"

"No, my sister is not married," Corey's ears come on point.

"She is skinny, but perhaps she wishes a husband." Palane looks toward the house. "I have many horses. How many would her father wish for her?"

Corey coughs slightly, even though he already knows what Palane is leading up to. The Indian way is to buy a wife, and in his world, what he has just proposed, is proper, and a compliment to the woman. Somehow Corey knows Ben Stallings would not take it that way and Judith, well she would laugh it all off in her own way.

Corey has to be careful here. He doesn't want to embarrass Palane or shame him outright with a straight no, for an answer. Corey knows he is not good with words. He always let his fists do his talking. This is a very delicate matter. Corey sure doesn't want to offend a man who has helped them get Colby back twice.

"Palane." Corey is trying to find the exact words he needs when Palane breaks into a wide grin.

"You see, white man; all of you rattle as you say. I do not want white woman. I just want see you rattle." Palane thinks it is a good joke.

Corey blows out a breath of air. "You had me there for a minute." He actually, in that minute, came to like this warrior. "My friend, you did have me rattled."

Lambert comes walking up as Corey is regaining his composure. "Palane, our horses are just scrub mustangs, but we were wondering if you had any running horses in your village?"

"You want to have race with our horses?"

"Well, since we're having a bet, we might as well." Lambert looks over sideways at Corey. "You know, everyone loves a good horse race."

"What you bet this time?" Palane acts unsure.

"Three more horses of your pick."

Corey straightens up. "Lambert did you ask pa about the horses."

"Why, me and Samuel caught 'em, broke 'em, and if we want, we can bet with them."

"Yeah, and if he wants, pa will tan your hides for you. If I were you, I'd ask before I wagered anymore," Corey warns.

Palane doesn't give Lambert a chance to back out. "We will come in three suns. You and me have bet; we race horse."

Somehow Corey feels Lambert and Samuel have just been suckered in. How, he doesn't know, he just feels it. He knows the Kiowa love their horses, and they weren't about to foolishly gamble them away. He also knows Palane noticed the tall thoroughbred stallion in the smaller lot. The warrior is no sucker. Palane was a horseman from birth. He could tell the big stallion could run a lick, yet he still took the bet.

Palane swings up on his horse and watches as Lambert walks away, a new strut in his walk.

"I brought you this." Palane turns his attention back to Corey and hands him a rolled up rabbit skin. Inside, folded up neatly, is a dried scalp, old and grey.

"Micah?"

"He fought the Mexican Hernandez. He asked the people to tell you how he died, so someone would know."

"He was an old man." Corey looks at the scalp. "Much too old, to fight."

Palane nods. "The warrior who brought me the old one's hair and watched the fight said Micah challenged the Mexican, then died fighting, trying to revenge his son."

"He was too old."

"It doesn't matter; we all die." Palane looks directly at Corey. "It only matters how we die, that is all."

"I should have ridden with him."

"He died bravely, and he almost killed Hernandez as the Mexican was taking his hair."

"Almost killed him, how, what happened?"

"The scar faced one thought Micah was dead and walked too close. As he knelt down to take the scalp, the old one's knife reached for the Mexican's stomach, but not far enough. It didn't kill him." Palane shrugs.

"I'll be, that had to have hurt, playing dead while you're being scalped."

"I brought his hair here for you to bury and sing his praises." Palane hands over the scalp.

"I will do that."

Palane starts to turn away, but stops. "The old man, I have known him all my life. He was brave. Sing loud so his grandfathers will hear when he travels the warrior's path to them."

Corey only nods grimly as Palane turns slowly and rides away. Looking down at the light bundle in his hand, Corey nods his head slowly. "I will sing very loud for you, Micah Halleck."

CHAPTER 11

B en Stallings' voice can be heard all the way to the corrals. "You what?"

Corey knows Lambert must be explaining how he managed to wager three more horses.

"It's a cinch, Pa. With Samuel riding him, they ain't got nothing that'll touch that thoroughbred stud of yours."

"Lambert Stallings, I ought to tan your backsides, and I will if you lose my horses." Ben Stallings chuckles to himself as Lambert walks away. With the threat of a good strapping, the lad is not quite as positive or cocksure of the wager's outcome as he once was.

Ben remembers betting six of his mother's good laying hens, one winter many years ago on a family coonhound, then the hound up and lost the coon hunt. Man, he took a strapping from her when she had to watch those six good laying hens head down the road into the arms of Jedidiah Beck. It wasn't so much, she lost her chickens, it was that their best hound had been shown up and outrun by that no-account blue tick dog of the Beck boys. He smiles, remembering that night. It was a bad night for him and his dog. The blue tick just got lucky. Those old time Ozark folks definitely had their family pride, and shucks, their hounds were family.

Several fistfights broke out over the results of the hunt when the judges of the contest awarded the win to Beck's dog. The next day, the chickens were still laying their eggs at the Beck house, and Ben's bottom was still stinging. His mama could sure handle a willow switch. He remembers he couldn't sit down for a week after that.

The next three days were busy around the ranch house. Palane implied Chief Cayuse and many other warriors would come to watch the match and they expect to eat as well. Corey killed and dressed a young bull buffalo, and the girls are now smoking hams and back-strap over a slow fire. How many Indians will show up, Corey doesn't know, but it wouldn't surprise him if the whole Kiowa Tribe arrives for the activities.

Samuel put front shoes on the tall thoroughbred and has been working him slowly, around the oval track. Lambert tries not to show it, but he is as nervous as a June bug in a henhouse. If he loses his pa's horses, he knows there is gonna be hob to pay, and it isn't gonna be Samuel or anyone else suffering the consequences, only him. Well, there's no sense crying over spilt milk, Corey certainly warned him.

The morning of the big race and buck out, arrives, and so does about thirty of the Kiowa elders, warriors, and Chief Cayuse. They came in about midmorning with the sun at their backs. All arrayed in their finest clothes, new deer hide, hunting shirts, decorated with porcupine quills, and the finest moccasins and leggings, all quilled and dyed. The elders are all wearing the long trailing string of eagle feathers floating on the air, each feather representing a feat of bravery, a mark of honor for the wearer. Their horses are groomed and painted with emblems of every kind.

They put on quite a show for the whites, charging their mustangs back and forth across the yard, yelling, and screaming. All are expert riders and eager to show off their skills, and to show they are proud to be Kiowa. The paint stallion, Corey gave Chief Cayuse, prances across the yard with his rider, and stands quietly, as the chief raises his arm in a gesture of peace. They definitely are quite something for the whites to behold.

At Ben's insistence, Corey reluctantly stays close to the ranch and does not ride out to check the surrounding grasslands. With the Kiowa present, Ben argues the Mexicans wouldn't cause any trouble at the ranch, but he really wants Corey nearby in case he needs him.

Palane is all grins and smiles as he rides into the ranch yard and slips quietly to the ground. Behind him, another warrior leads the ugliest, pigeon toed horse Corey has ever seen. The poor horse is sway-backed, his withers stand up sharp as a knife blade, and he is ewe necked. What an animal, but for some reason, Corey doesn't share Lambert's glee at seeing the poor thing. Something about the gleam in the horse's eye says beware.

Lambert, on the other hand, is finding it difficult to keep from laughing, as Palane presents his racehorse.

"Maybe you would like to wager a few more horses?" The Kiowa look over at Lambert, who is about to bust, trying to keep a straight face. Lambert is about to reply when he catches the scalding glare of Corey's eye.

"No Palane, I reckon not. Pa's not real happy now." Lambert turns down the bet. "Sides, if the old saying, winning by a nose, is true, that horse's head is so long, you'd win by several noses."

"Yes young one, his head is big, but look at all the brains it takes to fill it," Palane laughs.

"I never heard a horse needing brains to run a race." Lambert shakes his head.

"Ah, but there you are wrong," Palane laughs. "Brains in any animal make them more dangerous."

Pulling Corey off to the side, Lambert takes him by the arm excitedly. "Dang Corey, that poor thing can barely walk, much less run."

"Don't let his looks fool you, little brother." Corey looks over as the warrior leads the gelding away. "Look at that deep chest and powerful rear end."

"So?"

"That horse can run a lick, or my name ain't Corey Stallings."

"Shucks, he's so pigeon toed, he can hardly walk without tripping over his own feet," Lambert argues. "I doubt he'll make it to the finish line without falling down."

"Just cause a horse's feet are turned in, don't mean he can't run." Corey admonishes Lambert. "You do what you want to, but if I were you, I'd let well enough alone."

"You mean you wouldn't bet any more?"

"That's exactly what I mean," Corey nods. "I think your backsides will thank you for refraining from losing any more of your pappy's horses."

"I'll bet my good skinning knife against yours, old ugly is left in the dust by pa's thoroughbred."

Corey shakes his head. "You're just aching to bet ain't you?"

"Well, you know what they say," Lambert grins, watching the little horse walk away. "Every dog has his day, and brother, I feel like mine's today."

"They also say, a fool and his money are soon parted."

"You betting or not?"

"Alright Lambert, you got yourself a bet."

Cayuse and the elders of the tribe sit around in a circle and smoke as their women serve steaming hot dishes of buffalo meat, hot bread, and gallons of black coffee. The atmosphere around the ranch is jovial as everyone is in a good mood awaiting the upcoming horse race with enthusiasm.

Warriors dance and strut about, while telling of their heroic deeds in battle, and of the buffalo chases they participated in. The older men smoke their ceremonial pipes and insist Ben smoke with them. Corey stands alone, near the corrals, smoking and watching the proceedings. Feeling a presence near him, he turns to find Sarah close behind him.

"They are something aren't they Corey?" She smiles, "Wild and free as the wind."

"Yes, they are."

"Look at Colby. He's having a great time." Sarah points to where Colby stands laughing with Palane.

"Yes, he is. He has really taken to Palane."

"Oh, Corey, look. Here comes Papa Ben's horse." Sarah is excited about the race. "Isn't he beautiful?"

"I'll have to admit, he is a beauty alright." Corey watches Caleb lead the tall thoroughbred past.

The big thoroughbred is led prancing toward the throng of warriors who stare in admiration at him. He is definitely a thing of beauty, blood bay, with black up to his knees and only a spot of white in his forehead.

Long legs and a short back lead to a beautiful small head and sparkling eyes.

Next comes the smaller gelding of Palane. The skinny horse walks quietly beside the warrior leading him, never twitching an ear as the circle of warriors surround him. Watching him shy away from the bigger stallion, Lambert laughs, swearing the poor thing is embarrassed to stand next to the stallion. There definitely isn't any comparison between the two. Where the thoroughbred has a coat of hair that shines like a twinkling bright star, the gelding still has last year's winter coat, which is long, full of cockleburs, and dull. In looks, the two horses are as different as daylight and dark.

Corey stands off to the side and watches as Palane starts to harangue the warriors, trying to get them to bet against his horse. Several walk over to the thoroughbred and run their hands over his velvet smooth hide, shaking their heads and walking off. He knows Lambert might be in a little trouble when not one warrior bets against the little horse. Finally, as no one dare place a bet against Palane, Corey knows he is right. The warriors know this horse and they know he can run. Finally, Palane gives up in disgust and walks over to Corey.

"They will not bet," Palane frowns. "They are afraid to lose."

"Do you blame them?" Corey grins. "I'll bet they've seen your little horse run many times."

Palane looks innocently up at the taller man and laughs. "You are right, white man. This horse, well, he's not pretty, but the warriors know he has never lost a race."

"Yet." Lambert walks up and adds his two cents worth. "Today we're gonna change that."

"Never," Palane shrugs. "You wish to bet more, young one?"

"I ain't allowed, but I sure would if I could." Lambert kicks the ground, looking sideways at Corey.

Palane shrugs. "Your horse is sure to win. He is bigger, prettier. Surely you wish to bet more on him."

"Can't." Lambert shrugs and walks away.

Sarah carries out another pan of buffalo ribs and steaks. Setting them down on a table, she walks to where Corey is still standing, leaning against the corral. "Is it safe to have all these warriors right in our yard?"

Corey smiles down at her. "Scared?"

"No, not when you're close, but they seem so savage." Her eyes dart around the yard.

"They are our guests, Sarah. Now if I were to meet them out on the range, yes, I would worry, but not here."

"Why not here?"

Corey lets his gaze drift across the gathered Kiowa. "Because, they come as friends and would not disgrace themselves by any act of violence while here."

"They are heathens, Corey. I have heard they have no principles, when it comes to violence."

"You are wrong, young lady. In their own way, they have more principles than we do."

"Corey Stallings, look at me. I am a full-grown woman, not a young lady." Sarah's eyes flash at the insinuation she is a child.

Looking down at her, he recognizes the fire in her eyes. "My apologies Sarah, you are indeed a grown woman."

"Thank you," she smiles. "I'm glad you finally noticed the fact."

Quickly changing the subject, Corey nods at the warriors. "Right now, these warriors are our friends. Next time we meet, who knows."

"I know you are right, but what about Colby?"

"Colby, what about him?" Corey asks curiously, looking around for the boy.

Sarah points to where Colby sits laughing beside Cayuse. "He seems to be taken with the warrior, he sits by."

"He is, the warrior is their war chief, Cayuse, and he kinda adopted Colby as his own."

"Adopted, and you don't mind?"

"No, I don't mind." Corey looks down at her. "The Kiowa already saved Colby's life and maybe yours too."

"I should be getting back inside to help Judith." She lets her hand linger on his arm slightly, smiling up at him before she turns toward the house. "I am a full-grown woman, Corey."

Corey watches as she walks away. Yes, Sarah is a full-grown woman, but she is the wife of his dead brother. In Corey's eyes, she is still married to Eli. For him to think of her in any other way, seems almost disrespectful to his memory.

As the day wears on, several horse races have already been run. All are the prelude to the upcoming race that everyone eagerly waits for. Corey is about to walk toward the corrals when a whistle from the roof takes his attention. Samuel waves his hat and points toward the grasslands, off to the south. A lone rider sits his horse at least a mile out on the flats. Studying the horse and rider for several minutes, Corey strains his eyes to no avail. The rider is just too far away to make out, but he can tell the rider wears a huge Mexican sombrero.

Palane walks over to where Corey stands watching the man. "Who is he?"

Corey only shrugs and walks further out, away from the corrals. Waving his arm, he tries to motion the man in. "Whoever he is, he doesn't want to come in any closer."

Palane follows Corey, standing beside him. "This one, he waits for you to come to him."

"I know!"

"I don't think this rider comes for the horse racing." Palane turns. "I will ride out and see what he wants."

"No, my friend. You are a guest, but I thank you." Corey starts toward the corrals. "I think I know what he wants, anyway I will go see."

"Be careful, my friend, it could be a trap."

"No, I don't think so." Corey turns toward the corral. "I figure this may be a personal matter if Micah Halleck was right."

Palane looks sharply at Corey. "The old one?"

Saddling a horse, Corey quickly checks his pistols and kicking the gelding into a slow lope, he rides out, toward the waiting stranger. He knows this is the Mexican Micah warned him about. He can feel it and the closer he rides to the man, the surer he is.

Pulling the horse down to a walk, he studies the man as he rides up close to him. He is a big man, maybe bigger than Corey himself, Micah said he was. The face is smooth shaven, no facial hair, so familiar with the Mexican race. Corey can tell, by the straight set of the man's shoulders and his steady gaze, here is a proud man, a man of honor.

Pistols hang on the man's hips, plus two more attached to his saddle swells. A rifle is slung across his back. A heavy bowie knife finishes off the man's armaments.

Corey waits quietly. He knows, before him sits a real fighting man, a dangerous man. Intelligent black eyes, peer at him from beneath a large black sombrero. Across from him sits Señor Don Lorenzo, the Mexican Micah warned him about.

"You must be Don Lorenzo. I don't recall your Christian name." Corey speaks first.

"It is Ricardo. So you know me?" The voice is deep and strong, a voice of confidence. "That is good."

"Micah Halleck said you would be coming."

"The old hunter is dead. Hernandez killed him." The man's voice wavers on the last words. "He was a great hunter and tracker. He once led me on a great buffalo hunt. He was a good man."

"He said you were the only man he ever feared."

"Yes, he witnessed things I had to do to keep control of Santa Anna's army." Lorenzo shrugs. "Many, many bad things."

"I heard." Corey watches Lorenzo's eyes closely, as Micah warned him. His arm is tingling with anticipation of the man's draw. "Why are you here?"

"If you know my name señor, you know why I am here."

"I figure I know, but why don't you tell me anyway."

"I have come for the killer of my brother, Roberto." The man rides closer to Corey. "Send him out to face me."

"Your brother attacked this ranch, and was trying his best to kill all of us."

"That does not matter. This is Mexican land, and you have no right here." Lorenzo tenses. "You are trespassers."

"Our deed says we do."

"Sam Houston's paper is worthless, now send him out." Don Ricardo drops his hand downward.

Corey smiles. "The one you seek is here, señor. I am your man, Mister Lorenzo."

Corey watches the man as he straightens as if to draw. Slowly, his eyes roll backward in his head as he slides sideways from his horse. Dismounting warily, Corey walks over to where the man is lying on the ground, one foot still hanging in a stirrup. The dark eyes glare in pain as they watch Corey approach. The man's coat falls open, revealing a large blotch of blood on his right side. Corey didn't notice before, being engrossed in watching the man's eyes, but the shirt and right leg are drenched in blood.

"Peers like you've been shot." Corey kneels beside the man, examining the wound. "You've been hit hard."

"Si, I apologize." Lorenzo whispers hoarsely. "I wanted to finish with you before I fell from my horse like a woman."

Palane, Lambert, Ben, and several others, ride out to where the man lies, surrounding the Mexican, they stare down at him.

"Let's get him in the house. He's been shot bad." Corey nods at his brothers.

"Let me die, señor, or you will regret it later." Lorenzo pushes away the hands that reach for him. "Let me die."

Palane stares unemotionally down at the fallen man. "He is a dead man already. Leave him to die here. Let us have our horse race."

Corey shakes his head at the warrior. "Let's take him inside."

"When the old hunter passed through our village, looking for the Mexican Hernandez, he told the Kiowa this one would come one day and try to kill you." Palane argues, "Let him die."

"Pick him up."

Several hands pick Don Lorenzo up from the ground and start toward the house.

"What's he talking about Corey?" Ben questions.

Corey never spoke of the Mexican or the threat Micah warned him about. Explaining, as they walk toward the house, Ben only nods as the story is finished.

"Well, dat gummit, what's one more problem?" Ben shakes his craggy head. "I mean, we only got a few hundred now."

The bullet entered Don Lorenzo's back and exited the left side, leaving only a small exit wound. He has lost much blood and greatly weakened, he finally passes out as he is laid on a bed. Sarah and Judith go to work on their patient quickly, while he can't feel the pain. Growing up, with the feud going on for years, both women have vast experience with gunshot wounds.

The warriors outside are still in a festive mood. Men being shot, out on the plains, is just an everyday experience for them.

Corey watches as Sarah quickly washes the wound clean and sews up Lorenzo, wrapping his side tightly with bandages.

"He gonna make it?" Lambert asks curiously.

Judith shrugs. "He's lost a lot of blood, it's hard to say."

"We best get outside to our guests. It's about time for you to lose your bet." Corey pushes Lambert toward the door.

"What about him?" Lambert hesitates, looking back at the bed. "We gonna leave him?"

"I don't s'pect he'll be going anywhere for a while, if ever."

"Don't seem Christian to be gambling and horse racing with a man dying in our house," Lambert argues.

"To our way of thinking it ain't, but the Kiowa out there aren't Christians and will be highly insulted if we don't run our horse."

Lambert takes one last look at the unconscious man then follows Corey out to where Palane and the Kiowa are standing around.

"Cayuse want to know if Mexican alive?" Palane nods at Chief Cayuse.

"He is, for now anyway."

"My Chief knows this one, bad man, much fight, kill." Palane shakes his head. "Come here to kill you maybe."

"So I've heard," Corey nods.

"Then maybe you should kill bad man, while he sleeps," Palane grins. "Let him die as I told you."

Corey shakes his head. "Let's have our horse race."

Palane shakes his head again. "Palane think you no hear so good, white man."

"Palane, I can't kill a defenseless man."

"Me kill for you." Palane looks back at the house. "You go race horse. I take care of brown man."

Corey only shakes his head. "No, now let's have our horse race."

"You rattle easy, white man," Palane laughs.

As the two riders come up to what is designated as the starting line, Samuel dwarfs over the shorter Indian rider as the thoroughbred towers over the little horse. This doesn't faze Palane in the least, as he tries his best to get someone to bet with him. Finally giving up in disgust, he translates to his rider the rules of the race that he and Lambert agreed on. Lambert wants the race to be three laps of the oval circle where they work their horses, but Palane wants only two laps. Corey knows why, but this is Lambert and Samuel's horse race, so he keeps quiet. He figures the smaller horse would have great speed for a short distance, but if the race is lengthened, the thoroughbred would pick up speed and in the third lap overtake his opponent.

"Alright, two laps," Lambert gives up arguing with the warrior and lets him have his way.

"Bad mistake," Corey whispers to Ben.

"Why so?"

"You'll see, Pa, you'll see."

Ben laughs openly. "You telling me, that little runt can outrun my studhorse?"

"He will, at two laps."

"Not at a half lap, no sir."

"Have it your way, but don't say I didn't warn you." Corey shrugs.

The horses stand on the line marked off by Lambert's boot. The thoroughbred trembles and prances around, while the little horse stands there quietly, as if he is bored with the whole thing. Cayuse raises his riding crop for all to see and suddenly drops it. Corey only grins as the little horse springs forward like a rifle shot, his short legs working like pistons in the deep sand. Corey knows a jackrabbit has nothing on the little swayback horse of the Kiowa.

Lambert's eyes bug out, almost falling off his face, as the smaller horse jumps ahead by almost twenty feet. The scary part for Lambert is, those short legs are drumming a steady rhythm as they make the first turn, and the thoroughbred isn't closing the gap. The warrior lies flat on the little horse, clinging to the horse like a tick on a hound's back and hollering at the top of his lungs. Urging him on with his feet and hands, the little Indian is riding like a banshee, urging more speed out of the little ugly horse with every stride.

Corey already knows the result. In such a short race, the long legged thoroughbred, from the first jump, didn't have a ghost of a chance of catching the smaller horse. Another lap and maybe it would have happened, but he still isn't sure. The short distance and curves benefit the Indian horse considerably more than the Stallings' horse. The bigger horse closes the gap, his head almost to the smaller horse's tail, when they cross the boot mark designating the finish line.

Lambert kicks the ground in disgust as Palane walks up grinning. "Now we will have the riding."

"I reckon." Lambert still can't believe the ugliest horse in the country, the ugliest horse that ever existed, has just outrun the greatest racehorse in Arkansas. Who would have ever thought that little runt could run like that? Well, Corey warned him. Weren't no use crying over spilt milk.

"Sure looked like he was half jackrabbit the way he covered the ground, didn't he, brother?" Samuel slaps Lambert on the back, laughing. "Yes, sir, all ears and legs."

Lambert lets out with an expletive and follows Samuel toward the corrals. "You better win the riding or we better hide out, before pa gets ahold of us."

"We? I don't remember pa being mad at me," Samuel bursts into laughter again. "It's your backsides he'll be after."

"You gonna leave me hanging out to dry?"

"You worried?" Samuel grins, looking over where Sarah is standing with Judith.

"Yeah, I'm worried." Lambert shakes his head in disgust as the little horse is led past them. "What are them no-account Kiowa's gonna come up with this time?"

"Don't worry little brother. I'll pull your chestnuts out of the fire as usual." Samuel averts his eyes as Sarah looks right at him. "For your information, they're not no-account, Lambert, just darn good horsemen."

"Ok, brother Samuel, just how are you planning on saving my backsides?" Lambert studies Samuel.

"Don't worry, you just go plunk down some more bets with Palane and his friends, and I'll handle the rest."

"Not me, brother. I'm in Dutch with pa as far as I'm gonna get myself." Samuel shakes his head.

"Do it. Trust me."

"Trust you my foot. Last time you said that, pa like to beat us to death." Lambert watches as Corey and Palane choose horses for the riders. "No, sir, not me."

"That was different. I didn't know he was gonna drink that stuff we mixed up for Sid Wright at that dance."

"Well, he did drink it, and that stuff liked to have killed him, is what it done."

Samuel sighs in disgust. "Lambert it just gave him a little headache from being drunk and a few quick trips to the outhouse, now go get down as many bets as you can."

"Pa might have got a headache, but my backside got a bigger ache. I couldn't sit myself down to eat proper for a month."

"Git."

"Alright, but I'm a telling pa this was your idea if it don't work out like it's supposed to. I ain't gonna keep quiet like last time, no sir."

"Fine, fine," Samuel grins. It was kinda funny watching pa hurry to the outhouse every few minutes. Course now, when he found out why, it sure wasn't so funny.

Samuel beat a hasty trip over to where Corey and Palane were making their final selection for the bronc riding. Taking Corey by the arm, Samuel pulls him off, out of hearing, as Palane studies the milling mustangs that have never been touched by a human's hand, as of yet.

"Select the roan as your last horse." Samuel nods at the roan standing alone in another corral.

"Why, you've already broke him to ride." Corey looks dumbfounded at Samuel. "He won't buck a lick."

"Just do it, Corey."

Palane puts up a fuss as the roan is brought out, arguing he wasn't with the others to pick from. Corey shrugs his shoulders saying it was just an oversight, telling Palane he can choose the roan if he wants.

Smelling a trick, and noticing the saddle marks on the roan, Palane turns down the offer, picking a sturdy-built paint as his last horse. Three horses are chosen for each rider, the roan being Corey's last pick. No time limit is set and no rules applied except the rider would only qualify if he were still atop the bronc when the horse stops bucking.

The corral is crowded with Indian warriors sitting on the top rail, eager for the fun to begin. Samuel's opposition is the same small, wiry rider that rode in the race against him.

Palane is still eyeing the roan as Lambert walks up. "You have been betting again young one. I thought your father forbid you to wager more?"

"He changed his mind," Lambert lies. "I've still got a few items to wager Palane. You willing?"

"Perhaps it has something to do with the roan horse over there."

Lambert shrugs innocently. "He's the same as any of the others, I reckon."

They agreed the Indian rider would ride his horses bareback, while Samuel could use his scarred up old saddle. Chief Cayuse is master of ceremonies. He holds a stone behind his back, letting Lambert and Palane pick a hand to see who will ride first. Picking the hand with the stone in it, Palane wins and chooses to let his rider go last.

Watching Samuel, as he places his old bronc saddle on the paint, Palane shakes his head and looks over at Corey dubiously. "I still think there is something wrong with the roan."

"What about the little horse and two laps," Corey grins. "You know what they say?"

"No, me not know what white man say."

"Palane my friend, every dog has his day."

"Kiowa eat dog, pretty good."

Corey grins. "That's not quite what I meant."

Samuel eases into the saddle and pulls the blindfold off the paint, all in one smooth fluid motion. He can feel the power in the animal and he wasn't wrong. The mustang gathers himself and launches his body airborne as Samuel screws himself down into the high backed saddle and pulls his hat down. Even before he climbed aboard, he felt this was gonna be a wild ride.

The ground tilts in every direction as the paint lunges and kicks straight back, rolling hard when he hits the ground. Bawling and moaning, the horse sunfishes, back and forth, across the corral, plowing headfirst into the timbers. Knocking himself backward, he stands there on shaking legs, letting his head clear a minute before exploding into the air again.

Finally, unable to get the weight from his back, he flings himself backward, hitting the ground with a jarring thud. Samuel pushes himself from the saddle at the last minute, before the horse rolls on top of the saddle. Stepping back into the saddle, as the horse pushes himself up on his front feet, Samuel pulls his hat down hard again, and waits for the next lunge.

The paint banged his head hard against the ground in his last fall. This time, the mustang is finished. Winded and a little dazed, he stands spraddle-legged. When he finally manages to stagger to his feet, the fight goes from him. Samuel swings down, sidestepping a well-placed kick from the paint, and removes his saddle.

The onlookers all holler and clap, even the Kiowa. They know a good ride when they see one. The next horse belongs to the small warrior, and he too puts on a good show, even though the horse isn't as big and strong as the paint. Bucking the mustang out, the rider makes it look easy as he stands straight up on the bronc when it finally quit lunging and bucking around the corral, giving out and stopping.

Lambert is sweating bullets. He bet everything he and Samuel owns on this contest. Crap, he would be walking around naked if Samuel loses this contest. The little Kiowa rider is as Palane said, very good. Palane is grinning from ear to ear as he congratulates his rider, turning to where the next horse has been roped and is being drawn toward the snubbing post.

Samuel makes this ride look even easier as he rides the horse to a standstill. He uncinches his saddle and removes the heavy halter, then steps off the mustang. The warrior's second horse is roped, and again the small Indian rides the wild mustang like he is sitting in a rocking chair. Corey grins as he thinks Lambert looks sick when he notices Ben glaring at both him and Samuel. Lambert knows they better win, but even a draw would look good to him right now. At least Ben wouldn't lose all of his horses.

The last horse Palane picked for Samuel to ride is a palomino, slim of build, but stout. Turned loose, this one is more prone to run around the corral and kick up his feet than actually buck. Acting bored, Samuel wants to put on an extra good show for the Kiowa. Pulling out a pack of tobacco he builds himself a cigarette and lights it. As the palomino finally runs out of breath, Samuel throws his hat in the air and slides to the ground, all the while puffing away on a smoking cigarette in his mouth. The roar of the spectators, showing their appreciation for the good show, sounds again with Lambert's voice the loudest.

The roan is the last horse to ride. If the little Kiowa is able to best the horse, then the contest would be considered a draw, and all wagers would be off. However, if the Indian rider gets bucked off, Lambert and Samuel would be the winners. That would make it a draw for the day and Lambert knows that would save his bacon, not to mention his bottom.

The horse stands quietly as the warrior slips on the rawhide hackamore and removes the rope. Looking over at Palane, the rider grins, and bounces nimbly onto the red roans back. All eyes are glued on the roan as the horse turns his head slightly to look at the little warrior sitting on his back. Samuel grins over at Palane. He knows exactly what is fixing to happen. He has already experienced the ride himself, first hand. He only hopes it would turn out the same for the warrior as it turned out for him.

Suddenly the stout roan flattens his ears and goes airborne in a powerful lunge. The roan seems to reverse himself in midair, turning belly-up to the sky before ducking out from under the rider as he comes to the ground. On the very first jump, Samuel notices the Kiowa lost his death grip on the horse, slipping back a few inches from his withers with only a handful of mane holding him on. The next jump is a humdinger, as Samuel already knows, enough to sling the little rider off to the side of the horse. One last final lunge and a hard spin to the right, sends him flying through the air. It happens so fast and furious, the small warrior never has time to get into rhythm with the horse before he finds himself sitting headfirst, covered in dirt, on the sandy corral ground.

Lambert hollers and whistles, whirling Samuel around as he walks up. Palane has lost his grin, and he has lost the contest. Walking over to the boys, he nods, then laughs.

"The grandfathers told me I should never trust a white man. I knew there was something wrong with that roan horse." Palane shakes his head. "What a horse."

"We picked your rider the gentlest horse on the ranch Palane," Samuel speaks, winking at Corey who still stands there, dumbfounded.

"Gentle? Him bad horse, white man."

Samuel laughs again. While everyone watches, he catches the roan and saddles him. Looking over to where Sarah has been watching the riding, he motions for her to come into the corral. Holding the gelding, he waits for her to walk across the corral.

"Just get on him and walk him around the corral, Sarah." Samuel holds the reins out to her. "It'll be okay."

"Is he gonna buck me off?" Sarah looks at the roan suspiciously.

"Hope not, it's sure gonna make me look bad, if he does," Samuel laughs, taking her by the arm.

"Samuel Stallings, you get me bucked off in front of all these people and I'm gonna poison you."

"You promise?" His blue eyes stare into hers.

Pulling her eyes away from his, Sarah reluctantly steps into the saddle, looking down at him as he backs away. Nudging the roan with her heel, she walks him around the corral slowly, then picks him up into a trot as the spectators, both red and white, go wild with laughter. Even Palane has to laugh, as he knows the joke is on him.

"I would never have believed it." Corey watches Sarah ride the roan. "Why, what caused him to buck the Kiowa off like he did?"

"He'll ride with a saddle fine, but you better not ride him bareback," Samuel answers Corey's comment, never taking his eyes off Sarah. "I found that out the hard way."

"By golly, he can sure buck, that's a bona fide fact." Ben slaps his leg as he walks up. "What a horse."

All bets are settled and squared up as the Kiowa go back to enjoying the feast the women prepared for them. Judith walks out on the porch, holding her bloody apron in front of her.

Seeing her standing there, Corey walks over, stepping up on the porch. "How is he?"

Judith looks at him, "He's alive, for now, but just barely."

Corey looks over to the corrals where Samuel and Sarah are still standing beside the roan laughing and talking. Dropping his eyes, he enters the house.

CHAPTER 12

After the fiasco of the buffalo wallow, Manny Sharps and Josh Slocum ride hard and fast through the night and day for four days to reach the safety of the small village of Bowie. Entering the town, they study the streets closely for anything suspicious, and lead their ganted horses into the livery stable. Both men are spooked, not knowing the whereabouts of Hernandez or the Stallings men.

Three days after arriving, Slocum sits at a small table playing poker with two other men while Sharps sits alone, putting down shot after shot of Tequila at another table. Sharps turns surly and mean. Other customers avoid him like he has the pox. Both men are killing time in their own way, Slocum with cards, while Sharps nurses the tequila bottle and broods over the last few days of utter failure. Since their arrival, both men's attention constantly returns to the swinging doors of the saloon, each time someone enters.

With Slocum's luck at cards, and Sharps' moodiness, they soon wear out their welcome in the small town. Slocum refuses to leave as he has been on a winning streak at three card Monte, since hitting town. Sharps is afraid to venture outside the city limits without Slocum. The Mexicans could be anywhere, just waiting for him to leave the safety of the town.

Sharps is in a bad state mentally, not only because of the tequila bottle, several other things are responsible. Mostly, though, he is a coward and a bad case of the jitters keeps eating at him, gnawing at his insides. Restless nights, with no sleep, and the wicked, grinning face of Hernandez, waving the branding iron comes back to haunt him every time he closes his eyes. He was forced to watch, as the Mexican laughed wickedly, while branding Lon over and over, after his cousin was already dead. He knows the Mexican is sick. Sharps cusses himself as he knows he should have tried to stop the man. Sharps knows he is better than the Mexican with a gun, but he also knows he is a coward. He just can't face the man or look him in the eye.

The afternoon crowd in the saloon is small. Only a few town loafers sit around the well-worn tables, talking and tossing back drinks. None dare venture anywhere near Sharps or try to speak with him. His partner has been on a run of luck, that to most watching, has been unbelievable, even though they weren't about to accuse him of cheating. The gamblers finally gave up and left town as there is no other game in town. Besides, Slocum already took most of their money.

"Let's ride. Let's head back east to Arkansas," Sharps slurs his words, as he sits unsteadily, glaring over at Slocum.

"What's your hurry, Manny? We've got plenty of money now, why leave?" Slocum grins. He knows why Sharps is in a hurry to dust the town.

"You know why, Hernandez has had plenty of time to find us by now."

"He ain't coming here," Slocum shakes his head. "Relax."

"How do you know that for sure?"

"Why would he? What for?" Slocum shrugs his shoulders. "This town is too far east for the good health of Mexicans and they know it."

"We quit him, that's why, and there's still Stallings." Sharps looks toward the door.

"Quit worrying; Stallings ain't leaving his precious ranch, even if he knew where you were." Slocum throws down another drink. "Relax for Pete's sake."

"That's easy for you to say, he don't know anything about you."

Slocum is just about to say more when several Mexicans push through the swinging doors and enter the saloon, spreading around the room, their pistols out and ready. His empty drink is halfway back to the table when it stops in midair, his face a stunned look of disbelief.

Sharps' chair crashes backward on the floor as he lunges to his feet, his hand inches from the butt of his pistol. Seeing the futility of going up against so many drawn weapons, he lets his hand relax as Hernandez enters the room. His stomach feels like it turned to jelly as he gazes into the face of the Mexican. He looks down at the ever-present branding iron, clutched in the brown hand. Here he is, the devil who causes all his nightmares. Slocum stands up slowly, letting the shuffled cards, slide slowly from his chubby fingers.

Hernandez grins, making the scar widen as he watches the fear in their faces grow. "My friends, we meet again, eh?"

Sharps thinks he is going to be sick, he is so scared. Slocum recovers from the shock of seeing the Mexicans and steps forward, around the table.

"You're a long way from the canyon, Señor Hernandez."

"Si, I missed you and Señor Manny very much I think." Hernandez lifts one foot onto a chair, his big rowel Mexican spurs ringing out across the room.

"Missed us, why?"

Hernandez looks around the room at the hand full of loafers. Motioning at them, and waving his huge sombrero at the door, he laughs as they make a beeline for the door. Fear, in other men feeds his huge ego. Laying the branding iron on the poker table, the Mexican pulls out a chair. "Por favor my friends, sit and be comfortable while we talk."

Nervously, both men eye the heavy iron, and do as Hernandez orders. There is no escape and they are at his mercy. They can hear the noise of many horses, stomping their feet and moving about, coming from the street. Slocum knows Hernandez and how he operates. He would never come into a town like this unless he had it completely in his grasp. He knows without looking, several riders wait outside.

Smiling cruelly, as the two men sit down, Hernandez pulls out a chair for himself. "Now my friends, we have unfinished business."

Slocum looks across the table. "If you're gonna kill us, do it, and quit yapping."

"Señor Josh, my dear friend, kill you? Why would I do that to a compadre?" Hernandez pretends innocence. "We have shared many profitable ventures together, have we not?"

"We have," Slocum frowns. "Leastways, until this last ridiculous escapade."

Hernandez lunges forward, leaning over right in Sharps' face, causing the man to pale. "You ran out on me, but under the circumstances, that wasn't such a bad idea. We ran too. Is that not so Toreo?" Hernandez looks over at one of his men and relaxes into his chair. "Yes, we ran from the ones in the buffalo wallow."

"Si, patron."

"Tell me compadres, why did you kill my two men, and where is the young gringo?"

"We didn't kill them. We ran for our horses and found them already dead. The Stallings' boy was gone."

"Is this true Manny Sharps?" Hernandez turns his dark eyes on Sharps.

Nodding, the man swallows hard. "It's true. We also left your horses so you could escape."

"Who could have killed our compadres then? Perhaps, the others from the rancho?"

Hernandez looks puzzled. "Then they have the boy now."

"How would we know?" Slocum knows Hernandez plans to kill them, but he isn't going to show cowardice as Sharps is. "Like I said they were dead when we got to the horses."

"Toreo, bring me some of the Tequila that Señor Manny is so fond of."

"Si, patron."

"Señors, my dear friends, we have a problem," Hernandez acts sad. "I have lost many men and have gained nothing in return. This is a very bad thing, very bad. It makes me look bad."

"What about us? We lost money too." Sharps finally finds his voice.

"This I understand, but I have also lost face with my men." The Mexican downs a shot of Tequila and looks across at Sharps. "I would offer you some señor, but you look as if you've had enough."

"He has," Slocum growls. "Get on with it Hernandez, what do you want?"

"We are still partners, are we not?" Hernandez turns the branding iron with his finger. "We will go back to the rancho again, but this time we will succeed."

"Are you crazy? We can't go back there." Sharps looks stupefied at the man. "Corey Stallings will be ready for us."

"No, señor, I am not crazy. We will go back. Most of them burned in their casa, there are few left. First señors, you will tell me why you wished to attack this rancho so badly." Hernandez grins, spinning the branding iron again. "And please, don't tell me it was just to kill a man, or steal a redheaded woman, even though she was very beautiful."

Sharps looks over at Slocum, then down at the iron. "No, those are not the reason. There is money somewhere on that ranch, and now, since they sold their horses, there is more."

"Why you no tell me this before? Maybe we try harder to find this money." Hernandez pretends hurt feelings. "I would have waited and searched the rancho."

"I forgot about the money. I only wanted the woman." Sharps is scared. He knows Hernandez is just toying with him. The branding iron points straight at him. Sliding the bottle over to Sharps, the Mexican leader smiles. "Drink deeply Señor Manny, then we ride, it will be your last." Hernandez hesitates, grinning, "For a while, anyway."

In the corner of the saloon, a lone figure sits, watching and listening to the ongoing conversation between the arrogant, scar-faced Mexican and the two white men. Pretending to be passed out drunk, the listener has been completely ignored by everyone in the room when Hernandez ordered the saloon cleared. Picking up his head slowly, as the men exit the room, the tall man's blue eye focus coldly on the retreating back of Sharps.

He arrived in the saloon only moments before the Mexicans burst through the saloon doors. He started to call Sharps out and kill him, or die trying, when the doors swung open and several Mexicans entered with drawn guns. He heard Sharps is a coward, but he is still fast and accurate with the pistol strapped to his waist. Everyone in the mountains of Arkansas knew that for a fact. He is shocked as he watches the redhead stand there, his hands shaking, scared sick of the scar faced Mexican.

Only this untimely arrival of the Mexicans, busting into the saloon, spoiled his plans for Sharps. Frowning, he cusses his luck as he rises to his feet and follows the men from the building. Hatton Evans stares coldly at the bartender, who watches him curiously, as Sharps disappears through the swinging doors.

There would be another day, there always was. He will follow Sharps until hell freezes over, if necessary. It was Manny Sharps and that no-account Zeb Pike that were responsible for killing his brother Kyle, only a few days before he was to marry Judith Stallings.

Hat could remember the day, almost like it was yesterday. The events were burned into his brain. The two lovers were so engrossed in talking to each other on the street, they didn't notice Sharps and Pike slipping up behind them. The loud blast of the pistols, and Judith's loud screaming as Kyle was gunned down by the two men, is what caused Hat to run from where he was standing in the general store.

As he raced to Kyle's side, he recognized two riders, Manny Sharps and Zeb Pike, who were whipping their horses unmercifully as they fled west, out of town. That was four years ago and Hat Evans is still on Sharps' trail. He heard Corey Stallings killed Zeb Pike, and then later, Travis Pike as he was on his way to Texas. Sharps was harder to get to, not straying far from the safety of the Sharps' clan, or their mountain farm that was bristling with rifles. He also knew that word was out, the Stallings and Pikes made a truce, and Corey Stallings, the man killer, was headed for Texas. Now maybe Sharps would leave his safe haven and, unknown to him, Hatton Evans would be waiting somewhere along his trail.

That winter was severe. Hat Evans took refuge in town from the cold rain. Now he stands on the windblown main street of Fort Smith, Arkansas, watching for any sign of Manny Sharps or his friends. Suddenly, from the corner of his eyes, he notices Levi Pike, walking directly toward him. His hand, inches from his pistol, Evans waits calmly, wary of the approaching elder. He is suspicious as he knows of the volatile temper of the elder Pike, also of his hatred for Corey Stallings. Levi Pike himself is well aware of the close friendship of Hat Evans and Corey Stallings, something that made Evans very leery of the man.

The meeting turned to shock when the patriarch of the Pikes, without hesitation, stopped and informed him exactly of the whereabouts of Manny Sharps. Levi Pike told him the man he was after was now in a town called Bowie, Texas, a place he has never set foot in. Stunned, Evans stood there speechless as Pike wheeled around and walked proudly away.

Heading west, out of Fort Smith as fast as a good horse could travel, he has ridden hard to the town of Bowie. He arrives only minutes before the Mexicans bust into the saloon, preventing him from calling Sharps out and killing the man.

Now, torn between wanting to kill Sharps, or hurrying to warn the Stallings' about what he has overheard. Hat mounts his horse and follows the Mexican riders to a nearby livery where Sharps and the other white man have their horses stabled. He is unfamiliar with Texas and has no idea where the Stallings ranch is, only that it is somewhere north and west. Now his only choice is to lie back and follow the Mexicans until they lead him there, and that would be risky.

Corey Stallings is as close a friend as Hat Evans ever had. His brother Kyle, on the eve of his death, was to marry his friend's sister Judith. Now he wants Sharps dead by his hand and his hand only, but he owes it to his dead brother to see to the safety of Judith Stallings first.

He smiles from the dark alley that conceals him from the riders in the street. She was indeed a beauty. Kyle met her first and won her heart, but Judith Stallings won the heart of Hatton Evans forever, whether she knew it or not.

He would have followed her west to Texas sooner, but first, he had unfinished business with Manny Sharps. Now, with this latest news, he would again have to alter his plans and try to find Ben Stallings. He must warn him the Mexicans and Manny Sharps are on their way to his ranch.

Hat counts twenty Mexican riders and two whites in the group riding from the town. They are traveling northwest at a leisurely pace, seeming in no hurry. This is a curiosity to Hat, as he figured by their talk, that Hernandez would waste no time riding to the Stallings' ranch. All he can do is follow along cautiously, making sure to stay out of sight.

Hernandez acts like he doesn't have a care in the world. To the contrary, he seems in a festive mood, puffing on his ever present cigar and enjoying himself. Slocum looks over where Sharps slumps in his saddle and scowls. He detests the man more with every passing mile. Slocum has his own faults, many faults, but he is no stinking coward, and he hates one.

"He's taking us out here to kill us." Sharps whispers across where Slocum rides. "I'm telling you, we're dead men."

"Yeah, and after he kills a man he brands them all over." Slocum grins in the dark as he speaks to Sharps.

Slocum can't see it, but he knows sweat is breaking out on Sharps' face, even in the cool of the night. He has known many men like Sharps, brave men but bullies when they know they have the upper hand on lesser men. They turn coward when they know they have met their match, or weren't quite sure. He smiles in the dark, enjoying Sharps panic and discomfort.

The first night on the trail, after the Mexicans made camp, Hat tries to slip close enough to their camp to hear any conversation that might tell him where the ranch is. The shifting wind alerts their horses who smell him out, and stand with their ears pricked toward the spot where he lies hiding. Their actions alert the sentry who starts nosing around, causing Evans to retreat quietly to his own camp for the night. The second night is no better, but on the third, he hit pay dirt. As he crawls silently up to the Mexican camp, Hat finds himself luckily only feet from where Manny Sharps and another white man are whispering and discussing the ranch.

Two days later, Hernandez reaches the trail leading west to the ranch. Ignoring the cutoff, he bypasses it and rides on two miles further into the foothills where a small canyon is located. Smoke from several small fires drift slowly into the air and filter across the cliffs. Sharps, looks over at Slocum as they ride into the Mexican camp and dismount. Both men were curious why Hernandez passed the trail leading to the Stallings' ranch. Now they know, Hernandez has many more men camped here in the canyon.

Evans continues following cautiously. He knows, from the way the men are looking the trail over, and from what they said last night, this must be the road to the Stallings' ranch. He knew when Hernandez and his men passed the trail, he should turn off. However, he wants to try to find the Mexican's camp and what they are up to before riding to warn Ben Stallings. Now, as he watches from a small wash, he knows exactly what Ben Stallings is up against. The scar faced Mexican has a small army with him, camped in the canyon. Retreating to his horse, he turns back, along the trail.

"There must be fifty Mexicans in this camp, all total Slocum." Sharps is both impressed and scared at the same time. "What else is he planning?"

"Only one thing I can figure, the ranch." Slocum is also surprised. "I've been with him to their main camp several times. I recognize many of these wagons and men from there."

"Comancheros?"

"That's what they are alright," Slocum spits. "They'd as soon cut your throat as not."

"But why so many men?"

"That Mister Sharps, I don't know," Slocum shrugs as they walk through the camp. "I reckon he don't aim to fail again."

Sharps scowls, "With all these men, he shouldn't."

Slocum stops in his tracks, staring at a gray headed white man, so bowlegged he can hardly walk.

"Pesky, is that you?"

"Josh Slocum, you old horse thief." The drawl coming from the man's grizzled face is heavy with a southern accent. "Where you been keeping yourself?"

"Back east a piece." Slocum shakes hands with the man. "What's going on here, Pesky?"

The little man turns his head and looks over at Sharps before answering. "Hernandez is planning a job east and north of here, some ranch I never heard tell of. I didn't even know it existed, till Hernandez sent for me."

"Why would Hernandez send for you, my friend? Why are you here?" Slocum is curious.

"Seems this ranch was burnt clean to the ground, everyone in it kilt, and what do you know, these kilt people up and survived the fire."

"How does Hernandez know they're alive?" Sharps interrupts the man.

"Had men watching the ranch after he tried to burn it and lost many of his men, that's how he knows." The man called Pesky grins, showing a face empty of teeth. "You know Hernandez, he ain't about to lose face in front of his men, no sir, can't afford to with this bunch."

"Why would he send men back there to watch a burning ranch?" Slocum mutters. "We thought they were all done for. He wouldn't even wait around for daylight to make sure they were dead. Why did he let on, to us back in Bowie, they were mostly dead?"

"Some bigwig from Mexico showed up here the same day I pulled in. One bad hombre, I hear tell, and he looked it, to me." Pesky looks over at Sharps again.

"He's okay, go on and finish your story." Slocum had seen the curious way the man was looking at Sharps.

"This bigwig sits his big black horse and looks down his nose at Hernandez. Then he asks where the ranch lay, and tells him in no uncertain words, to leave the ranch alone, that it was his to deal with personally." Pesky snorts, then laughs. "Funny thing, Hernandez already burnt the place, but he wasn't about to tell this highfaluting Mexican. I think he was scared of the man."

"Hernandez scared?"

"For a fact, and so was these others. They were all fetching and jumping through themselves, waiting on this feller, and funny thing about it, he was alone."

"What happened next?"

"Well Hernandez, real quick like, sent Toreo back to this ranch ahead of the bigwig to check it out. When old Toreo arrives, he finds the place is being rebuilt and he sees men and women cleaning up the yard, all very much alive and kicking."

"How in the world did they survive the fire?" Slocum shakes his head. "The way that place was burning nothing could have lived through it."

The man grins. "Probably a root cellar. Smoke and fire do funny things in a hole. That's why Hernandez brought me along this time."

"Why?" Sharps asks curiously as he doesn't know anything about the one called Pesky.

"He's a hot man," Slocum scowls.

"A what?" Sharps asks.

"Dynamite; this stuff." Pesky pulls a stick of dynamite from his shirt.

"He's gonna have you blow the place up?" Sharps' is shocked. "Cripes."

"Yes, siree bob, if'n they don't come out this time, he sure is." Pesky makes a swooshing sound with his mouth and laughs. "It'll be a show for sure. Just like the fourth back home."

"Hernandez is crazy," Sharps swears.

Pesky only laughs. "You two should come with me and watch the show."

"Oh, we'll be there, I'll bet." Slocum's hooded eyes look over at Sharps.

"What about this bigwig Mex, where'd he get off to?" Sharps' is curious.

"Left here headed east the next day." Pesky shrugs "Ain't seen hide or hair of him since. Funny thing though, when he rode down there by that watering hole, his men all appeared like magic out of the washes and grass."

"His men?"

"Yep, he came riding in here alone, like old Santa Anna himself," Pesky laughs. "He sure didn't need his men to scare the pants off this bunch, no sir."

"How many men did he have with him?"

"Reckon about ten or so. Count 'em yourself, they're still camped out down there." Pesky nods off toward a small grove of trees.

"He didn't take his men with him?" Sharps asks curious.

Pesky grins his toothless smile. "Sonny, let me tell you; from what I seen, that man could go hunting grizzly bears with a switch; he's a bad one."

"Don't call me, sonny, old man," Sharps glares.

"Youngster you think that popgun of yours scares this old man?" Pesky pulls out a stick of dynamite and lights the fuse with the cigar stub in his mouth. "Pull that hog-leg; let's see how you dance to this jig."

"Boys, we got enough trouble without this crap." Slocum reaches and jerks the fuse out of the dynamite.

Sharps breathes a sigh of relief as the fuse is tossed to the ground. He was about to run backward. He thinks this crusty old character may be crazier than Hernandez.

Slocum looks where Pesky pointed at the big Mexican's camp, and then back to where Hernandez is talking with a Mexican, the one called Toreo. Both men are deep in conversation, both shaking their heads. He knows these men are arguing about something. The shorter man keeps looking over to where they stand.

He is shocked about the dynamite, but he knows Hernandez wouldn't blink an eye if he had to use the stuff to get his revenge on Stallings. The lives of the women at the ranch mean nothing to any of them, except Sharps himself. He knows Hernandez must save face somehow, and now he knows about the money. Just one more reason to raid the ranch. He shakes his head. Doesn't the dang fool realize or care that if he blows the place to smithereens the money could also be lost?

The two Mexicans start his way, frowns on their faces and the deliberate unhurried way they walk, tells him they have something serious on their minds.

"Keep your yeller mouth shut and let me do the talking, if you know what's good for you," Slocum hisses out of the corner of his mouth.

Toreo is staring coldly at them from under the brim of his sombrero as they approach. Hernandez though, is still wearing the same grin across his scarred face. Slocum figures he is studying on some devious plan. He also knows, when Hernandez stops smiling, look out, he is at his most dangerous.

"By now you've probably heard your friends at the rancho survived the fire unharmed." Hernandez looks across at the three white men. "Also, now we have another problem."

"They're not our friends!" Slocum snaps. "So what other problem do we have?"

"Don Ricardo Lorenzo."

"Lorenzo!" Slocum knows the name and the man that carries it. "What's he doing way out here?"

"One of the peons killed at the buffalo wallow was his youngest brother." Hernandez looks over at Toreo and shrugs. "He rode with me. It seems Don Ricardo is looking for the man who killed him."

"Why did he come here, señor?"

"It seems someone told him who the killer was," Hernandez grins. "Someone told him it was a gringo from a white ranch nearby."

"Who?" Slocum already knows the answer to that, he just doesn't know why.

Hernandez looks over at Slocum. "I sent a fast rider to my brother in Mexico City. I had the messenger tell Señor Lorenzo."

"So, Lorenzo now thinks that man is Stallings?"

"Si, señor, it was Stallings, was it not? After Lorenzo came here, I sent Toreo back to check on the rancho of the whites. On his way there, Toreo discovered the tracks of a single man on foot, walking away from the buffalo wallow. Toreo followed the man back to the white rancho. That is when he found all the gringos very much alive.

"Just one man went back to the ranch?"

"Si, tracks of only one man walking."

"But, there were more," Sharps speaks up. "There were at least two men down in the wallow."

"Si, señor, and after you ran out on us, more men were shooting at us from the ridge behind us. We did not have time to see where the others went." Hernandez looks hard at Sharps. "We ran like rabbits, just like you and Señor Slocum did."

Slocum tunes out the talk. His thoughts are on Lorenzo, a man he knows well. He is Santa Anna's right hand man and executioner. He is one man Slocum fears. Utterly ruthless, the worst cold-blooded killer he has ever met. Once at the battle of Chaco Canyon, Slocum watched as Lorenzo personally executed over one hundred prisoners, smiling all the while he shot them down.

"Where is Lorenzo now?" Slocum already figured out Hernandez's motives for sending word to Lorenzo. He is, as the saying goes, covering his own trail. Lorenzo knows his brother Roberto rode with Hernandez, who technically, got him killed. Hernandez wanted to put the blame on Stallings, pointing the Don and Santa Anna away from him. In Mexico, those two were like kings. It didn't pay to have them mad at you.

"He rode east, toward the Stallings Rancho," Hernandez looks over at Toreo, "If he lives."

"If he lives?" Slocum is curious at the remark the Mexican leader made. "Tell me what has happened to Lorenzo?"

"Toreo is supposed to follow and make sure the Don did not reach the white rancho, but maybe he missed and maybe Lorenzo lives."

"You ambushed Don Lorenzo, Santa Anna's right hand man and good friend?" Slocum can't believe his ears. "Why, have you gone mad? You're just asking for trouble."

Hernandez glares over at Slocum. "Lorenzo is a thorn in my side, coming in here ordering my men around."

"So you had him killed?"

"No, señor, the gringos at the white rancho killed the Don's brother, not I. I sent word to the Presidente, telling him this." Hernandez smiles. "Now, these hated gringos have killed Don Lorenzo as well, poor man."

"But, now you're not sure the Don is dead?" Slocum knows most of the riders with Hernandez are renegades and deserters, but their true loyalties lay with Santa Anna and Mexico. They ride with Hernandez, but their fear of Lorenzo and their loyalties to Santa Anna would cause them to side with the Don, providing of course he is still alive, and returns.

Hernandez shakes his head. "No, Toreo says he hit Lorenzo hard, but isn't positively sure he killed him."

"There was no body, or were you afraid to look?"

"Be careful my friend." Hernandez holds the smaller Toreo back as he starts toward Slocum. "I ordered him not, under any circumstances, to follow. We could not chance letting Lorenzo recognize him, if he lives."

"So now, we don't know if Lorenzo is alive or dead, or if he might return here, knowing you had him ambushed." Slocum shakes his head. "His men camped down there; they're almost as mean as Lorenzo."

"In the morning, we ride." Hernandez looks over at Sharps. "When they find out their precious Don Lorenzo has been killed by the gringos, his men will ride with us."

Sharps cusses under his breath. How many Mexicans is it gonna take, to kill five men and two women? Dividing the money among so many, there will be nothing left for him, just scraps. This is what he is risking his life for?

"Soon my friends, we will attack the white rancho," Hernandez laughs. Then, with Toreo following, he turns and walks off.

Slocum spits as they move away. "I hate it when they use the word friend."

"Wonder what he's got in store for us?" Sharps shakes his head worrying.

"Killing us probably." Slocum takes enjoyment in keeping Sharps scared. "That's what happens to most men that run out on Santiago Hernandez."

"You think they're setting us up?"

"I'll tell you this, Hernandez isn't bringing us along this time because he needs us." Slocum rubs his chin thoughtfully. "No, he's up to something, but for some unknown reason, he still wants us with him, or wants us to see what he intends to do to the Stallings."

"When will he attack?"

Slocum shrugs. "Who knows about that one?"

"We should have ridden on to Arkansas while we had the chance."

"Well, it's too late now."

Sharps tosses a stick of wood into the small campfire and looks over at Slocum. "Yeah."

CHAPTER 13

Late evening arrives and the ranch is quiet. The Kiowa departed early in the afternoon and now, as dusk settles across the yard, Samuel and Lambert are laughing on the front porch as they settle their winnings. The horse race was a set-back, but they more than made up for it in the bronc riding.

Samuel is glad he won, but he feels guilty about using the roan horse the way he did. Of course, he knows Palane outfoxed them on the horse race and that eases his conscience somewhat. Lambert, on the other hand, is just happy they came out of the day ahead, with his backsides still intact.

Admiring a skinning knife he won from one of the Kiowa warriors, a knife to replace the one he lost to Corey, Lambert smiles at Samuel. "You know brother, I've got me an idea."

"Oh no you don't," Samuel fires back.

"You ain't heard my idea yet."

Samuel shakes his head. "If it's got anything to do with gambling, I don't want to hear it either."

"Just hear me out," Lambert pleads. "Let's swap Palane out of that ugly little old horse of his. We could make a killing back in Arkansas."

"You pull that stunt on them boys back home, they'll skin you alive."

"What stunt?" Lambert acts shocked. "It'll just be a horse race for Pete's sake."

"No," Samuel shakes his head. "The boys back home are not as easy going as we are."

"What's easy going got to do with it?" Lambert laughs. "Shucks Samuel, it was a fair and square horse race."

"No, it wasn't. Palane ran a ringer in on us. You try that on the boys in Arkansas and they'd have your hide nailed to a barn door. Now forget about it."

"Ok, ok, I forgot it." Lambert grins and looks up at the stars with his hands clasped behind his head. "I still would have loved to see the look on their faces."

"No, I don't think you would, brother."

Corey walks across the yard and enters the house, just as Lambert is fixing to put up another argument. Samuel is always amazed how small the door looks every time Corey passes through it. He knows his brother is a big man, but when he is astride a horse or sitting in one of their kitchen chairs, he realizes just how big. He shakes his head as Corey passes. His brother could have at least said something as he walked by, but then Corey hardly talks to anyone except Colby.

Pulling up a rawhide chair, Corey takes the coffee Sarah offers. Ben sits straddle on a chair at the far end of the table, cleaning his old Kentucky long rifle. Sarah walks around him and sits down across the table from Corey, quietly sipping coffee.

"It was quite a day, boy." Ben never looks up, "Quite a day."

"Yes, sir, it was," Corey acknowledges.

Ben chuckles, "Scared Lambert out of half his fun though. That boy thought he lost my horses for sure."

"Is Colby still up on the roof?" Corey looks across at Sarah.

"You want I should fetch him, Corey?" Her green eyes wrinkle at the corners when she smiles.

"No, I was just wondering where he was."

Judith enters the room and sits down at the table. "Mister Lorenzo is breathing easier, but he's green as a gourd."

"Any bleeding?"

"No, Sarah, I got that stopped. If he doesn't catch blood poisoning or a fever, he should pull through the shooting, okay." Judith sipped on her coffee. "We'll know in a day or two."

Corey knows his sister. Something is bothering her. "What is it, sis?"

"That bullet hit him hard, close to his spine. He could be paralyzed, like Cousin Elvin was after them Pikes up and shot him in the back." Judith looks over at Sarah. "Sorry Sarah, I shouldn't have said that."

"Paralyzed? Why do you think that?"

"Cause, he ain't moved his legs a hair since we put him in that bed."

"Maybe he just ain't tried," Corey argues.

"He thrashed around good with both me and Sarah holding him, and he didn't move 'em then."

"I'd rather be dead than paralyzed like Cousin Elvin is." Samuel overhears them talking and speaks up as he enters the room, taking a seat alongside Sarah.

Corey knows Samuel is sweet on Sarah. He doesn't blame him, she's a beautiful woman. He doesn't want to admit it, but he is taken by her too. He can't help being a little jealous of his brother.

"At least Elvin is alive," Ben speaks up.

"Is that being alive, Pa?" Samuel looks at Ben.

Ben lays the rifle down and looks down the table. "Samuel, he is alive. If the good Lord wanted him dead, then he'd be dead; he ain't."

"Lambert go relieve Colby. I'll be up in a while." Corey looks over at Lambert as he comes in the house.

"Yes, sir."

Stepping to the bedroom door, Corey enters and looks straight into Lorenzo's eyes. "You're awake."

Nodding weakly, the Mexican moves his head. "Si, señor, I am awake."

"I reckon you overheard our conversation?"

"Yes, I did, and the young one is right." Lorenzo nods his head slightly as if answering his own question. "If I were condemned to this bed for life, I would rather die."

"You have any idea who shot you?" Corey pulls a chair up next to the bed and rolls Lorenzo a cigarette.

Lorenzo blows smoke in the air, ignoring the question. "I hear the señorita speak also. She says I am paralyzed too, maybe."

"No, she meant she hadn't seen you move your legs." Corey watches the big man lying helpless as a baby. He almost feels sorry for him.

"I have tried; they will not move."

Corey looks into the pale face. "Give yourself a few days to heal. Don't try to move or you could damage yourself worse."

"Why you no kill me?" The words are barely a whisper. "I came here to kill you. I hear the Kiowa tell you to kill me."

"Tell me who shot you."

"I do not know for sure, maybe you gringos."

Corey shakes his head. "Weren't us, we were all here on the ranch."

"Maybe Indians."

"Most Injuns don't have rifles, especially a Mexican smoothbore."

"How do you know this? The bullet went clean through me."

"Yes, it did, but only a smoothbore will leave a smaller, neater exit wound like you have." Corey leans on the back of the chair. "I think it was some of the Hernandez bunch, or perhaps Manny Sharps."

Lorenzo grins feebly. "You are a student of warfare señor?"

"No, I ain't, but I've seen a few gunshots in my day."

"You killed my brother."

"I did."

"He was just a niño, a young boy."

Corey stands up. "He rode with the men who attacked this ranch and my family, then burned our house and tried to kill my family, and the women. No, señor, he was no boy." Corey turns and walks toward the door.

"Señor."

Corey stops and turns. "What?"

"When I leave this bed, I will kill you." Lorenzo drops the stub into a coffee cup. "I must, its family honor, you understand?"

"You can try."

"Until then, I thank you." Lorenzo lies still on the bed. "Tell me, who is this Manny Sharps?"

"He rides with Hernandez."

"Many whites ride with Hernandez."

"This one is tall, red curly hair, wears two pistols."

"I no see this man."

Corey shrugs, walking from the room, closing the door quietly behind him. Walking around the table, he sits down and picks up his coffee cup. Looking back at the closed door, he thinks about what the

Mexican said and shakes his head. Family honor, the man said, the same honor that caused him so much trouble back in Arkansas.

From the roof above, Corey hears Colby stutter as he calls down to them. "Someone's coming."

Samuel sprints to the ladder and quickly climbs onto the roof where Colby and Lambert are watching a single rider approach. "One man Pa, coming in from the southeast."

"Come on down Samuel. Lambert, you and Colby stay put, and keep a close eye out for a trick."

Ben and Corey walk out onto the porch and separate, covering both ends of the ranch house. They can barely make out the rider who stops momentarily to look the ranch over, then waves his hat. He rides slowly across the flat ground toward the house.

Corey steps down from the porch grinning. "If I ain't gone plumb blind, I know that rider."

Samuel can barely make out the man's silhouette. "Who is it? I don't recognize him."

"It's Hatton Evans, if I don't miss my guess. No one sits a horse like he does." Corey grins. "You remember Hat, tall, gangly, and ugly as homemade sin?"

Ben nods. "Sure I do, but what's he doing way out here, and how did he find us?"

"Can't say, but it's him for certain."

Judith overhears Corey's remark and smiles. "Hatton Evans is tall, but he's definitely not gangly or ugly, Corey Stallings."

Evans rides slowly up to the men and sits his horse, grinning down at them. "Well, are you jaybirds gonna ask a tired, hungry man down, or are you just gonna stand there gawking?"

"Hatton Evans, you old son of a gun, what are you doing here, and how in the world did you find your way out to these parts?" Corey is pumping the man's hand so hard, he all but jerks him from the saddle.

Dismounting, Hat shakes hands with Ben. "It took some doing, but a little bird led me here."

"A little brown bird named Hernandez?"

"I do believe you are correct there, and he had a helper; the one and only Manny Sharps and some other white man."

"So, they're still together are they? I was hoping the Mexican would put him out of his misery."

"Peers to me, they were scared of the Mexican, cause they sure went along with him, meek as lambs."

Stepping on the porch, as Samuel and the rest of the family walk out to greet him, Hat shakes hands all around before his eyes glimpse Judith. Smiling, he removes his hat and greets her.

"Miss Stallings, it's been a while."

Momentarily shocked, at seeing him up close, she hesitates briefly. Hat and Kyle Evans had an uncanny family resemblance. Both men are tall, broad shouldered, with dark hair and flashing deep blue eyes. Seeing him standing there brings back untold memories washing over her.

Ignoring the outstretched hand, she embraces him instead, kissing him lightly on the cheek. "Hatton, what a surprise. It's so good to see you."

"It's good to see you, Miss Judith." Hat is momentarily embarrassed. He didn't think she would remember him.

Ben takes charge and ushers them all back inside, out of the brisk wind that starts to pick up. Curiosity shows on everybody's face as they take seats around the long table.

"Lambert, you're supposed to be on guard; git." The youngster wants to stay in the warmth of the kitchen and listen to Hat Evans talk, but he knows better than to complain. Wouldn't do him any good anyhow, Ben wouldn't listen. He had already been told to stay on the roof.

"Yes, sir."

"Colby boy, would you put Hat's horse in the corral? And feed him."

"I'll take care of my horse, Ben." Hat starts to stand.

Ben motions him back to his seat. "Not tonight you won't. Tonight you're a guest."

Hat watches as Lambert quickly climbs the ladder and exits onto the roof. "So that's how y'all knew I was riding in so quickly; mighty ingenious."

"What brings you way out here, Hatton?" Ben addresses him as Sarah pours coffee.

"Does a man need a reason to visit friends?" Hat smiles that contagious smile of his.

Ben sips his coffee. "No, if that's why you came and nothing else."

"Well, sir, there is another reason." He looks over at Judith and Sarah. "Maybe we should speak outside?"

"No reason pard," Corey answers. "They know what's coming, and I'm thinking you do too."

"Alright, here it is. A Mexican called Hernandez and that skunk Manny Sharps are on their way here with fifty riders, maybe more." Hat goes on to tell about his years following Sharps around, trying to get to him, and finally finding him in Bowie.

Everyone sits in silence as they absorb the bad news Hat has presented to them.

"I brought all of you out here to get away from trouble. It seems I've just got you in more." Ben shakes his head.

"It's not your fault, Papa." Judith stands behind Ben, patting him softly on his shoulder.

"Hat, how long do you figure we have?" Corey looks across at the tall man.

"Hard to say, for some reason they want this place bad, real bad." Hat sips on his coffee. "But, their leader doesn't seem in a hurry."

"Hernandez lost a lot of prestige with his men the last time he was here." Ben speaks up softly. "He ain't about to make the same mistake again."

Hat looks across at Judith. "Why did they attack your ranch, Ben?"

"Sharps knows we got money from the sale of our land and cattle back in Arkansas, and more from the horses we just sold."

"Well, they're coming, and folks, that's a fact." Hat speaks up again, looking over at Judith. "I'm here to help if you want me."

"Ain't your fight, Hatton," Judith speaks up.

"I'm making it mine." Hat notices Judith smiled at him. Just maybe he is home.

Palane lies prone, behind an outcropping of rock and dirt. He crawls unnoticed, through the tall grass and weeds, to reach a vantage point. Below him lay the encampment of the scar faced one and his brown men. Normally he would ride in unnoticed to trade with the Comancheros, but not today. He wants to spy on the camp, unobserved, to see what their intentions are. He already has his suspicions, but he wants more.

He knows if he rides in, many of the Mexicans would recognize him. He has been in the larger encampment, in the big canyon further west, many times. On the day of the race, he wondered, if any of them spied on the ranch of the whites and saw him there. He knows these men are dangerous. If they suspect he is friends with the whites, he might not be welcome in their camp.

Mexicans, whites, even Indians, move freely about the small encampment. Palane knows this is a war party as few women are present. Mexicans like to eat and dance. Rarely would they travel without women to do their cooking and camp work. He also recognizes the tall, scar faced Mexican called Hernandez, who now walks about the camp laughing and talking to his men. He has seen the scar faced leader on many occasions at the big canyon camp, further west on the staked plains.

Three white men sit huddled around a fire, talking together. He can tell, even from a distance, the redheaded one acts scared, looking anxiously over his shoulder every few minutes. There is only one reason they are camped so close to the ranch of the whites. They are here to raid.

Slipping back quietly, the way he came, Palane is almost to his horse when several riders surround him; Comanche warriors. Palane raises his hand in peace and walks to where they surround his horse.

"My friends, you have found my horse I see."

A short, portly warrior, stares solemnly down from his horse. "Why do you spy on the brown warrior's camp?"

"I do not spy. My horse threw me and now you have recovered him for me."

"You lie, Kiowa," the warrior points his finger. "You lie; your horse is tied. He didn't tie himself."

Palane starts toward his horse, only to have his way blocked, the long lances of the Comanche pointing at him. Turning, he looks into the dark eyes of the squat warrior.

"The Kiowa and Comanche are brothers. I have ridden with your people many times, against your enemies."

"I know you, half-breed dog. What you say is true, but you are not Kiowa and not my brother. So tell me, why do you spy on the Mexicans?"

"I wasn't."

Motioning to the horse, the warrior waits as Palane mounts. "We will go into the camp. We will see if you tell the truth."

Comanche warriors, coming and going from their camp, is no surprise to the Comancheros. They come frequently to trade or sell prisoners. From where they sit, Slocum and Sharps barely pay any attention to the mounted riders as they pass.

Dismounting, the squat warrior walks to where Hernandez sits in the shade of a wagon. Pointing where Palane sits his horse, the warrior speaks a few words to the small Mexican sitting with Hernandez. Several words are exchanged and the taller Mexican stands up, walking toward Palane.

"Get down; I do not look up at people who spy on me."

Palane slips easily to the ground and stands quietly, waiting on Hernandez to speak. He notices the three whites walking in their direction.

"Translate for me, Toreo." Hernandez looks over at the Mexican. "Coyote here, says you were spying on my camp. What do you say?"

Palane turns his eyes on the Comanche, before the words can be translated. "He lies."

Hernandez is surprised. "You speak our language?"

"Yes, and English and Kiowa."

"I see, you are an educated man for a," Hernandez doesn't finish.

"For a heathen?"

"Yes, for lack of a better word, señor. I did not wish to be rude."

"My mother was Spanish, the daughter of a Spanish aristocrat she said."

"Uh huh." Hernandez looks closer at Palane. "And your father?"

"Kiowa."

"Tell me, señor; how did this come about?"

"She was on her way to her wedding in Santa Fe when she was captured by my father and the Kiowa people."

"I see; does she still live?"

"No, the Kiowa were on a wild horse hunt when Apaches attacked their camp. My father was killed trying to protect her. The Apache killed many that day, but since then, they have paid as well."

"Your mother; tell me her name." Hernandez motions Palane away from the others.

"Donna Isabelle Carmen Baca is what she told me."

Hernandez pales for a moment, before recovering himself. "How old are you?"

"Nineteen summers."

"Were you spying on my camp?"

"I wanted to see who you were before I came in to trade," Palane lies. "I have been taught to look a strange camp over twice before you enter."

"A good idea out here; anyway, we will see." Hernandez walks to where the Comanche and Toreo wait. "Tell the Comanche, this one says he was on his way into our camp when they rode up."

Translating, Toreo barely got the words spoken when the Comanche, known as Coyote, steps forward. "He lies."

Palane steps forward, smiling. "Perhaps fat dog, you will prove I am a liar."

"You are a liar half-breed." Coyote throws out his chest, pointing at Palane.

"Your words are harsh, even for a Comanche dog, now we will see." Palane pulls his knife.

Toreo starts to step forward, between the two warriors, until Hernandez restrains him. The insult has been spoken, now the knife will see which man speaks the truth. Hernandez has traded with, and ridden among the Comanche and Kiowa for many years. He knows their law. Once an insult has been spoken, only blood by trial and knife, will tell who speaks the truth.

Coyote pulls his knife and faces the east, then turns to the west, north, and south, holding up his arms to the sun. Finally finished with his totem ritual, he turns to where Palane waits.

"I say Palane lies, now he will die."

Palane crouches, no longer a smile showing on his face. He waits, the razor sharp knife held in his right hand, blade up, ready to rip the stomach from the Comanche. No longer is this just insulting words. The knife will say which warrior speaks the truth. The warriors advance toward each other, both ready to strike, to kill.

Hernandez puffs quietly on what is left of his cigar and watches as the two warriors slowly circle each other. He would not stop the fight. This is a personal grudge between warriors of different tribes. If he interferes, they will think he is choosing sides, and in his business, he cannot afford to lose the trust of these people.

The ranch ahead, is just a sidetrack for him. Afterwards, he still needs their friendship and contraband they bring to trade.

The Comanche is the much heavier of the two warriors, and he is still in his prime, moving with the speed and grace of a young man. Palane retreats quickly from his rushes, sidestepping, and parrying every blow. Blood flows down the Comanche's arm from a long gash. The warrior looks down at his arm and grins, before lunging forward.

Palane is methodical, as he repeatedly circles, leaping forward, swiping with his knife, then retreating. He is the much faster of the two and both know it. The Comanche also knows, he has to end the fight quickly. He is a horseback Indian, used to riding, not walking. Rushing in low, Coyote catches Palane off balance for once, and manages to leave a deep cut across his left leg. Blood flows heavily from the wound.

"Now Kiowa, you are a dead man. You cannot run any more like a rabbit." Coyote holds up his bloody knife and tastes the blood on its blade. "Now I will eat your heart as you die."

The Comanche rushes forward to the attack recklessly, but this time, Palane fools the bigger warrior. He doesn't retreat. Lunging forward, he ducks under the arm of the tiring Comanche, swiping his knife across the warrior's stomach, utterly cutting the man in two. Coyote takes two unsteady steps forward, looking down at his ripped stomach and intestines.

Palane limps around to Coyote's face and looks the warrior in the eye. "Now dog, now I will eat your heart." The knife plunges deep into the Comanche's chest, making a sucking sound, as Palane cuts the still beating heart from his body. A grumble goes out from the watching Comanche as Coyote collapses and dies.

Hernandez stands back, puffing slowly on his cigar and watching the faces around him. Sharps, standing off to the side, almost throws up. He has seen many men die, many from his own hand, but never has he witnessed anything as savage as this. He gags as the warrior holds up the dead man's heart and bites into it.

Palane lies on a blanket in front of Hernandez's tent where he could be guarded. His leg has been stitched up and a Mexican stands watch over him. Many Comanche are still in the camp and openly threaten Palane. The fight was fair. The one called Coyote challenged the Kiowa causing his own death, but the hostile Comanche want revenge for their fallen tribesman.

Hernandez pulls up a box and sits down in front of Palane. "So tell me, why were you watching my camp?"

"I told you, I wanted to see who you were before I rode in."

"Is that all?" Hernandez studies the Kiowa. "Coyote believed differently."

"The Comanche was a fool." Palane looks into the dark eyes unflinching. "What else would I be doing?"

"Describe your mother to me."

Palane looks at the scar faced Mexican curiously before answering. "She was very beautiful, slim, long black hair, big brown eyes."

"Tell me of her mouth."

"Her mouth?"

"Si, what did you see when she smiled?"

Palane nods. "She had a small dimple that smiled deeply when she was happy."

Hernandez nods his head. "Your mother was my youngest sister."

"Your sister?" Palane is shocked.

"Si, she is the reason I am out here in this wilderness instead of taking my rightful place as my father's eldest son."

"Tell me, why would she cause you to be so far from your country?"

Hernandez seems to look far away. "My father ordered me to come here many years ago and try to find her. My other brothers were too young at the time. I have remained here since then."

"You have been here twenty years?"

Hernandez nods. "Yes, my father's last words to me, were not to come back until she came with me."

Palane only shakes his head. "Then you are my uncle?"

"Si."

"I have been to your rancho in the big canyon many times. I have seen you, but being a lesser warrior, I was never permitted to come near you."

"We should have met sooner." Hernandez nods. "I am sorry we did not."

"What will you do now?"

"I have unfinished business with the white men in the bend of the big river, east of here."

"You will attack them?"

"They have made me look like a poor leader. I must attack their rancho if I am to lead these men." Hernandez frowns. "Even more nephew, I do not like being made a fool of, by anyone."

"Why do you not return to your father, now that you have found her?"

Hernandez looks at Palane. "It is too late; my father is dead. Toreo brought me word of his death. There is nothing back there for me now. I have made my life here."

"And your father's lands?"

Hernandez smiles coldly. "My loving brothers have taken all the land."

"You will return to the canyon soon?"

"When I am finished here, you will accompany me and live there with me," Hernandez smiles. "We will have great times."

Palane watches as Hernandez stands and walks away, after Toreo summons him. His uncle is a proud man, an aristocrat in his own country. He has acknowledged Palane as his nephew, but nothing was said of his Kiowa blood. Palane knows he could never return to the big canyon with him. His place is with the Kiowa people. He does not know this uncle and he would not be happy in the village of the brown men. His leg will take several days to heal enough to ride, but when it does, he will return to his people. Hernandez is a stranger to him, and finding out he is his uncle means nothing to him.

The news of his uncle's intending raid on the white ranch is disturbing to Palane. The whites are, no matter to him, but the young one called Colby, must be protected. He has given his word to his chief. It must not be broken, his honor is at stake. Palane lies back and rests. First, he will let his leg mend and then slip silently away from the

Mexican camp and his uncle. His eyes follow the tall form of Hernandez as he walks with the smaller Mexican, the one called Toreo. Palane has a decision to make. Will he tell the whites of the intending raid and betray his own blood, or will he remain silent and try somehow to get the boy away from the ranch before the raid.

CHAPTER 14

Two weeks have passed since the horse race and the Kiowa's visit to the ranch. Everything has been quiet and the everyday routine of working the ranch returns to normal. Corey, with Hat Evans beside him, rides out every day, scouring the outlying countryside for any signs of Hernandez or his men. Ben and the boys resume their labor. They return to breaking the mustangs, already in the corrals, and bringing in the wild ones from the canyons scattered throughout the ranch land.

One person is always watching from the lookout atop the ranch house as Corey instructed. Judith and Sarah take turns watching, cooking, and tending to Lorenzo. His wound is healing, but Judith's prediction comes true as his legs do not work. The women massage them and work them in vain; nothing helps. As his wounds heal, Ben and the boys carry Lorenzo, every morning, into the front room and place him in a comfortable chair Ben fashioned for him.

Sundown is coming on and Lorenzo watches as Sarah prepares supper, working over the hot wood stove. "I wish I could thank you more for your kindness."

"There is no need."

"You do not like me much, señorita."

"Should I?"

"Perhaps you will tell me what I have done that has caused your dislike of me," Lorenzo smiles. "I do not remember meeting you before, and I would never have forgotten such a beautiful woman."

"You came here to kill Corey." Sarah never turns around. "I heard you say so from your own mouth."

"I see, but señorita, he is responsible for my brother's death. How am I supposed to treat him?"

"You are wrong, Mister Lorenzo. Your brother came here with others, to kill and burn this ranch."

Lorenzo shrugs. "He was young. He should not have ridden with Hernandez, but he did."

"Maybe you should kill Hernandez as well."

"Perhaps I will, when my legs are better."

"I hope that is soon."

"Señorita, I see you have feelings for Señor Corey."

"Why do you say that?"

Lorenzo smiles. "Only a woman in love would go to the trouble of defending the man as you have."

Sarah ignores the remark and doesn't turn around, but he knows he hit a nerve. Her hands move nervously, kneading the bread she is making, much more than is necessary. Lorenzo sits back in the chair and smiles. Yes, he knows she is a woman in love.

Corey rides in at dark, unsaddles and turns his horse into the corral. Samuel steps out of the dark, almost at Corey's shoulder.

"Where's Hat?"

"We split up about noon. He should be riding in soon."

"See anything out there?"

"No, the range is quiet as a churchyard, nothing moving, only the night creatures."

Samuel can only see the shadow of Corey in the dark. "Then why do you two ride out every day?"

"They'll come soon. I feel it in my bones."

"Is that the only reason?"

"What other reason would I have?"

Samuel looks toward the house. "Sarah."

"Leave her out of this brother."

"She thinks a lot of you, Corey." Samuel steps closer. "Why do you stay away from the ranch so much, away from her?"

Corey ignores the remark, turns and walks toward the house where the coal, oil light glows in the window. At sundown, it is always there, beckoning him to come inside, out of the cold, into the shelter of the warm room. Entering the house, Corey looks to where Sarah stands before the stove, her back to him, and then over to where Lorenzo sits in his chair. The Mexican smiles and nods as Corey walks to where he sits.

"Good evening, señor."

"Don Lorenzo, how are you feeling tonight?"

"It is kind of you to ask. I am doing as good as expected, for a cripple. I feel useless, of no help."

"This is your home as long as you wish it to be." Corey nods, "You are welcome here."

Lorenzo looks into Corey's face, confused. "I came here to kill you. You know that, but yet you welcome me into your house."

"Tell me, Señor Lorenzo, will Hernandez ride against this ranch again?"

"I forbid him to do so," Lorenzo shrugs. "I also heard the words of your new guest when he arrived. Yes, I think he will come soon."

Corey pulls up a chair. "If you told him not to attack this ranch, it would be a good reason for him to turn on you. Perhaps that is why you were shot."

"Si, señor. I have been sitting here for many days, thinking the same thing." Lorenzo studies the fireplace. "Señor Hernandez thinks he is the patron out here and will tolerate no interference."

"And you came here and interfered?"

"Si, I forbid them to raid this rancho until you were dead by my hand alone."

"Your legs, have they moved?"

"No, I fear they will never move again." The big Mexican looks down where his legs are covered with a thick blanket. "This, Señor Corey, is no way for a man to live."

"Give it time. Like I said, you are welcome here."

Lorenzo looks over where Sarah places a hot cup of coffee on the table. "She is your woman, yes?"

"No, señor, she is the wife of my brother Eli."

"But señor, I understand he is dead."

"Maybe so, but she is still his wife."

Lorenzo smiles, shaking his head. "I do not think so my friend. A dead man can be remembered, but he cannot hold a woman in his arms."

"That is none of your business, Lorenzo." Corey looks hard at the Mexican. "Leave it alone."

"As you wish, señor," Lorenzo bows his head, "As you wish."

Fall is in the air and the nights are turning colder. Judith walks to the closed window several times, looking out at the shadowy corrals.

Corey watches her and smiles. "He'll be along soon, sis."

"It's dangerous for you two to ride alone. Why don't you stay together?"

"We can cover more ground by splitting up, that's why."

From where he sits, Ben smiles. Maybe his daughter has found love again. She smiles more every day Hat is here. He is glad. Every woman needs a man out here, far from civilization, but good men are as rare as hen's teeth.

It is almost an hour past dark when Hat and Samuel come laughing through the door. Judith wants to scold him, but she is so relieved he is back safe. She returns to getting their supper on the table. Only Lorenzo notices the look of relief on her face.

Palane rides silently out of the Mexican camp, heading for the Kiowa village. Hernandez finds him missing and sends men to follow him, but he manages to evade the Comanche trackers. "Comanche dogs!" He mutters the words in pain as he watches them follow a false trail he laid for them.

The wound seemed healed when he rode out of the canyon, but it has lied to him and now the leg is swollen. Palane rides into the Kiowa village and dismounts in front of the old medicine man's lodge. He can barely walk and falls to the ground, his body wracked with fever.

Lying back, against the backrest in Grey Owl's lodge, he calmly watches as the old one opens the festered wound with a sharp knife. Pain sears through his brain as green pus flows down his leg. Palane closes his eyes, trying to shut out the pain. Not a sound utters forth from the fevered warrior.

Watching, as Grey Owl sprinkles healing powder on the open wound, Palane wipes sweat from his forehead. Cayuse enters and sits across from Palane, watching as grease and bandages are wrapped around the leg. Palane quickly tells him of Hernandez and his plans to raid the white ranch.

"He will ride against the white man's ranch again?" Cayuse shakes his head. "This is foolish. His medicine was not strong enough the last time he fought the whites."

Palane nods. "He says this time will be different, and I believe him."

"Why? The whites will be hard to defeat. They are watchful. Why would he attack them?"

"The scar-faced one is an arrogant and proud leader. He believes he has lost face with his men. He thinks they will not follow him anymore if he does not destroy the whites on the river." Palane looks wearily over at his chief. "This time he has many more warriors, enough to defeat the few whites, I think."

"Maybe, but the whites have the evil one, the one with the cold heart."

Palane frowns. He knows Cayuse speaks of Corey. "One man, against fifty?"

"These warriors who come into our lands, both white and brown, are hard to understand sometimes." Cayuse watches as Palane stiffens, when the medicine man raises the bad leg and places it on top of a buffalo robe. "When will you be able to ride?"

"Tomorrow, my chief."

"He will not ride soon," Grey Owl speaks, almost in a whisper. "Perhaps many days."

"I must protect the Faraway One at the white man's ranch. Nothing must happen to him."

Cayuse looks at Palane. "You are the only one that speaks the white man's words."

"Tell me, I know it is not polite to ask of another's medicine, but why is this young white man so important to you?" Palane has to ask and he was curious.

Cayuse looks over to where the old medicine man is mixing some herbs in a wooden bowl.

Grey Owl looks up at the chief, nodding, then resumes his work.

"When I was a boy, my father took me on my dream quest, the same as the one you went on with me as your advisor, after your father was killed. In my dreams, I met a spirit person. The spirit person was a faraway person, a man with no mind. It was a troubled dream. I watched as the spirit person died from an enemy arrow. Then I watched as I too died. Then all of our people fell dead about their tepees. Dead Kiowa were lying everywhere around the village with our enemy all around, dancing, singing, and rejoicing. My spirit medicine had spoken. If my spirit person dies, then I, and all our people, shall also die."

"You think the white boy is your spirit medicine?"

"Grey Owl, many years ago, said this, and I know this." Cayuse nods. "The white one with the faraway mind is the same as the one in my dream, the very same."

"Your dream, person was white?" Palane is confused.

Cayuse shakes his head. "In dream, people many colors and no color."

Palane has grown up with the Kiowa. His father was Kiowa. He respects their ways, and wears the sacred medicine bundle, with his secret charms, around his neck. He believes, as the Kiowa, but he remembers his mother's influence and teachings, even though he was very young at her death. He believes Cayuse speaks the truth about the white youth. He does not dare anger the spirit world. It does no harm to placate both worlds, his mothers and his fathers. Only a fool would do less.

"What would you have me do, my Chief?"

Cayuse looks into the small fire. "I will hold council with Grey Owl and look into my medicine. You rest and heal, then we will talk more."

Palane knows Cayuse worries about the safety of the white youth. He feels the tribe's future is intertwined somehow with the destiny of the one called Colby.

"How long does Grey Owl think I will be weak and unable to ride?" Palane looks over at the medicine man.

"Leg bad, much bad spirit inside; maybe ten sleeps, maybe more."

Palane shakes his head, ten sleeps, he would have to lie here helpless. How soon would his uncle attack the white ranch? He knows the only reason Hernandez has waited, was for Palane's leg to mend and he wanted to know for sure if Lorenzo still lives. Hernandez practically told Palane, he ordered Lorenzo's death when Lorenzo ordered them not to attack the white people. Hernandez also told him, Lorenzo carries much power in Mexico City. He would not disobey an order from him, for fear of coming in direct conflict with Santa Anna. He had to know if Lorenzo was dead, as Toreo believes. Then, and only then, would he proceed. Frowning to himself, after putting much thought into the problem of his uncle and the white boy, Palane lies back, trying to relax, but his thoughts are troubled.

Several days later, Hernandez paces the floor of his tent like a caged animal. His nephew is gone, vanished like a thief in the night. His best trackers have been unable to find and return Palane to the canyon. He has delayed attacking the white ranch until Palane could recover from his wounds and be able to accompany them. Why did he leave? Did he not feel welcome here? Perhaps the Comanche was right. Perhaps his blood nephew was spying on him. No matter, there is nothing anyone can do to help the whites, except warn them, and that wouldn't help them against so many.

Hernandez looks over to where the old white man sits making fuses for the dynamite, and nods. Against the might of the dynamite, nothing will help them. The log house will be splinters when he is through, then maybe they will surrender. He would like to take the white woman with the red hair as his. He smiles, Sharps will become enraged, and then, in front of his woman, he would kill him. This is the only reason Sharps still lives. Hernandez is a cruel man as this would be just payment for Sharps running out on him.

Toreo slowly approaches the tent. He does not trust Hernandez when he is in these black moods. The man is unpredictable and violent. Toreo has seen him vent his rage and kill good men, men who were loyal to him, when in one of these crazed, temperamental moods.

Stepping inside the tent, the short Mexican finds Hernandez sitting at a small table. The man is engrossed in writing a letter and does not look up. Toreo doesn't interrupt. He waits uneasily, for Hernandez to address him.

"You will send a fast rider with this letter to Mexico City. Comprende? A very fast rider."

"Si, Patron, I understand, a fast rider."

Hernandez turns his cold, bloodshot eyes, on his second in command. "Tomorrow, I wish you to find Señor Lorenzo, even if you have to ride into the white rancho to do so."

"Si, Patron, but why not attack the rancho now?"

"Toreo, you are a fool."

"Si, Patron, I do not have your brains."

"I must know for sure if Lorenzo is working for El Presidente Santa Anna, or just for himself. We cannot go against Santa Anna. It would be certain doom for us all."

"Why? We are way out here and the Texans ran Santa Anna from Texas."

"Because, we are still Mexicans and loyalty to Mexico comes first." Hernandez strikes a match to his cigar. "I must know before I strike, if Lorenzo is working for Santa Anna or just for himself."

"Why would these whites concern Santa Anna?" Toreo shrugs.

Hernandez exhales. He heard rumors of Mexico's impending invasion of the new Republic of Texas. Whether they were true or not, he didn't know for sure, but he knows Lorenzo is Santa Anna's second in command. Perhaps he is here on a mission, concerning the invasion. He must know for certain. To cross Santa Anna, and spoil his plans, would be disastrous. He would never be able to return to Mexico again, even if he wanted to.

"Tomorrow you will find Lorenzo." Hernandez ignores Toreo's question.

"Si, Patron."

Toreo watches his dispatch rider leave, as the drumming of the horse's fast running hooves slowly fade into the night. Toreo is curious, why has Hernandez sent a letter to his brother in Mexico, when Lorenzo's brother was killed, and now this second letter. Why is it so important? Why did he bother? He always denounced his brother, swearing he'd never return to Mexico, or his father's hacienda.

Many things are unclear to the small Mexican. No one in Mexico would know if Lorenzo accidentally died or just disappeared. This is a huge land with many hazards. The only answer that makes sense is, Hernandez is keeping the way open for him to return someday to his father's home in Mexico. Toreo frowns, where would that leave the rest of them, including himself? Most are deserters and traitors to Santa Anna, unable to ever return to Mexico if they treasured their lives. Is this what Hernandez has in mind, to desert his men, to leave them here leaderless? No other leader is as strong or as cunning as Hernandez. The men would fall apart. No other leader could hold them together.

The thought is still on Toreo's mind as he leaves camp at the head of five men and an Indian tracker. Two of the men riding with him, are the gringos, Slocum and Sharps. Why Hernandez insisted they go, he has no idea, but he did.

He knows the search for Lorenzo is senseless. He and his men have already crossed and recrossed this land, searching out everyplace that could conceal a man and horse for twenty miles in every direction.

No buzzards soar in the sky, nothing shows the location of a dead body anywhere. If Lorenzo is anywhere near, he has to be at the rancho of the whites. Hernandez ordered if Lorenzo is not found on the grasslands, he is to ride straight into the white ranch, and see for himself if the Don is there.

Toreo knows he wounded the man. He saw him jerk sideways in the saddle, before riding out of sight, below a small hill. He had his orders from Hernandez, he was not to follow Lorenzo if the man was only wounded and able to ride away. Under no conditions, was he to allow himself to be identified by Lorenzo. This was fine with Toreo. He is no coward, but Lorenzo is a very dangerous man. Some thought him almost superhuman like a spirit. He waited, hoping the man would bleed to death or at least pass out from lack of blood.

He did as ordered, he waited two hours before following the trail of the wounded man. All he found was a few spots of blood and horse tracks. He followed the trail northeast, until it crossed over a hardpan of rock and clay where he completely lost any sign of the man. Toreo is no tracker. By the time he returns with an Indian tracker, two days later to pick up the trail, the wind would erase all signs.

Toreo has his own ideas. He knows Lorenzo had to be at the white ranch, or dead. He could not have survived a wound like that out here, alone in the elements. He doubts whether the man is still alive at all, hit as hard as Toreo thought he was.

Hernandez ordered him to ride into the ranch in daylight and ask the gringos if they had seen Lorenzo. Ride right in and ask them; madness, a foolish idea. Toreo shakes his head, to do as Hernandez ordered, would sign their own death warrants, if the whites recognize them. Why did Hernandez make the two white men ride with him to the white rancho? Toreo knows Hernandez well. He is cruel, and has a sick way of amusing himself. The redheaded one is already scared to death, knowing he would have to face the white men at the ranch. In a fight, Toreo knows the man would be useless.

Hernandez only laughed when Sharps first refused to go along. Shrugging, the Mexican gave the gringo a choice, go with Toreo, or die right there. When Hernandez produced the branding iron, the redheaded one nodded grimly, mounted his horse, followed Toreo and the others from camp. Toreo knows the white men, would be afraid to desert him. Hernandez told them his men would be watching. If they desert again, and were caught, the branding iron would be used.

The white rancho lies only twenty miles to the north, less than a day's ride to the big river, the river the whites call the Brazos. Toreo knows the location well. He has been there many times, trading with the tribes of the North Country. He planned himself a rancho in this very country, pictured it in his mind, a dream of raising a family, but Hernandez always talks him into staying a while longer. Now, others have come here and taken the land, his land. Perhaps, when the whites are finally destroyed, he would marry and settle here. Yes, he thinks, he would leave Hernandez before his leader could leave him.

Judith spots the riders, almost at sundown, coming in from the west, under the setting sun. Sounding the alarm, she watches as the five riders advance boldly, straight in, like they hadn't a care in the world. Lambert takes his position beside her on the roof, his rifle primed and ready.

Ben stands on the front porch while Samuel, Colby, and Sarah, watch from the windows of the house. Lorenzo sits as straight in his chair as possible, straining to see the riders.

"Pa, come on back in here with us." Caleb calls, seeing no sense in Ben showing himself.

"There's only five of them." Ben watches as the men approach closer. "They won't try anything with all these rifles pointing at them."

"I wish Corey was here," Sarah speaks from the window, looking over to where Lorenzo sits.

Ben nods, "Me too gal. He should be along directly, it's almost dark."

Toreo rides straight up to the front porch, within a few feet of where

Ben stands, before reining up. "Good evening, señors." Seeing Sarah at the window, he smiles, "And señoritas."

"What do you men want here?" Ben is short and to the point.

"Por favor my friends, we are looking for a compadre of ours, a Señor Lorenzo."

Sarah hears Lorenzo whisper behind her and looks back. He is shaking his head vigorously, trying to tell her something. Calling to Ben, she watches as he retreats backward to the window.

"Señor Lorenzo is trying to say something. I don't think he wants you to tell them he's here."

Ben nods when she finishes whispering. "I ain't about to tell them nothing." Returning to where he was, Ben answers the short Mexican. "No one by that name is here."

"Señor Lorenzo is a big man. He rides a big black horse, exactly like the one you have in your corral over there." Toreo cocks his head toward the corral.

"Manny Sharps, is that you under that Mexican hat?" Lambert calls out from the roof.

The hammer of Ben's rifle can be heard cocking all over the yard. Sharps was trying to hide his face by keeping his head lowered in the oncoming darkness.

"Is it you, Sharps?" Ben growls.

Toreo looks behind him, where Sharps sits his horse and then turns back, toward the house. "Señor, about our friend, we think he has come here, maybe he is wounded."

"If he ain't answered or looked up before I speak again Lambert, knock that Mexican hat off his head."

"Yes, sir, but it might take a little hide with it, hard to judge with that much hat."

"It's me, Stallings," Sharps looks straight at Ben, his eyes wide with fright.

"Well now, last time we seen you, our house got burned and our family almost went with it."

"Weren't me that done it."

"You're a liar Sharps," Caleb speaks from the window, "A black liar. We heard you and them dead cousins of yours."

Toreo swears under his breath, why did Hernandez send the white men with him, to be recognized? Why did he insist the two gringos ride into the ranch yard with Toreo? "Por favor, señor, our friend, have you seen him, the one that rides that black horse?"

"Mex, you got three seconds to ride out or die; whichever." Ben raises his rifle. "It's your choice."

Toreo looks into the hard face of the man on the porch. "We only look for our friend."

"Two seconds, hombre."

"We go." Toreo starts to turn his horse.

"Sharps!" Hat Evans walks around the corner of the house, moving slowly toward the riders. "Turn around."

With a look of fright, Sharps whirls, grabbing for his pistol as two shots sound only a fraction of a second apart. The rest of the riders take off, in a dead run, as a Mexican falls to the ground, stone-cold dead, two slugs dead center of his chest. Corey steps into the light from the other end of the porch, firing both pistols as fast as he can pull the trigger at the retreating riders. Manny Sharps returns their shots, firing wildly at the house as he follows the retreating Mexicans and Slocum.

Ben walks out to where the man lies, his black eyes wide open staring into nothing. Looking to where Corey stands, he shakes his head. "You didn't give them much of a chance."

"Didn't aim to, they would have done the same for me."

"You like to kill, don't you, boy?"

The dark eyes settle coldly on his father. "It don't bother me much, killing the likes of them."

Ben flares at his son. "Didn't make any difference to you that they just came in to talk?"

"No, I reckon it didn't." Corey hesitates. "Maybe you don't remember the last time they came visiting?"

Hat walks over and looks down at the dead man, and then over at Ben, then at Corey. "I shot the Mexican Ben. Sharps was reaching for his gun and the Mexican's horse lunged in front of him. I meant to kill Sharps."

"You shot him?" Ben stares hard at Hat.

"Yes, sir, it should have been Sharps lying there. He must have nine lives, like a cat."

Ben only stares at his son's back as Corey turns and walks out of sight, around the house, without waiting for an answer. Cussing himself, he knows he accused Corey again of being a cold-blooded killer, and again he was wrong.

Corey walks back to where he left his saddle horse and leads him toward the corral. Catching a fresh horse, he is switching the saddle over to the new mount, when Samuel and Caleb walk out to where he is.

"You heading back out?" Samuel leans on the corral.

"I am." Corey looks to where his brothers stand. "You two drag that Mex off somewhere and let the coyotes finish him."

"Kinda unchristian ain't it, Corey?" Caleb looks back to where the body lies.

"I don't figure he's worth the sweat it'd take to dig a hole for him." Corey jerks his cinch strap tight. "But you boys suit yourself."

Caleb stares over at his brother. "Pa didn't mean anything by what he said, brother."

"He could have fooled me."

"Corey, he just worries about the family, that's all." Samuel opens the gate into the corral. "I'll ride with you."

"I don't need you."

"Is that a fact? Well you got me anyway." Samuel ropes a bay gelding and leads him out. "Caleb will you go to the house and have sis put us up some biscuits and side meat?"

Caleb looks at both brothers, expecting more words, and then nods, walking away mumbling. "I'll get your food."

"Where we headed?" Samuel swings his saddle on the horse and cinches it down.

"I aim to find where Hernandez is holed up. If we can find the trail of the ones that just left here, we may get lucky." Corey steps up on his gelding as Lambert trots up with a sack full of food. "Anything beats waiting on them to ride in here at their leisure."

"Caleb and Colby are dragging that dead Mex off. He asked me to bring you these vittles."

Samuel takes the sack and nods at Lambert. "Thank ye kindly, brother."

"Tell pa to keep a sharp look out. This very well could be a trick to draw us away from the ranch." Corey speaks down to Lambert.

"I'll tell him." Lambert looks up at his brothers. "Y'all be careful."

"Lambert, you stay on the roof tonight and have Colby and the girls stay inside."

"Yes, sir," Lambert nods. "Soon as I finish helping Caleb."

"Samuel," Hat Evans walks up, "You stay here and let me go with Corey. Your sister and Ben need you here to look after them."

"Hat, I should go," Samuel protests. "It's my family, my place."

Hat smiles, taking the reins from the protesting Samuel. "If them Mexicans circle us from behind, you'll have your hands full right here. Stay alert."

"We'll be close." Corey turns his horse. "Not over a stone's throw away."

"Anything I should tell pa?" Lambert speaks up.

"Nothing." The words are like ice, coming from the big man.

Lorenzo sits in his chair, looking across the room at the table where Ben sits drinking coffee. Sarah slams the cup down on the table and retreats to the roof to sit with Judith.

Ben looks over at the Mexican. "She thinks I'm too hard on him, I reckon."

"What do you think, señor?" Lorenzo smiles knowingly, as a father would.

"I think my son is a coldblooded killer, that's what I think."

"Perhaps he is, but out here a man like that is needed." Lorenzo shrugs. "These killers do not respect anything but strength."

"Señor Lorenzo, they shot that man down in cold blood," Ben argues. "I didn't argue with Hat, but there were two bullet holes in that man's chest."

"Tell me señor, did not the Mexicans and whites come here to do the same to your son, given the chance?"

"My son has been killing men since he was sixteen years old." Ben sips on his coffee. "It has turned me cold."

"Have you not killed?" Lorenzo stares at Ben. "Were you not prepared to kill those men tonight?"

"It's different, I gave them a chance to ride out," Ben argues. "You don't shoot a man down in cold blood, with his back turned."

"I would señor," Lorenzo smiles. "You will one day, learn out here, it is different. You don't let a man get up once he's down. I believe they shot the man tonight in the chest."

"That's not my way, señor."

"It should be," Lorenzo nods. "Out here, the only man that can't kill you is a dead man."

Ben sips his coffee. "Like y'all did at the Alamo and Goliad?"

"Si, the very same."

"Were you there?"

"Si, señor, I was there." Lorenzo leans back in his chair. "You gringos do not understand. Santa Anna did not kill those men because they resisted him, he killed them because he feared them. They were great fighters and brave men. Dead, they could fight him no more."

Toreo rides hard through the night, distancing himself from the white rancho. One of his men lies dead, back at the ranch. This itself, is of no matter to Toreo, but he knows this is Hernandez's way of getting rid of the redheaded one, but the dead man got in the way. Hernandez knew this would happen if Sharps was recognized. Toreo wonders when it would be his turn. When will Hernandez decide to get rid of him and send him into a trap?

Pulling up, on a small hilltop, Toreo dismounts and walks back and forth, kicking the small rocks that were in his path. Slocum steps from his blowing gelding and loosens the cinch. Walking the horse in circles, he cools him out slowly. They have run a good five miles through the night, maybe more. Sharps stands nearby, reloading his empty pistol.

Slocum stops as Toreo walks in front of him.

"What do you think, Señor Slocum?"

"I think Lorenzo is in that ranch house. His horse is there in the corral, and the big man on the porch is a poor liar."

"You have a good eye. Si, I think the same."

"I also think the one that killed your man will soon be on our trail. He will try to follow us back to where Hernandez is camped." Slocum looks off in the dark.

"There were two men shooting at us when Reuben rode in front of my horse," Sharps spits the words out. "I was just lucky he took the lead and not me."

"One, two, it does not matter. Should we let these men follow us to Hernandez, or wait here and ambush them?" Toreo rolls a smoke and lights it.

"Do you think Hernandez sent us into a trap on purpose?" Slocum picks his words carefully. "Perhaps he wanted us all dead. If that's the case, I say let them follow."

"Señor, Hernandez does not care about us. He only worries about what he wants, and right now, it is the gringo's ranch." Toreo blows smoke. "Si, he knew if the whites recognized the red headed one he would probably be killed, but he figured we'd find out if Don Lorenzo was at the rancho, before the shooting started."

"I'm next, is that it?" Slocum glares at Toreo.

"Do not blame me, señor. You can ride out now if you wish."

Slocum is shocked that Toreo would speak so frankly about his leader, but no one was here to hear him. Toreo could deny everything later.

"What do you want to do?"

"For me, I would allow the gringo to find Hernandez, but this, I cannot do. I need Hernandez to lead us. Without him, the men would leave and go home, so I must stay here and ambush this man, if he is so foolish to follow us here."

"Maybe you are right," Slocum nods. His fortune has been made with Hernandez. He wouldn't desert him now, there was plenty more money to be made. Slocum doesn't even bother to look over at Sharps for his opinion, as it means nothing to him. They are staying with Toreo.

Corey and Hat separate, casting back and forth, trying to pick up the trail of the hard running horses ahead. During the night, when the darkness keeps them riding blind, they follow the stars, tracking due west. Now daylight comes again and they try to pick up the lost trail.

Finally, crossing the tracks of the running horses, they come back together and stop to down a few biscuits and meat.

"They're still moving fast." Hat looks at the way the deep tracks are cut and the dirt thrown up with the horses running stride.

"You have a good eye for tracking, Mister Evans."

"Those horses can't keep that pace up much longer." Hat tilts his canteen. "It must be six or seven miles back to the ranch, maybe more, they've run them horses hard."

"Scared men don't think sometimes." Corey wipes his mouth. "But, I don't think these men are that scared."

"You think they're trying to lure us into a trap?"

Corey nods. "There's always that possibility. Let's go see."

After sunup, Toreo spots the two riders from his vantage point atop a rocky outcropping, and whistles down at the others. He was about to give up and ride on to the canyon, thinking no one was following them. Slocum labors up the steep grade, sending the small stones and gravel under his feet, rolling to the bottom.

"Well now, what do we have here?" Slocum hisses at Toreo as he looks cautiously over the ridge of the hill.

"I think the big man in the lead is the one who shot our compadre last night."

Slocum glares, "He had help. There was another tall man standing in the yard, but I think you're right, he was one of the shooters. There couldn't be any more men that big in these parts."

"Hernandez will pay us well for killing these two." Toreo grins, checking the priming on his rifle.

Slocum slips back down the small rise and waits unseen, behind some large rocks where the two riders would have to pass. Directing the other two Mexicans, where they could be of the most use, he checks his weapons and waits. Toreo will fire first then he and the others will finish off the two men. Sharps looks at the two approaching riders and then slips behind another sandy outcropping, checking his weapons.

Hat rides in front, checking the ground and tracks as they cross the flat ground that slowly starts upward. They ride toward the ridges and ravines common in this part of the country. Corey let Hat do the tracking, while he concentrates on watching the flat ground directly in front of them. He would have liked to go around, but the trail they are following, leads straight ahead, right into the rough country. He has ridden this country before, looking for wild horses and scouting for the Mexicans. He knows instinctively, this country holds countless places that are perfect for an ambush.

Everything seems quiet, as they ride forward. Doves and other birds fly from under their horse's feet, and the call of a meadowlark sounds. Everything seems peaceful. Only the wind breaks the silence, blowing sharply across the flatlands, making the tall grass, that stands almost belly deep on the horses, sway back and forth, its dry stems making a rustling noise.

Their horse's ears suddenly perk up, as they catch the smell of a dozen or so wild ones, running off to their right. Hat looks after them and points with his finger. Little does he know, his arm moving, saves his life. One of the Mexicans thought he was spotted and fired prematurely, grazing Hats arm, knocking him from his horse.

Several shots ring out. Corey feels a slug pull at his own sleeve and dives sideways from his horse. Grabbing Hat under one arm, he drags him bodily into a shallow gulley. The small cut in the ground is barely deep enough to protect them from the steady rounds of hot lead that come pouring into the ground all around them.

Pulling Hat's woolen shirtsleeve up, Corey examines the wound, pressing a folded up piece of his own shirt over the shallow furrow.

"How bad is it Mister Stallings?" Hat props himself up on one elbow and looks down at his bloody sleeve.

"Not bad, it'll be sore as the dickens for a few days, but I reckon you'll mend, providing of course you don't get any new holes in you."

"Man, it burns like the devil."

"I believe you." Corey nods, his side still throbbing from the fall, as it hadn't completely healed yet. Corey eases over where he can get a look at their attackers and cautiously pushes his rifle barrel upward, through the tall grass that grows along the gully. Hearing Hat moving, he whispers across to him. "Save your energy and let that wound stop bleeding. You can't see anything from here anyway."

A bullet whistles by, only inches over their heads. Hat can swear he feels the air move as it passed over. Removing his hat, he peers over the top of the gulley, trying to find a target. Nothing moves along the ridges. Only quiet, blankets the landscape. A rifle roars, making Hat duck instinctively, just as another bullet whizzes by overhead.

Corey nods and then looks to where Hat lies crouched in a ball. "Do that again Hat, I spotted the smoke of that critter's rifle.

"You're talking about my head here." The white teeth gleam as Hat grins, rising slowly from the ground.

Both weapons fire, almost at the same time, the one from the ridge and Corey's. A muffled scream sounds just before a body pitches forward and rolls slowly down the slope. Corey laughs loud enough for the ones on the hill to hear, and then reloads.

Toreo cusses under his breath. The one below has the eye of an eagle, and he is dangerous as a striking rattlesnake. Few men could shoot like this one. His rifle reaches out and touches its victim with the kiss of death. He listens as the man below laughs again. He knows if he remains, his life could be forfeited next. Toreo is no coward, but he believes in choosing his own battleground, this place is no longer to his advantage.

Slipping backward from the crest, he slides down the gravel slope and walks to his waiting horse. Slocum, Sharps and the remaining Mexican, join him quickly.

"We go." Toreo mounts, turning to Slocum, "Hernandez will not hear of this, do you understand? We lost both men at the gringo rancho?"

Slocum only has time to nod as Toreo kicks his tired gelding into another hard run to the west. He knows, as Toreo does, the temperamental moods of Hernandez. Getting another of his men killed and running again from only two men, would send the Mexican into one of his killing moods, but who would he kill.

Corey waits several minutes and slowly makes his way from the gulley and up the small hill. The dead man is a Mexican, probably one of the ones that came to the ranch the night before. He has no way of knowing for sure. The others left him where he fell and were hurrying to the west.

Retracing his steps, he gathers their horses and helps Hat mount. The wound is still bleeding a little, but Corey knows they have to ride for home. The wind is picking up, blowing in gusts. Corey can smell the dampness in the air as the temperature falls steadily. He can see the black clouds rolling in. The first cold rain of the early winter is racing toward them, across the prairie. Corey knows if the rains hit, they would lose the trail of the Mexicans quickly. There is no need for Hat to suffer any further.

CHAPTER 15

Hernandez is in a rage, not only because Sharps survived, now he has lost two more of his men, and Toreo failed to find Lorenzo. Toreo, Sharps, and Slocum stand inside the tent, watching, as Hernandez paces back and forth, rubbing his hands together in a fury.

"Tell me, gentlemen, where do you think Señor Lorenzo is now? Do you think he still lives?" The man's cruel eyes leap out at all three men. "Surely you can tell me something?"

"I do not know for sure, Patron." Toreo shrugs.

"And you, Señor Slocum, where do you think he is?"

Slocum looks into the dark eyes. "I think he is in the Stallings' house."

"Then why does Toreo not think this?"

Again Toreo shrugs. "It is possible, but I did not see him with my own eyes as you instructed me to."

"And you, señor, what do you think?" Hernandez is furious, glaring coldly at Sharps.

Sharps' is tired, hungry, and out of sorts. For the moment, he has lost his fear of Hernandez. He saw Sarah in the shadows of the house, but he was no closer to getting her or the money than he ever was. "I don't know, he could very well be at the ranch."

"The rancho was expecting you?"

"They were expecting somebody for sure. They were armed to the teeth and had us dead to rights the minute we rode into the ranch yard," Slocum answers the man. He is tired of Hernandez and his games.

"And my nephew, the Kiowa?"

"Nothing, Patron. We saw nothing of him."

Hernandez quits pacing and sits down on his cot, staring at the floor. "Then my friends, you leave me no choice, we will attack the rancho in two days."

Slocum looks over at the man. "Señor, the ranch is heavily fortified. We will lose many men and maybe gain nothing."

"You said the whites have much gold. We will gain that, will we not?"

"Perhaps we will, but we only have the word of Sharps. Maybe the money does not exist." Slocum shrugs, looking over at Sharps, daring him to say anything.

"I have known men like Señor Sharps. Our friend may be a little fainthearted, but he is not stupid. No, Señor Slocum, he would not gamble his life if the whites did not have the money he spoke of." Hernandez smiles over where Sharps stands, eyeing them all with disdain.

"I did not lie about the money."

"Perhaps he only wants the red haired woman," Toreo speaks up.

"No, señor, the man is a coward. He would not put himself in danger for a mere woman," Hernandez smirks. "Isn't that right Señor Sharps?"

"Then you are going to attack the ranch?" Slocum doesn't wait for Sharps to answer.

"In two days we will ride on the rancho, two days, no more. Have the men ready." Hernandez looks around at the three men. "We have wasted too much time already."

Toreo smiles, "This is good, Patron, when the white rancho is destroyed, we can go back to the canyon and resume our trading."

Hernandez looks over at his Lieutenant. "Toreo, we must succeed this time or our men will desert us, do you understand? When the gringos are all dead, then you can have the place you've always wanted, and maybe one of the white women for your new esposa?"

"Si, Patron, but I do not think the men will leave your side." Toreo is shocked. How did Hernandez know of his dream? He has never mentioned wanting the Brazos River Bottoms for his own.

"Do not fool yourself my friend. Their loyalty lasts only as long as I make them money, and they fear me."

"Perhaps you are right."

"I am right. Remember, two days; have the men ready." Hernandez looks over at Slocum and adds an afterthought. "Men, who have no fear of their leader, do not respect him."

Palane sits upright against a backrest in the lodge of Grey Owl, the medicine man. His leg is healing, and the swelling has gone down. Yesterday, he walked around the village with just a slight limp. Cayuse visited the lodge several times over the last few days. The chief is anxious. What are the Mexicans doing, and when will Palane be able to ride?

Palane sent two of his friends to watch the camp of Hernandez. He has no idea what Cayuse will do if the Mexicans start toward the village of the whites. He knows his chief will not let anything happen to the mindless one, even if it means sending a war party against the brown men.

To some, it seems foolish, but Palane knows his chief fears for the safety of his people, should any harm befall the Faraway One. His medicine people sent him a dream, a dream that cannot be ignored. To tempt the spirits, by doing nothing, and let harm come to the Faraway One or his people, Cayuse fears, would be disastrous to the Kiowa. Did he not see this in his dream? Was it not foretold? It would not pay to ignore his spirit dream.

The warriors of the tribe have been told to prepare for battle. Arrows have been prepared, knives sharpened, and war axes rewound with fresh buffalo sinew. The fastest and strongest horses are brought in and painted for war. The Kiowa are a warlike tribe. It matters not, that they always traded with the brown men of the big canyon to the west, and considered them friends. Their chief has called a war council. The elders have listened and agreed the warriors should follow Cayuse.

Palane is still uncertain. To ride against the Mexicans, just for the sake of the Faraway One seems risky to him. The Kiowa would lose many men. The brown men are good fighters and they have guns, something the Kiowa have few of, and the ones they have been able to trade for, are clumsy and misfire more than they fire.

Palane looks into the small fire. It is not his decision. He is a low ranking warrior, unworthy of speaking his opinions to the elders. Cayuse he knows, has already made up his mind. The Kiowa will fight, if the Mexicans ride against the white ranch.

Palane straightens as a single horse trots up to Grey Owl's lodge. Looking out the flap, Palane watches as one of the warriors, he sent to watch the Mexican camp, slides from his horse, and walks toward him.

"You are back, my friend." Palane motions to a seat across from him.

Grey Owl stops what he is doing and calls to his woman to bring food for their visitor. Palane is eager to hear the news Pony's Tail brings, but protocol calls for a guest to eat and rest before any talk. Even though this is Pony's Tail village and his own family and lodge is nearby, Grey Owl observes Kiowa manners.

Finally, the warrior finishes eating and nods his thanks to the old woman. Looking over at Palane, he glances down at the leg.

"Your leg looks better. It is not swelling as it was."

"It is healing." Palane brushes off his leg. He is anxious to hear the news the warrior brings. "Tell me, you bring word of the brown men?"

"Yes, they are preparing to ride against the whites."

"What do they do?"

"Me and Little Calf met a Comanche that was paid to track for the Mexican Toreo and two white men. He told us they rode to the white village, looking for another Mexican. He scouted along the trail, the Mexicans told him the man was taken, but he found no tracks of the one they searched for. As they neared the white lodge, he held back and waited, afraid the whites would shoot a Comanche on sight."

"What happened?"

"The Comanche said the men were not gone long. He only waited a short time when gunfire rang out and the men rode back fast. One of the Mexican's horses was running loose. The rider was killed. The Comanche warrior could see the fear in the redheaded white man as they rode past where he waited. Only two Mexicans and two whites passed, fleeing to the south, not stopping to speak, not waiting for the Comanche to catch up.

Pony's Tail smiles, "The Comanche thinks the fleeing men cowards, so he would not ride further with them. Instead, he took a different trail back to the canyon and joined the other Comanche waiting in the Mexican's camp."

"Go on," Palane is anxious.

"Four Mexicans and two whites left to search for the big Mexican. Only two Mexicans came back, and only one was killed at the white's village, so there must have been another fight after they fled the ranch of the whites." Pony's Tail shrugs. "This I do not know for sure. The Comanche did not follow, so he didn't know what happened to the other Mexican. Perhaps he ran away."

Palane nods, "Go ahead, my friend."

"The men entered the camp and went straight to the scar-faced one's lodge and held a council. The next morning, the camp started preparing to ride north. I was told they would ride in two days. They invited the Comanche to fight with them, but their chief said no." Pony's Tail shakes his head. "The Comanche will not ride with cowards."

"Where is Little Calf?"

"He stayed behind in the Mexican camp to watch. He will come here when the brown men start their ride to the north."

"You have done well Pony's Tail. I thank you." Palane nods, "You and Little Calf will be well rewarded."

"I have heard, from our warriors on the trail, our Chief Cayuse will make war on the brown men if they attack the whites."

"This is so."

"The Mexicans are strong fighters. They have many men and guns." Pony's Tail shakes his head. "Why would Cayuse wish to fight them? We have always traded with them in friendship."

"This is true, I know, but our chief thinks we must fight the Mexicans. We must protect the Faraway One."

"I am Kiowa; I will ride with my chief," Pony's Tail nods. "The Mexicans have many guns and ponies for us to take. It will be a glorious fight, but I do not think the Mexicans will be easy to defeat."

"This is good, my friend," Palane nods. "I have one other task I would ask of you."

"Ask."

"I wish for you to ride to the ranch of the whites and warn them."

"The whites by the river?" Pony's Tail is curious.

"Yes."

"They shoot plenty quick at Indian," The Kiowa looks over at

Palane, doubtfully. "Why do you wish me to do this thing?"

"I want them to know our people, the Kiowa, are on their side in this one fight only."

"It is many miles. I will need a fresh horse."

"Take the paint tied outside," Palane points. "Be careful my friend. Show yourself and alert them, before you ride into their camp."

"I will return quickly," Pony's Tail smiles. "If the big warrior of the whites doesn't kill me like he did the Mexican."

Palane nods. "Why did the big white named Corey kill the Mexican so quickly?"

The warrior shrugs, "The Comanche says the Mexicans tell him, this one is mucho loco, crazy, one who likes to kill."

Palane shakes his head. "I do not think this."

Pony's Tail grins, "If he kills me, you will believe then. I go."

Spotting a lone rider sitting in the early morning dim light, Colby opens the hatch and whistles down to where everyone is eating breakfast.

"There's a rider sitting out on the flats, Pa."

Everyone knows their job. Instantly, the room is abuzz with activity as the men gather weapons, closing and barring the window shutters. Corey, Ben, and Caleb walk out onto the front porch and stare out, past the corrals, where indeed a lone rider sits his horse, unmoving.

From where he sits, the rider can see them plainly and starts turning his horse in tight circles. Pulling the horse to a stop, the warrior raises his right hand and holds it up, palm forward, as he starts forward toward the waiting men.

"I think he wants to talk." Corey steps into the yard, walking toward the approaching warrior.

Pony's Tail pulls his gelding to a stop in front of the huge white man. He heard these men were big, but he had no idea how big, until he looked upon the white. The Comanche described this one exactly, a huge man, with cold hard eyes. Maybe this one is like a lobo wolf, kill crazy. Yes, there is no doubt this was the one that killed the Mexican. Pony's Tail wonders would he also die by this white's hand before he could speak.

Corey listens as the warrior speaks in a guttural tone, but he can't understand the words. Pony's Tail watches as the man shakes his great head and shrugs his shoulders. Palane forgot these whites do not understand the Kiowa language.

Lorenzo sits beside one of the windows, listening. "He has a message from someone called Palane."

"You understand their talk?" Ben is surprised.

"Si, I have traded with these people for many years," Lorenzo nods. "It helps to know what they say when trading. It helps that they trust you."

"I reckon it would come in mighty handy at that." Ben looks back to the warrior. "Motion for him to come closer Corey, and for Pete's sake, don't shoot him."

Corey only frowns at the last remark and motions at the window where Lorenzo sits. Understanding the gesture, the warrior dismounts lightly and walks toward the house. He was not with Palane and the Kiowa Elders when they came here to race the little horse, but he heard about their great lodge and these huge white men.

Lorenzo manages to pull himself to the window and make the sign of peace toward the warrior. "It is customary to give him something to eat and drink before he speaks."

"Do we have to follow their customs?" Corey is eager to hear what the man has to say. "Just tell him to say his piece."

"It would be better, señor," Lorenzo nods. "He has ridden far to give you a message from Palane."

Sarah brings bread and side meat out on the porch and hands it to Pony's Tail along with a hot sugary cup of coffee. Smiling gratefully, the warrior gulps the food down and nods at Lorenzo.

"Now, señors, we can begin."

"Ask him what words Palane sends to us?" Corey fires the question at Lorenzo.

"He says his name is Pony's Tail. He asks first to see the Faraway One." Lorenzo is curious at this request. He has not been told anything about Colby and his experiences with the Kiowa.

Colby steps quietly through the door, at Corey's beckoning, and smiles brightly at the warrior. Pony's Tail steps backward, away from the youth, and nods.

"He's scared of the boy. He thinks he is big medicine," Lorenzo volunteers. Now he is beginning to understand the strange relationship the Kiowa have with these whites.

"We've been through all that before," Corey is impatient. "Ask him about Palane."

Nodding, as Lorenzo speaks, but not taking his eyes from Colby, Pony's Tail takes two more steps backward, away from the porch, and stops before speaking. "He says Palane sends word the Mexicans ride against you in two sleeps. He says Chief Cayuse wants him to bring the Faraway One back to the Kiowa village so he will be safe," Lorenzo translates.

Ben pushes Colby back inside the house. "Tell your chief we thank him, but the boy will stay here with us."

"He says many men come here, many bang bang." The warrior looks at the window where Colby reappears. "You send him with Kiowa. We take good care of Faraway One."

"I know your people would." Ben waves his hands flat in refusal. "But no, he stays here with us."

Lorenzo waits until the warrior finishes speaking and swings up on his horse. "He says Palane will come soon with many warriors and help you fight these brown men."

Corey steps up near the warrior and nods his head. "Tell Palane, he is always welcome here, but we will fight our own battles."

"Señor, maybe you should let them help you." Lorenzo does not think it wise to offend the Kiowa by turning down their offer of help. The Kiowa are notorious raiders and rarely, if ever, offer to help someone other than another Kiowa or Comanche tribe. For their help to be refused by the whites could be taken badly. The big man can still not believe the Kiowa have offered to fight against Hernandez, who they have traded with for years.

"Tell him we do not wish our friends, the Kiowa, to be killed by the brown men," Corey raises his hand and turns toward the warrior.

Lorenzo finishes translating and relaxes in his chair, exhausted, as Pony's Tail turns his horse and starts back west. "Why wouldn't you let them help?"

"Have them at my back with you Mexicans attacking, no thank you."

"I have never known the Kiowa to make a treaty of war with the white man." Lorenzo wipes sweat from his brow. "I have never known them go back on their word when they did go into battle with other tribes."

"Sounds like a good idea to me," Hat speaks, leaning back in the bed they moved into the kitchen by the fire for him. The weather turns colder by the day, and Judith pampers him like a newborn.

The ride back from the ambush made the wound in his arm to start bleeding again, taxing his strength greatly. Corey tried to stop the flow of blood, but when they reached the ranch, Hat was too weak to make it in the house alone. For three days, Judith has been fussing over him like a mother hen with chicks.

"Hatton Evans, lie back on that pillow and rest," she chides him good-naturedly.

Lorenzo laughs. "Si, señor, you may need all your strength before long."

"You think they'll come soon, Don Lorenzo?"

"It is not Hernandez you will need your strength for, I think." Lorenzo throws his head back and roars laughing, as Judith blushes beet red.

Corey has been preparing for the attack for the past few days since his return with Hat. All the mustangs, except their riding horses, have been turned back into the canyons. Lambert and Colby are kept busy with the bullet molds and hot lead. Ben cleans and recleans the rifles, checking them over. There will be no time for repairs later. Water barrels are filled and firewood brought in. The ranch house is like a fortress, getting ready for a battle.

The evening sun dips low in the western sky as night draws near. The days are still warm enough, but with the coming of sundown, the air becomes chilly, and after dark, it turns cold. Corey and Ben sit on the porch smoking and listening to the whippoorwills along the river. Lorenzo leans from the window, his broad shoulders almost filling it.

"Tell me, Señor Lorenzo, when do you think they'll come?" Corey looks up at the man.

Lorenzo shrugs, "Perhaps tomorrow or the next day, no later. The warrior said two days."

"Why do you think this?"

"It is quite simple. Hernandez needs a kill. He must show his men that his luck is still strong, or they will desert him like rats."

"Are you sure?" Ben puffs his pipe.

"Yes, tomorrow or the next day, they will come."

Corey exhales. "How will they attack us?"

"At daybreak, they will come in from the east, with the sun at their back. First, they try to talk you into surrendering, then they will attack."

"How, horseback, afoot, how?"

"This señor, I do not know for sure, perhaps both." Lorenzo repositions himself. "Were it myself, it would be afoot as there is no cover at all around your rancho."

"Corey, how many men are going to be on the roof?" Ben asks.

"Two is all we can spare."

Judith steps out on the porch. "And that will be me and Sarah."

"Señorita, por favor, no. You cannot do this thing," Lorenzo protests. "It is far too dangerous."

"No, you sure ain't," Hat yells from the bed.

"Hatton Evans you ain't my boss yet, and I can shoot as good as any of you." Judith wads her apron and glares at Corey. "And that's final."

Corey grins. "Reckon that settles that then."

"But, señor."

"It's settled Don Lorenzo," Judith smiles at the Mexican. "But, thank you for worrying about us."

Ben looks over at Corey. "Well boy, I guess even you will get your fair share of killing tomorrow."

Corey rises slowly to his feet, and without a backward glance, he walks off into the dark. Before he tosses it aside, only the glowing butt of his cigarette shows the direction he walks.

"You are hard on your son, Señor Ben," Lorenzo looks out the door, "Very hard."

"Yes, I am, and I'm sorry, but he's a born killer." Ben walks to the stove for coffee. "Bless his mother's soul. She's probably turning over in her grave at this moment."

"Aren't we all, my friend?"

"Not like him."

"He's my brother, Pa, not a killer." Colby looks his father in the eye.

Ben gazes around the room at his children and swallows his coffee. Nodding, he lets his shoulders slump.

CHAPTER 16

Palane sits listening as Pony's Tail gives his report of what the whites have said. Nodding slowly, he smiles slightly, as he understands the white man is too proud to ask for help, but haven't the Kiowa always been the same way.

It does not matter, Chief Cayuse will fight beside the white people, whether they like it or not. He knows the prophesy of his dream. The Faraway One must be protected. The existence of the Kiowa people, depend on it. If the one called Colby is lost, the Kiowa people would be lost also.

Palane stands and tests his leg. Tomorrow, Chief Cayuse will ride to the east and he will be at his side. He doesn't understand why, but for some reason, he has come to like the big white man called Corey.

Hernandez looks back at the long line of riders following him. The few Comanche scouts riding with him reported Kiowa warriors on both sides of the column, following the procession. Why, he doesn't know. Perhaps they are waiting to get in on the kill. They have always been friendly, always traded with him at the large canyon so he considers them no threat. The Mexican's destination now is certainly obvious. The white rancho is the only thing this far toward the north worth attacking with so large a force.

When his scouts ride in and report the white's rancho is only five miles distance, Hernandez makes camp for the night. In the early morning hours, he will cover the remaining distance and be ready to attack at first light.

Sharps paces back and forth nervously. Hernandez already ordered the two whites to lead the attack. He knows first hand, the accuracy of a rifle in the Stallings' hands. He and Slocum will be the first targets the rifles find when the shooting starts.

"If that fool charges straight up to the house, we're dead men Slocum," Sharps whines. "Sitting ducks are what we'll be."

"He'll talk first."

"And then? Them Stallings are hill folk. They ain't about to give up their womenfolk, unless they're dead," Sharps spits. "You can count on that."

"One stick of dynamite will change their mind." Slocum grins as he leans back on a saddle. "I'll guarantee it."

Sharps snickers. "You my friend, do not know the Stallings clan very well."

"Well then we'll blow them back to Arkansas, won't we, friend." Slocum drags out the word, friend.

"Sure we will Slocum. We're dang fools, that's what we are," Sharps frowns. "If he has us lead the attack, we won't be around to see the dynamite do its work."

"Maybe, then maybe not, we'll see." Slocum closes his eyes.

Sharps isn't ready to give up the argument. He is scared of dying and he knows death is only hours away if Hernandez charges the ranch house. Why did he ever leave Arkansas and the safe haven of his kinfolk? "Not to mention the fact, if he uses dynamite, he'll blow the money to bits."

"Not to mention your woman either, huh Manny?" Slocum laughs.

Little Calf, the Kiowa warrior Palane sent with Pony's Tail to watch the Mexicans, rides his sweat stained mustang hard through the village of his people, pulling up at Grey Owl's lodge. Disregarding all protocol, he doesn't wait the usual time, good manners require, before he enters the lodge and starts talking.

"The brown men are moving." The young warrior and friend of Palane, kneels inside the lodge. "They rode from the canyon at dawn when the sun rose. I followed beside them for a few miles to see if they were indeed heading for the big river."

"Then they will be there in one sleep, if they do not fall asleep as Mexicans are prone to do." Palane nods figuring in his head.

The Kiowa, on several occasions, rode into the Mexican camps and found all the men sound asleep in the early afternoon, taking their customary siesta. From this they had come to believe the brown men were lazy, and sleep all the time.

"We must warn the whites immediately." Palane stands slowly to his feet. "You, Pony's Tail and Little Calf will ride to the whites now. Take two spare horses with you and ride hard my friends. Warn them of the brown men and fight with them until Chief Cayuse arrives. You must guard the Faraway One at all costs."

"We go." Pony's Tail walks from the lodge. "You have Pony's Tail's word. We will protect the Faraway One with our lives."

Palane follows them outside. "Choose the best horses from my herd, my friends, Palane thanks you."

The three warriors clasp forearms. "We are brothers; we go."

Palane watches as the warriors race away, then hobbles slowly over to Cayuse's lodge. Bending painfully, he enters.

Hernandez has Toreo kicking the men from their bedrolls as the moon stands high in the night. Not a cloud is visible in the sky above. Only the millions of stars twinkle brightly in the cold night air. Frost glitters on the canvas bedrolls as the men grumble when they wake up and forced out of their warm beds. Horses are saddled quickly and the caravan of riders mount, heading northeast. Steam blows from the men and horses' nostrils in the early morning, cold frosty air, giving off an eerie shadow.

Hernandez knows the unprotected ranch lies waiting only a few miles distance. He smiles as his men would fall on it like a pack of wolves, devouring the ones that dare to fight. He looks over where the whites ride quietly, neither uttering a word. The fat one has guts, but the redheaded one, the coward, will be dead before the battle finishes. It is no loss to him, but the one called Slocum is different. Hernandez is undecided about his future. In the past, the man was useful and they had a good relationship. The two of them had stolen plenty of money and trade goods.

Hernandez feels no remorse about losing Slocum, but at the same time, he doesn't want to lose a man that has been so profitable to him. Lighting one of his small cigars, the Mexican sneers. He believes in fate. If the white survives the battle, that would be good, if not, oh well, he could be replaced. The redheaded one, Sharps, is another matter entirely, and he will die.

Pony's Tail and Little Calf race their worn out horses into the ranch house yard, two hours before the sun is to break over the horizon in the east. A warning shot from the roof brings everyone inside, wide awake, and rushing to man the firing portals. Corey opens the door slowly. Recognizing Pony's Tail, he crosses the porch.

Gesturing wildly, the two Kiowa point first to the east, then toward the sky.

Corey looks behind him at the window.

"They're trying to tell you the Mexicans are near." Lorenzo crawled to where he can see the warriors.

"Ask them how much time we have?" Ben speaks from a nearby window.

"They say two hours till the new sun comes up, and the brown men will be here."

Sarah and Judith are already dressed and climbing the ladder onto the roof. Lambert and Samuel, who have been on guard, are sent back down to fight below.

"You ladies keep your heads down when the shooting gets hot." Hat speaks from where he is trying to get dressed.

"One of us will come back down and throw together some breakfast," Judith hollers from the roof.

Ben shakes his head. "There's no need, we'll make out until this is over."

"Better let her cook, Pa," Caleb speaks up. "This could take a spell and I'm hungry."

"Suit yourself then, reckon I could use a cup of hot coffee," Ben grins. "Round up something for the Kiowa."

"The warrior says they will fight to protect Colby, but they do not like house."

"Tell him we thank them. Ask them if they know how to shoot guns." Corey walks back inside the house.

Lorenzo shakes his head. "They say no, they will use their own weapons."

"Bows and arrows," Lambert scoffs. "They'll be a great help."

"They've probably killed more men throughout history than guns, my young friend."

"Yes, sir, but that was before guns were invented," Lambert scoffs.

Lorenzo smiles, he can't argue that point with the boy. "Señor Corey, may I speak with you?"

Corey walks over to where the big Mexican is sitting on the floor. Kneeling down beside the man, Corey looks him over. "You hurting? You want me to help you back to your chair?"

"Hurting?" Lorenzo looks down at his useless legs. "I will not live like this. I feel nothing."

"I'm no doctor, señor," Corey shrugs. "Perhaps when you go home a real doctor can help you."

"You will listen to me now." Lorenzo takes hold of Corey's thick, muscled forearm. "I will never go home and señor you cannot defend this place against Hernandez."

"We can try."

"You do not understand, my friend."

"Now you call me your friend. Only days ago, you said you would kill me when you were well." Corey doesn't trust the man, now that other Mexicans are near. "What happened?"

"This I will do, but now, for the women's sake, you must listen."

"I'm listening," Corey nods. One thing he has learned about the big Mexican, the man is a gentleman, and has a soft spot in his heart for both Judith and Sarah, almost as if they were his own children.

"I was in the camp of Señor Hernandez. I saw an old man there, I remember." Lorenzo looks over at the others. "He is a dynamite man."

"And?"

"He has no conscious, none at all."

"And we're supposed to fear an old man."

"He is a dynamite specialist. He will blow this place apart, just like that." Lorenzo snaps his fingers.

"Dynamite!"

"Si, señor, just like that," Lorenzo nods. "One stick will blow this rancho to pieces."

Corey looks up, toward the hatch, visibly shaken. "What can we do?"

"I have a feeling my men will be with Hernandez." Lorenzo twists slightly, easing himself. He has probably told them, you whites killed me. They must see me before Hernandez gets close enough to use the dynamite."

"And how do you propose to do that?"

"We will tell them, when they ride up."

"We?"

"You have no choice in this señor, we must protect the women." Lorenzo shrugs.

"What do you have in mind, Don Lorenzo?"

"You will get my horse, señor." Lorenzo glances up as Judith starts down the stairs. "Saddle him and bring him close to the house."

"You can't ride. You can't even sit up straight," Corey protests.

"Get my horse, Corey Stallings, we haven't much time," Lorenzo grins. "I have heard you were a man of courage and liked to kill. Well, señor, now we will see."

"You may have been told wrong."

Lorenzo smiles, "I do not believe that either. Get my horse, then I will tell you what I have in mind."

Corey looks over where Ben sits rechecking their extra weapons. "Reckon you been talking to pa."

CHAPTER 17

Palane knows, as he rides out of the Kiowa Village at the head of a hundred warriors, they will not be in time to help the whites. He shakes his head, but he believes in the medicine people. If their medicine is strong, the whites at the river will live, if not, he shrugs his shoulders.

Hernandez sits his horse in front of his men. Slocum and Sharps sit to his right and left. Only the dim silhouette of the high tree line is visible in front of the gringo ranch house. Now, he waits only for daylight to come over the flat prairie, then he will attack. First, he will give the whites a chance to surrender. He will demonstrate the dynamite's usefulness, its power, and then it is up to the white men. If they come out of the house, they will live, at least for a couple more hours. If not, then he will have the old man set the charges. Hernandez doesn't want to dynamite the house. He wants the women alive. They are both beautiful, but if it is not to be, well at least he would have the money and his honor back.

"Do you wish to ride forward and talk with your friends, Señor Sharps?" Hernandez glances over at the man. "Perhaps you can convince them of the futility of resistance."

Sharps can't tell if the man is serious or joking, but he wants no part of riding into Corey Stallings' rifle sights. Looking over at the scar-faced Mexican, he shutters despite himself.

"You didn't answer, señor."

"They would shoot me on sight, and you know it."

"Perhaps, and that would be such a loss," Hernandez laughs evilly. "Such a loss."

Corey and Ben lift the heavy Mexican onto the back of the huge black horse. The animal dwarfs the other mustangs, standing at least seventeen hands tall. Corey double checks the ropes and belts, making sure Lorenzo is securely strapped to the tremendous animal, preventing him from falling from the deep saddle.

"Now, señors, my weapons and my sombrero, please."

Corey checks the loads in the three pistols, he has strapped to his saddle, then the ones around his waist, and he discards his rifle. This morning there will be no long-range shooting.

Somehow, Hat Evans is astride a horse and comes riding around the corner of the house with Samuel following.

"Samuel, you stay here and protect the women." Corey looks over at his brother. "And good hunting."

"Not likely," Samuel rides forward. "I'm going out there with you."

"Samuel, if they get past us, you're all that stands between them and the girls."

Hat kicks his horse closer. "We're counting on you Samuel."

Nodding, Samuel dismounts and slaps the rump of his horse, sending him out of harm's way. "Good luck, boys."

Corey nods at his brothers, and brushes Colby's hair, before looking up on the roof at Judith and Sarah. His dark eyes look deeply into the Sarah's green eyes for only seconds, but to her, it seems like an eternity. Nodding, he smiles, and turns his horse next to the black.

Lorenzo smooches to the black and starts a slow walk toward the flat ground west of the house where the dark forms of many men sit their horses in the early morning fog and mist. Corey and Hat Evans, follow closely behind him.

"Three against fifty, Pa, that sure ain't good odds." Samuel looks over at Ben, "Even for Corey Stallings."

"No, it ain't Samuel, but you may be needed here, like they said, to protect the women."

"Yes, sir."

Ben watches the broad back of his son riding calmly alongside Lorenzo and Hat toward the line of Mexicans. Raising his arm, he wants to call to Corey, but he knows there is no use. Nothing will call him back. He knows what he wants to say, should have been said many years ago. Now it's too late.

Lorenzo pulls his horse to a stop a hundred yards from the waiting Mexicans. Corey and Hat halt their horses alongside him. Ahead, the Mexicans sit strung out in a long line, waiting for Hernandez to give the word to charge the house.

"Amigos." Lorenzo's booming voice yells out, across the flat grassland. "It is I, Ricardo Lorenzo, your Don."

Several men spur their horses forward a few feet, stopping as Lorenzo holds up his hand. The scar-faced Hernandez, pales slightly, as he recognizes, first the voice of Lorenzo, and then the man himself.

Lorenzo clucks to the black and starts forward, riding to within talking distance of the Mexican line. A lone horseman races his horse forward, sliding to a stop in front of the black.

"Don Ricardo, we were told the whites had killed you." A small dark skinned rider salutes Lorenzo. "Praise the saints, Patron. It is a miracle you are alive."

"No Pablo, my friend, it was not the gringos, it was Señor Hernandez."

"Is this possible, Hefe?" The man turns in his saddle and looks back at Hernandez.

"Si my dear friend, it is true," Lorenzo nods. "He had that pig Toreo shoot me."

"What do you wish me to do?" The slight man asks. "I will fight with you to the death."

"No my friend, we have always fought side by side, but not this time." Lorenzo motions to the men beside him. "These men will side me today."

"But, Patron," the slight one looks over at Corey and the others. "One is wounded. He has a bad arm and there are only three of you. This is sure death against so many. Por favor, I beg you, let me fight."

"Do as I ask my friend."

The Mexican studies the belts and ropes holding Lorenzo in the saddle and nods. "What do you wish?" Looking at the way Lorenzo is tied on, he knows something is wrong.

"Tell the men I live. Tell the ones who are loyal to Santa Anna and Don Ricardo Lorenzo to ride away from this place, now."

"Patron." Tears come to the Mexican's eyes as he studies Lorenzo. "Please Hefe, please, let me ride with you."

"Pablo, my good friend, one other thing, por favor."

"Hefe."

"Tell my esposa and my niños that I think of them this day."

"Si, Patron."

"Now go, my friend."

"Are you hurt bad, Patron?" Pablo can't tear his eyes from the ropes.

"Si my friend, I am paralyzed. My legs are useless," Lorenzo nods. "Now, I am only half a man. Toreo has killed me where so many others have failed."

"But Hefe, you still have your life."

"This isn't life, Pablo."

"Si, Patron, you are too much of a hombre, too proud to live with no legs." Pablo nods sadly. "I am sorry."

"Adiós, my friend."

"Vaya con Dios, Don Ricardo."

Hernandez watches as Lorenzo talks with Pablo Garcia, his longtime compadre and second in command, then looks on in shock as the slight Mexican rides back to the Mexican line and approaches Toreo. No words are spoken, only the blast of a pistol shot and the falling body of Toreo as he pitches from his saddle, stone dead. Every gun is drawn and pointed at Hernandez and the men that remain loyal to him.

Hernandez watches as Garcia turns his back and rides slowly away, with almost all the Mexican riders following him to the south. Only ten Mexicans and the three whites remain behind to face Don Lorenzo and the two whites.

Looking across the flat ground, Hernandez cusses in disbelief, three against thirteen, but still good odds. His men are all veterans of many battles and well-armed, except for the two whites, all are willing to fight.

The other white, the dynamite man, will do what he was paid for when the fight is over.

"My friends, there are your enemies. If we ride through them, the women and gold are ours." Hernandez pulls his pistol. "Are you willing Manny Sharps? There will be more for all of us?"

Sharps looks across the grass field at his hated enemy Corey Stallings. He knows if he refuses, Hernandez will kill him outright. If he fights and wins, perhaps Hernandez and many of his men will be dead and he would be in charge; at least he would be alive.

The only ones left in the house are two men, two young boys and two women. Nodding his head, he looks over at the Mexican.

"Right behind you Hernandez," Sharps grins nervously.

"No, señor, you and Slocum will have the honor of leading the charge against our enemies." Hernandez points the pistol right at Sharps' belly. "Señor Pesky, you will wait here with the dynamite. When this is over, you will be needed."

"Why not use the dynamite on these three now," Pesky grins his toothless smile.

Hernandez looks off to the south, the direction most of his men left. He knows if Lorenzo's men hear the dynamite go off, they would return. "No, we must face these three and fight with the pistolo."

"I'll be right here, señor." Pesky grins as he looks over at the sweating Sharps, relieved he doesn't have to charge forward against Lorenzo.

Ben Stallings, his four remaining sons, and both women stand on the roof, helplessly watching the drama unfold in front of them. Sarah's eyes are trained on Corey as the Mexicans fan out in a line, ready to charge across the open field.

"I wish we were in rifle range, Papa Ben." Sarah speaks as everyone in the field seems to freeze in time.

Ben looks over at his sons, and back at Corey, the one he called a killer so many times in the past. Fear grips his heart, fear for a son, he turned from, and fears he will never be able to tell him his true feelings. In the few fleeting moments that pass, he knows the truth, it dawns on him. Yes, Corey has killed, there was no arguing that, but he was only protecting his family as best he could and the only way he knew how.

Tears come to Ben's eyes as he looks at the back of the proud son he turned away from. Would he ever get the chance to redeem himself?

Lorenzo looks at the men beside him and smiles. "Well compadres, if I am to die, this day, I can think of no men I would rather be with."

Corey nods and looks over at Hat. "Hatton old friend, here's where we separate the men from the boys."

"I'll be right beside you, Corey."

Corey smiles, "I know you will."

Hat Evans swivels in his saddle and looks back, toward the house where he knows Judith would be watching. Waving his good arm, he thinks he sees movement on the roof of the house.

"Hat you should marry that girl, providing we get out of this mess." Corey watches Hat wave then laughs.

"I aim to, you can count on it," Hat nods. "And my first son will be named Corey Stallings Evans."

Corey's eyes never waver from the figure of Manny Sharps. Hat straightens in his saddle and looks over at Corey, seeing where his eyes are focused.

"Huh uh, Mister Stallings, that bird's mine and mine alone." Hat nods across at Sharps. "I've got a big score to settle for Kyle and Judith."

"Okay Hat, he's yours, don't miss."

"I ain't planning on it. If I don't get the job done, you finish it for me."

Palane and the Kiowa ride to a small knoll, overlooking the flatlands just as the two lines form and prepare to charge. Cayuse looks toward the house and then back at the men in the field. Hernandez has his attention focused on the three men in front of him and never spots the Kiowa warriors watching from the knoll to his left. Seeing most of the brown men leaving, Cayuse holds his brown arm up, holding the eager warriors back, not letting them go forward.

Palane is beside himself. "My Chief, we do not help the whites."

"The Faraway One is not in danger. It would offend the medicine people if we interfere with these whites fighting each other. There is no need to get our warriors killed." Cayuse looks over at Palane. "My son, you can help your friends if you wish."

Palane nods, kicking his horse into a hard run over the knoll, toward the two lines of men. Screaming his war cry, Palane races to where Corey, the big Mexican and another one he does not recognize, sit their horses. Corey looks at the screaming warrior and smiles.

"You were almost too late, Palane." Corey speaks as the warrior slides his horse to a stop beside them.

"No, I came in time to save you from the brown men." Palane grins solemnly. "I don't think you whites fight well. Maybe you fight like you race horse."

Hat looks over at the warrior and nods. "You wanna bet?"

"Well, I hope I am wrong. I hope you are great warriors. This Kiowa thinks you get yourselves into a real fix this time. I see many warriors against you." Palane looks over at Corey and laughs. "Where is Pony's Tail and Little Calf?"

"Back at the house, protecting Colby."

"Seems even to me," Hat grins. "Only four to one since you arrived, not bad odds."

Corey grins. "Hatton Evans, meet Palane, but don't bet with him, he's kinda crooked."

"I heard that already from Lambert." Hat nods at Palane and grins.

"It is not my fault the white man's horse can't run fast like Kiowa horse."

Looking across the space, separating the two parties, Hernandez watches Palane, his blood nephew, speaking with the white men, raising his strong bow at the Mexican line, screaming his war cry, mocking them. The scar-faced one scowls, seeing red. His own nephew, one he offered to let join him, now sits on his horse, jeering at him, making a fool of him, his own blood.

Hernandez glares sideways at his men then raps Sharps' gelding across the rump with his riding crop. Both sides charge at the same time, yelling at the top of their lungs as they come closer together. The Mexicans are strung out in a long line as they close the gap, the hooves of their horses plowing up great clods of dirt as they pound across the sandy ground.

Sharps' horse is terrified with all the shouting and weapons being fired, plus, Hernandez is whipping him across the rump with every stride. With the animal lunging and rearing, it is hard for him to get a good bead on any of the four riders charging straight at them. Riding off to the side of the charging lines, Slocum watches, fascinated as the two sides slam together, firing as fast as they can cock their weapons.

Looking across at the hard charging men, Slocum catches his first glimpse of Corey Stallings as the big man races his mustang with a vengeance toward them. Beside the big man, another huge man rides, Don Lorenzo, a man he knows well, the one man he fears above all others. Slocum feels a cold shiver pass through his body. He knows they are all dead men; he feels it.

Hernandez has forgotten about whipping Sharps horse. Now, all he thinks about is killing the hated gringos, and the traitor Don Lorenzo, who are charging on his men. Lead and powder smoke hang in the air as both sides clash together, firing round after round. Terrified horses plunge and rear as hot lead pours into them unmercifully. Hat pulls his horse into the path of Manny Sharps and fires as they come eye to eye, less than five feet apart. The two horses crash into each other.

Hernandez picks out Lorenzo for his target as the big man fights his way through the lines, but with all the confusion, he fires at the big white man instead. Firing, almost point-blank, as Corey races past, he can't miss. Several saddles are empty, as loose horses careen about the field, some wounded and dying, others trying to escape the noise. Corey takes steady aim and pushes his way through the line of smoking guns, making every shot count.

The Kiowa lets out with his screaming battle cry as he rides beside Hat, shooting arrow after arrow into the hapless Mexicans. Guns roar, men scream and fall under flying hooves. Horses stumble and go down as the watchers on the roof see everything from their perch on the house.

They are not close enough to see in detail, the bloodbath that is taking place as the two sides fight, or near enough to feel the hot lead flying about. All they can hear is the death struggle going on. Each stares in anxiety as they watch Mexicans blown from their horses, and their loved ones falling from their own mounts. Judith cries out in despair as she watches the pistols of Hat and Sharps spitting out flame and smoke as they fire at almost point-blank range. She gasps as Hats horse goes down, under the horse of Manny Sharps.

Ben clenches his fists tight as he watches Corey fighting like a madman, firing both right and left as he passes through the line of Mexicans.

The scar-faced Hernandez sees the plume of smoke from Lorenzo's pistol and feels the red-hot lead pass through his left side, almost lifting him from his racing horse. Returning fire, as Lorenzo passes within touching distance of him, Hernandez watches as the black horse runs several feet and stops. Firing again at the broad back, he sees Lorenzo slowly slip from his saddle. Puzzled the big man didn't fall, he raises his weapon to fire again, when Corey fires at point-blank range, knocking him from his horse.

Palane is almost out of arrows, so he reverts to his war club, which requires him to get in close to his enemy. In a fighting frenzy, he never realizes how many times bullets have barely missed their target and pass him harmlessly. Slocum has shot twice at the screaming Kiowa, cussing himself for missing, taking slow, deliberate aim at the raging warrior. Corey snaps off a shot from behind Slocum, hitting him through the lungs. Turning slowly in the saddle, Slocum looks at the big man in disbelief, as he slides from his horse, dead before he hits the ground.

Palane looks around as Slocum falls, knowing Corey had just saved his life. Waving his bloody war club, the warrior glances around for another victim, but all the Mexicans are down. Looking around for Hat, he sees him lying beneath the body of the redheaded one, and thinks him dead also.

The noise of battle and gunfire subside, almost as quickly as it began. Corey slumps in his saddle, surveying the carnage lying before him. Manny Sharps' body lies across Hat Evans, not moving. Mexican bodies lie everywhere on the ground, some dead, others moaning, dragging themselves across the bloody ground, calling for help.

Corey looks to where Lorenzo's horse stands, head down, blood dripping from several bullet wounds, his master dangling headfirst from the saddle. Don Ricardo was a proud man. He found death as he had intended.

Corey nods, it is good Lorenzo welcomed death. He was a warrior, too proud to go through the rest of his life without his legs or pride.

Palane sits his horse quietly, watching as Corey looks around at the carnage. "The enemy are all dead, white man."

"Not all, some of the Mexicans live my friend."

Notching his last arrow, Palane drives the shaft through a man crawling across the ground in pain. "Now, they are all dead."

"Well, I'm not, get me outta here." Hat hollers from where he lies, pinned under Sharps.

Palane looks over to where the two bodies are piled atop each other and smiles. "It seems you are still alive white man. Why were you hiding?"

"Hiding?" Hat cusses. "With two hundred pounds of dead beef on top of me, it was hard to get up."

Corey steps slowly from his horse, taking Sharps by a leg, pulled him bodily from Hat. Releasing his grip on Sharps' leg, Corey slumps backward on the ground, into a sitting position. Hat struggles, but finally sits up slowly, using his left arm, as his right is completely useless.

Looking over at Corey, the smile of thank you slowly fades from his lips as Corey falls sideways. Crawling over to the big man, Hat lifts Corey's head, and pulls it onto his lap. Looking down, he discovers blood oozing from at least three bullet holes.

"You stay with me now, Corey Stallings." Hat looks toward the house and hollers for help. "You hear me, don't you die on me."

The dark eyes of the big man open slowly and look up. "Did we get them all, old friend?"

"We did at that, pardner."

"Lorenzo is dead, isn't he?"

Hat looks over to where Palane is bending over, looking into the face of Lorenzo. Turning back, Palane shakes his head, and walks to where Hat holds Corey.

"The big brown man is dead."

Corey nods, looking up again at Hat. "You marry Judith. She's a mite hardheaded, but she'll make you a good woman, after all, she's a Stallings."

"I'll do that Corey, providing she'll have me." Hat looks up to see everyone running toward them.

"She'll have…" The words play out as Ben runs up, out of breath. Falling to his knees, he takes Corey in his arms, pulling him close. "No."

"He's gone Ben." Hat looks away, hiding his own tears.

Sarah sits down on the ground beside Ben and touches Corey on the face, while tears run down her face. "He was a good man, Papa Ben."

"I know girl, now that it's too late, I know."

Cayuse and the Kiowa Warriors ride up slowly and sit astride their horses, looking over the battlefield. They watched from the hilltop as Palane fought like a wildcat, making them proud. No more would he be, just a warrior. He has proven himself as a great warrior of the Kiowa. They will sing his praises tonight over their campfires. Someday, he will be a great leader, a chief of the Kiowas.

A lone rider approaches the battleground and dismounts beside Lorenzo's body. Kneeling down, he crosses himself and silently weeps, his shoulder's shaking. Pablo looks over to where the others stare solemnly at him.

"I will take Don Ricardo's body with me, if you will permit it?"

Ben stands slowly. "I would be honored to have him buried here on this ground, beside my son."

The slight Mexican stands slowly, turning to his horse. Mounting, he looks once more at Lorenzo. "He was a great man, señors, a great warrior, and a great friend. It will be as you say you may bury him here. I know he will be honored; thank you." Crossing himself once more, Pablo Garcia looks down at Don Lorenzo then spurs his horse, riding at a lope out of their sight.

Palane asks several warriors to help carry the bodies of Corey and Lorenzo back to the house. Judith supports Hat, helping him back across the wide field. Samuel, Lambert and Sarah follow slowly in the rear.

"Corey's dead, Papa." Colby has tears running down his face as he stumbles along. "I will never get to talk to him again, never."

"Yes, son, your brother gave his life to save us all today, but he'll never be dead, never."

The End